beat

beat

Amy Boaz

THE PERMANENT PRESS
Sag Harbor, New York 11963

For information, address:
    The Permanent Press
    4170 Noyac Road
    Sag Harbor, NY 11963
    www.thepermanentpress.com

Library of Congress Cataloging-in-Publication Data

Boaz, Amy
    Beat / Amy Boaz.
        p. cm.
    ISBN-13: 978-1-57962-186-5 (alk. paper)
    ISBN-10: 1-57962-186-4 (alk. paper)
        1. Married people—Fiction. 2. Americans—France—
    Fiction. 3. Adultery—Fiction. 4. Self-realization—Fiction.
    5. Paris (France)—Fiction. 6. Domestic fiction. I. Title.

PS3602.O25B43 2009
813'.6—dc22   2009010680

Printed in the United States of America.

For

Charlotte and Terence

"I raced to find that Tarzan," I'm thinking, remembering boyhood and home as they lament in the Mexican Saturday Night Bedroom, "but the bushes and the rocks weren't real and the beauty of things must be that they end."

—Jack Kerouac
Tristessa

I

We spy a lost girl in the Louvre today. She must be about Cathy's age, maybe a few years younger, surrounded by three dark-suited guards with walkie-talkies pressed to their ears. They lead the abject child through the galleries; she is crying, her hands at her face. Cathy grips my arm, slowing my restless pace. She twists her whole body around to see through the crowded room. "What's wrong with her?" Cathy gasps, trying to make sense of the strange, sobbing girl. "Where's her mother?" I tell her I don't know, that her mother is no doubt looking frantically for her, too. "I'm sure they'll find each other," I say, and pull Cathy along, though I add, slyly: "You see how you must stay close and not lose your mother."

Cathy is pensive. She has tossed in bed during the night at our hotel, feverishly, and I have allowed her to sleep well into the morning. It is already late in the afternoon, and though we have been traipsing for hours through Northern European and Renaissance paintings, Egyptian antiquities, and the medieval dungeon of the museum, she does not complain. She sits on the central benches and sketches in her notebook. She has copied an Arcimboldo portrait made up of vegetables and flowers and labeled it: "Rodolfo II as Fruit Face." On another page she pencils the contours of the Winged Samothrace. I sit down beside her to watch, though briefly, since I am aware of the latening of the day and distracted by the constant stream of visitors through the galleries. I glide along the polished floors in the lofty rooms and I know that Cathy is aware of just how much distance to lapse between us before she gets up to follow.

Toward evening we take the métro to St. Michel. Cathy pockets our tickets in a slender compartment of her yellow anorak. She will hoard these artifacts of our journey and discover them only months later. It begins to rain; we choose a café along the busy boulevard. The place is objectionably smoky but the music is jazz, and there is an empty booth next to the bar.

Cathy writes in her Scooby-doo pad, big block letters that take up the whole page. She is imitating me and the scribbling I do in my own notebook.

"What are you writing?" she asks, her round, dark eyes flashing with the excitement of the new experience. She has never before been allowed to sit with me long hours in a café, "having drinks," she mimics me with her wicked sprite's smile, eating dinner unconscionably late, and bathing in the big hotel tub at night with her mother. Then we fall into bed at the same time, near midnight. She enjoys an *infusion*, pronounced with an accent that always makes her snicker, while I sink into an aromatic *pichet* of Bordeaux. She'll ask the waiter anything I tell her, as I coach her on pronunciation; she is direct, adorable with her brown boy's-cut hair and thin, assertive body, and when I miss her for a while I know she's made friends with the establishment's big dog or she's sitting at the bar shooting craps with the skeletal, chain-smoking locals.

But the eyes are too shiny, from fatigue or the stress of keeping up with me, and there are faint bluish shadows underneath.

"I'm jotting down observations from our day," I tell her. "Are you feeling all right? Do you want to eat now?"

"I'm feeling *great*," she replies with some exasperation, since it's a question I put to her often. "And it's too early to eat," she adds smartly.

She wears her blue cotton zip-up sweater that has a "2" stitched at her breast. It's a present from Joseph, sent for her birthday in January. He found just the right size, a slender six, with sleeves to grow on her long arms, and there are yellow and red racing stripes up the sweater's sides. Cathy went crazy for the racing stripes up the side. I don't know how Joseph managed to find something so right for her after having met her only once. He has told me he has dreamed about her. And he hears about her from me, of course, and studies photographs. I have sent him many pictures over the last year, of me and the children, and I'm pleased that he peruses them with care. Does he really? Joseph is wise—his learned Buddhist sagacity—and also thoughtful, a little foxy. I see him standing in the morning light at his kitchen counter in Boulder, mixing up his erection elixir. He wears jeans and a thick cotton shirt rolled up at the sleeves. He is regal, lean, and turns sideways to fix on me his enigmatic smile. His eyes tawny and glinting. What is he thinking? Does he want me to take him in my mouth, fix an omelet—or is he already planning where he has to drive his teenaged daughter this day? I wonder whether I truly know the man. He's a specimen of wild creature—now trapped, however, struggling to expiate his *bad karma*. And I, too, seek something like resolution—absolution. We are both battered, limping, beat.

We discuss the Parisian fashion of pointy, high-heeled shoes. Cathy has begged me to buy a pair for myself but I tell her we don't have the money.

"Then comfortable shoes, like those bowling shoes all the students wear," she sniffs, with uncanny maturity. She has been gaping after the Parisian *jeunesse*. She wants me always to look my best: she grimaces when I appear at her school-bus stop in our small town wearing Harry's sadly depleted down jacket from the seventies, my hair in uncombed knots; she won't allow me to denigrate my ravaged skin next to the perfection of her milky complexion. And the skin of my chin peels hideously after a weekend spent chafing rapturously against Joseph's beard. A daughter believes fervently in her mother's beauty. "You can't walk in those *boots*," she says, sounding like me.

"When you're a famous violinist you can come back to Paris and go into any store and buy whatever you want," I tell her.

"Yes, but with a dog and my *husband*."

"Husband!" I cry. For this is the first time I've heard of a husband in her scenarios.

"You mean Abner," I say. "You want to marry Abner. I knew it. And all along I thought he was just your best friend and soccer buddy. Forget it, now I won't agree to another sleepover with that boy." I don't mention her best friend's carrot-top head or his speech impediment, which Cathy imitates by way of some peculiar maternal sympathy.

"No, not Abner," she intimates mysteriously.

"Husbands are such a nuisance."

"I'll choose one that's not. That's *funny*," she says, challenging me.

"Your daddy *was* funny."

"He's only fun when you're not there. You never laugh together."

I sigh, audibly. I also roll my eyes and grimace and shrug exasperatedly and then wonder where my daughter picks up these mannerisms. "Daddy and I did laugh a lot when we first met, I guess," I say.

"Then why did you stop?"

"We lost our sense of humor. Or he did. Oh, I don't know."

"He picks on you."

"Does he?" I ask, genuinely surprised, since I always believed Cathy blamed me for the estrangement from her father. "I thought I picked on Harry."

But she's lost interest in me, engrossed in watching the group of youths at the next table, guffawing amid big clouds of cigarette smoke. They are probably in their teens, intent already at the adult-like tasks of conversing, ordering their snacks solemnly from the waiter, throwing back their heads at witty remarks, and scrutinizing new arrivals. A serious young lady installs herself alone at another table under the light, placing around her a pack of cigarettes, her markers, and books. She wears a striped sweater in the style of actress Anna Karina, heavy glasses, and those damn bowling shoes that are the fashion this year. She smokes and draws, evidently a student at her homework; it's only mid-March, after all, and in full *année scolaire*. I watch her and think of myself, once a student in Paris also, serious and seated alone, rarely looking up from her notebook, undeterred at her work despite the attention a solitary café-goer attracts, especially a young woman. I keenly felt that attention, was frankly terrified by it, exhilarated by its power, too. The power of youth that youth knows nothing of. I sip at my wine and feel immensely pleased that we have come in early spring, escaping the tourists who invade in warmer months: pleased to share the city I love only with the prickly French, and my memories. I am old enough to have my secrets.

Cathy doesn't ask about these. She stares at the solitary girl for a while, but since she won't look up and meet my daughter's gaze, Cathy decides against pursuing her. Instead she says:

"I want some olives."

"All right. Go ask. You say, Je voudrais des olives, s'il vous plaît."

She repeats the phrase and trots to the bar for our waiter. I watch my daughter deliver her speech directly to the young man, who gazes down at her, fascinated; she has her finger at her cheek, then her chin, in the way she has learned from her beloved school companion Abner; scrapes her heels, hunches her shoulders, never taking her liquid, enchanting gaze from the waiter's face. He stares, quizzically, until comprehension brightens his face, and he turns back to the bar. In a moment she returns triumphantly, holding up a small bowl of black oily *olives*.

"Well, just don't eat them all. You'll be sick."

She sets her attention on the olives, spearing each one with a toothpick and devouring it greedily. I thrust the napkin in front of her, then her cup of *infusion*, which surely now must be cold. She touches neither in favor of the olives. I have to worry about her, and the free-wheeling pleasure of moments before swiftly vanishes. I've had to worry about her since the day she was born, naturally; it's my job. I've kept her from breaking any bones, though she's an athletic kid; I've kept her from running in front of cars, falling from the precipice of the Grand Canyon, and gorging on sweets until she vomited (though it happened once, at four); she made it through scary high fevers and other sicknesses, and the only operation she's undergone was for the removal of a glandular lump on her temple at age one. She's taken innumerable falls from bikes, scooters, skateboards, and skates without scarring, and she's never ingested anything to poison her, though she did once get scalded when she brought down on her head a steaming bowl of pastina I had set on the kitchen counter. But I have hurt her, many times and more than I want to recall, by smacking her in a flash of rage at her sassiness, or spanking her buttocks at her misbehaving, though the reasons faded more quickly than the soreness of my response. I have been angry and critical of my daughter, and I've yelled at her enough times to press her flat against the wall. These years of child rearing have made me sick with worry; being a mother has not softened my edges, as seems to happen gracefully with other women, but rather rendered me shrewish and cross. I watch my daughter stab the last of the wrinkled, shiny olives and pop it into her mouth, savoring it with greasy lips and half-closed eyes in a manner remarkably and distastefully like her father, and I recognize that nothing will change between us that hasn't been established since her infancy, when we wrangled over breast-feeding—she demanded more, always more, and I couldn't give it to her. This trip alone together will not turn us into an ideal mother-daughter team.

"Did you leave one for me?" I ask her.

"You didn't want one."

"How do you know?"

She snorts and sits back, surveying the bar, her arms crossed behind her head. This is also the way she sleeps, lying back on the propped pillows with her arms looped behind her head and a sassy little smile pushing up the curves of her lips. It is this smile that enrages me: how can she be so confident, so arrogant? Is she making fun of me? With a frown I shift my attention to the room: the headlights darting in from the glistening boulevard ricochet off the bright copper fixtures. The clumps of youths have drifted out and others, dressed for the evening and smelling like fragrant bath water, wander in two by two. A man has entered the place, remarkable because he is powerfully built and black skinned, well dressed, with cropped graying hair and an interesting face. He greets the wait staff with a nod as if previously acquainted and slides into a booth in front of us, his back to me. Cathy doesn't notice him since she is facing me, though I find myself straining to listen to him speak to the waiter. He speaks well, fluently, with only a hint of an accent, probably American, and I wonder whether he might be a jazz musician, an old-timey from the Miles Davis days when young Americans flocked to Paris for their artistic initiation. Or maybe he's a writer.

"Cathy," I muse, feeling unstrung by the wine and the waning light. "Baby?" I say, and sigh; she watches me narrowly. We don't have to be anywhere tonight and if we are to have this conversation, it might as well be now.

"You know, we don't have to live in New York our whole lives," I begin, arranging my features in a hopeful expression. "I mean, we could live anywhere. Imagine. We could live in Paris, for example."

"I don't want to live anywhere but the U.S.A.," Cathy replies.

"How do you know? Don't you like Paris?"

"I don't speak French."

"Oh, but you'll learn quickly, such a smart girl as yourself."

She runs through her objections while displaying her repertoire of facial contortions. She does not like to speak French; I have not started her early enough and with the proper immersion. She won't leave her daddy, she won't leave her little brother, Bernard, and she won't leave Abner. Also, she's stubborn and I've learned to pick my fights, as the mothers in my circle like to say: the arguments we have and remember are over issues of violin practice.

"All right, we don't have to live in Paris. We could live in . . . Colorado," I venture, as a point of departure, because she knows I have been traveling to and from Boulder over weekends for the last year and a half. "The Rocky Mountains? Camping?" She crimps her lips together severely. "Okay, Boston?" I concede. "It's only a few hours north of New York and a wonderful city with a really famous music conservatory, as good as Julliard."

She scowls, squints her eyes suspiciously. "With Daddy and Bernie?"

"Of course with Bernie. Your brother goes where you go. But Daddy won't leave New York. His work is there. He won't live anywhere else."

"Then I won't go."

"But you'll have to come. I can't go by myself."

"Why not?"

"Why not?" I frown. She is outfoxing me. "Darling," I say, moving faster than I have intended. "I can't live with Daddy anymore."

She sets her mouth angrily. "No," she says, and shakes her head.

"But Cathy," I plead. I remind her that her father and I have arguments and sometimes we throw things—that is, I have thrown many things such as pieces of luggage and single shoes out the small rectangular bathroom window of our house—and we yell and make her and Bernie cry. And that for over a year Harry has been sleeping on a mattress in a hut he has constructed in the backyard. How does she explain this to Abner, whose parents surely sleep in the same bed and were actually spotted holding hands at the public swimming pool last summer? The vision of holding hands with Joseph intrudes before I can stop it, and with it, a warm surge of unbearable longing. We are strolling the streets near Harvard Square, and I am wearing a summer dress. We feel light, happy, with a whole weekend together in front of us. We don't mind the looks we attract—a handsome, graying man walking hand-in-hand with a younger woman—by the flicker of his eye I know he notices these looks. He grows solemn. We stop in the bookstore and Joseph surveys the shelves of Asian literature, letting a page fall open from the *Treasury of Court Poetry* (1100 A.D.). He intones a melodious line. I am stunned with delight: has he done this before, led his lover around the neighborhood where he grew up? Or am I truly "the jewel of his heart"? We will return to his brother's apartment in Cambridge and make strenuous love over the futon mattress, but I am not allowed to meet the brother, among other relatives here, as Joseph grew up in Boston. Later we pass the Grolier Book Shop and he catches sight of an acquaintance inside—someone who also knows his companion who is not his wife, and sees that I am not she—and he will drop my hand, leaving me smarting and sullen.

I demand of my daughter, somewhat sharply: "Then where should we live?"

She glares at me with darkly welling eyes. "You and Daddy will live together in our house just like before," she decrees in clipped Abner-like utterances.

"But I'm not happy there. Look, I'll get a job in Boston and we can move to a nice apartment in the city and then Abner can come visit—"

"No," says she.

"Oh, Cathy, for heaven's sake. I could even start a new life," I insist softly, pulling her arm so that she gets up and nestles next to me on my side of the booth. "With someone new, who loves me and cares about me. Don't you see, darling? Maybe we could all be happy. Can't we try at least?"

"I don't want a new life *or* new friends *or* a new school. And I don't want a new dad. No." She retreats into incoherent sobs, knocking against me as she cries.

The man in the booth in front of us turns around because we are making unseemingly weeping noises; the waiter darts a nervous glance in our direction. I pat my daughter on the back and smile tearfully, nodding at the seated man in front of us. He has an open, sympathetic face; he is older than I thought at first. He stares for a moment, then turns back around.

The waiter offers us a menu. The clatter and hum return to the café.

"Who is that man?" I mouth quietly to the waiter, pointing discreetly. "Is he an American? A musician?"

The waiter is young, with a hunted look. He shrugs. "He is rich," pronounces the waiter. "A rich man."

I order roast chicken with fried potatoes for Cathy and a glass of Orangina to cheer her up. She is pleased not to have to drink milk. And the fish special for myself, though I can't remember what *hareng* is: I know I'll be sorry for not asking.

THE TUBE through London lumbers slowly, jolts, and sways; it is packed with commuters at rush hour and Richmond is nearly the last stop in the western suburbs. I miscalculate time and distance. Cathy has dozed momentarily on the greasy cushioned seat. She wakes suddenly when the doors hiss open. She sits up, blinking and looking around. "What did I miss?" she cries, and I have to laugh at her bright-eyed confusion. I am holding a map of London, following our progress through the tunnels. People in nicely tailored suits and sturdy raingear smile indulgently at us. Ah, the Amurricans, they seem to say, and nod in an understanding way.

We emerge from the train at Richmond station almost a half-hour later than I have planned. Because of our lateness I am afraid I have missed my American friend Darla Worthington, but I spot her instantly seated on a stool in the waiting lounge. She is reading a newspaper, very blond and ladyish in a long camel-colored coat, her long legs crossed, pointed high heels kicking the air under her; she has written that she is four months pregnant. We greet effusively and embrace (I haven't seen her since Cathy was one and Harry and I came through Scotland), and I realize I don't exactly disapprove of the heels, or the violently blonded shoulder-length hair (a concession to British fashion?), because I have loved Darla since we first met at the fashion magazine where we both worked ten years ago. When I first became aware of this stylish young woman, she was escalating a steep set of subway stairs at 50th Street and Broadway, and a man on the step below her reached up her very short skirt and goosed her. I knew he goosed her from the whelp she let out, before scampering up the stairs and into our steel high-rise building. Then we became friends, lunch pals, confidantes, because she is kind and gently accepting of me, and I know she loves my daughter without knowing her. I have come this long way to watch Darla's beatific face.

Richmond is a stately town, a city really, with many shops along bustling streets—London's most desired suburban address. My friends are snobs this way. Darla owns, with her husband, Saul, who is English, half of a house on a choice corner in the town proper. The ceilings of Darla's house are high, the rooms narrow, molded, and charmingly appointed, and she explains they have been making drastic repairs and renovations since Saul's father died, when possession of the house fell to them. Its tall meandering staircase forms the artery leading to four lofty stories. Darla allows Cathy and me the top room, which is also my friend's study, full of galleys she's editing for her publishing house and also pictures of Darla smiling next to Asian gurus and yoga masters. She has a Wheaton terrier with a gigantic head, and his noisy barking and aggressive friendliness enchant my daughter, who is not afraid of dogs. The kitchen is new, astoundingly modern and sleek. We drink wine—that is, I do—and they sip at neon-bright glasses of Orangina.

"She is adorable," Darla says of my daughter, as one would of a toy or favorite pet. We have brought Darla a large rectangular tin from Paris etched with pretty lettering; we stumbled upon it in a store in Les Halles. I'm thinking already of the baby's room, on one of the upstairs stories of the house, and Darla is beaming at the tin, delighted by the presence of my daughter. Still, I feel I have to put Darla straight about child rearing. "She is stubborn and sassy and greedy for sweets and presents," I say of Cathy, who provokes the large dog to fits of frenzied yelping. I scowl and cower next to them.

Darla laughs. "You're afraid of dogs, Frances? Should I take him out?" she asks me, but doesn't do it. Cathy is absorbed in a game of fetch and retrieve with the dog's slimy milk bone—a child who dearly loves animals but isn't allowed to have any. Fish, I promise, maybe a bird, but who will clean up after a dog? Darla continues, "You know, we've been trying for three years to have a baby after all the turmoil around the time I lived in my Paris ashram, then I finally tried acupuncture—they worked on my feet, can you imagine? And also inserted pins in my abdomen. Saul is ecstatic: did I tell you it's a boy?"

She looks at me intently, with perhaps more *presence*—if I may borrow a word that her yoga master might use—than she used to, though forgivingly, lovingly, and I wonder about her newfound psychotherapy training. She will become a therapist after years of working through her own complicated personal history and eventually quit her job as an editor, she says, and devote herself to her patients. Also, her baby. Her aged Catholic mother still lives in Philadelphia; however, Darla and Saul look to be staying in London indefinitely, and I feel the familiar tinge of envy at the possibility of roads not taken. What if, I secretly entertain, I had married an Englishman—nay, a Frenchman, more likely—and my Cathy, capricious, irrepressible flirt, were espousing French idioms with killer ease?

"A boy! Oh Darla, how wonderful."

The mention of giving birth to a boy, the mention of her ashram: these subjects make me wistful, nearly weepy. Once I sat with Darla over a long, stolen night from our husbands in a bar in Greenwich Village and we allowed ourselves, after a couple of glasses, to indulge in confessions of wayward yearnings. Why were we feeling unhappy in our marriages? Hadn't we been rushing to be married, feel settled, have babies? Darla was flirting with a fellow student of her Buddhist guru in Paris—scandalized, thrilled, I was almost afraid to ask more. What would she say, that they were having an affair? Perhaps they had discussed leaving her husband, Saul Worthington, whose marriage to Darla I—and Harry—had witnessed at Columbia when Saul was teaching film studies. They lived in an apartment on 110th and Broadway then, and Harry's own student apartment had been right around the corner. Harry and I used to go over for dinner. Saul presided, skinny, critical, the relentlessly articulate film adjunct, and railed about many subjects, such as the sharp-C of Whitney Houston, or the superfluity of women's magazines. Saul always had an opinion. Darla was fair skinned, long legged, and bright headed as copper, then; she brushed off the tabletop, frowned with forbearance at Saul's insouciant demonstration of working-class manners, and asked, somewhat caustically, "Where did you go to charm school?" I wasn't convinced they were entirely compatible. In her embittered remark I recognized the chasm in their marriage— the desirous, hyper-attuned wife and her insensate mate—and saw my own. Once the subject of marital discord was broached we rarely spoke of anything else. Had we dreamed we would end up so conventionally? Pretty girls working at a glamorous fashion magazine, writing copy about necessary purchases and stepping out cheekily: weren't we being trained to assume the straight life of our parents? While I had been convinced, that night at least, when we drank together on Bleeker Street and discussed the insatiable achings of our young-wife hearts, that it was only a question of time before we would outgrow our stifling marriages, husbands who tended to be emotionally constipated (we would whisper and giggle), and homes as cold as the crypt, only to start over again with passion and honest conviction—these were my grand words!—we hadn't done it. We stayed where we were, sealing our fate by buying houses and having children. Or in my case, another child: Bernard, my boy, whom I had been waiting for all along.

Harry could never understand why I couldn't be happy with what we had.

But if I think about Bernie I won't be able to hold together any longer, so I don't talk about him. I don't even offer to show the pictures I have brought. Anyway, Cathy is jealous and won't let me. This is our trip, hers and mine, or at least I have presented our journey this way to her, and no one—neither Bernie nor Joseph, nor even Joseph's nemesis, Arlene Manhunter, his companion who has it in for me—can get between daughter and mother.

SAUL JOINS us for dinner at the restaurant, which stands on a deserted windswept canal along the river Thames. He is still slender, briskly officious in a tie, and quickly divested of his jacket, though his hair has grayed considerably, and the curve of his back is more pronounced; I recognize that more time has lapsed than I know and I feel again the stab of regret. Yet Saul's face, small and wryly pleasant, remains unshadowed, unchanged, and overall he looks a little like a kid actor who tries to make himself fit into an older part by powdering his hair. Saul won a local election as alderman and plans to go on to run for Parliament, a nearly impossible task for a Labor official who talks far too fast.

"What is your favorite museum in Paris?" he rattles off to Cathy, giving a swift, efficient swipe of his butter knife over the bread. He bobs his head at the selection of wine I have ordered. "Did you visit the Thomas Eakins exhibit at the Musée d'Orsay? Very enlightening. Which parks have you visited? Did you see the *guignol* in the Luxembourg? Do you speak French? Let's hear some words."

"J'ai quatorze ans," replies Cathy, to snorts by Saul and Darla's bright peal of laughter.

Saul is pleased to hear that I have been bickering with French waiters and postal officials, and as the chauvinistic Englishman he likes to tell this joke: "When God created Eden he created France, but then He realized it was too beautiful so He created the French."

Cathy twists and fidgets on the banquette next to me. Her eyes are glassy, fiery, and flashing (it is after nine o'clock), her cheeks flushed a similar feverish puce as the walls of the restaurant (*puce*: a pinkish tint much like flea-bitten flesh); she is delighted and flattered by the attention of my two friends and reluctant to relinquish the limelight. She is talking off the top of her head, interrupting the adults, rolling her eyes heavenward. "Have I really been to England before, Momma? Well, I don't remember. And I'm not having fish, take that away please—it smells. Do you know what Abner says?" she says, moving in with a conspiratorial air, and my friends have no idea whom she is talking about but they move in with her. They find her flighty gestures and mimicry *hilaire* (Darla tilts back her head and hoots silently, very ladylike), and Cathy likes nothing better than stealing the show. She is an actress, a comic, and as I push aside the glasses and plates from her spastic movements, I wonder if indeed acting would suit her better than the disciplined act of performing her violin pieces in concerts. I shush her, even physically restrain her flailing arms to hold her down on the seat, but to no avail.

Soon she will crash, and she does, upstairs in Darla's house, as I read her one of the French books I purchased in the Gare du Nord and slipped surreptitiously inside our traveling rucksack.

She is too exhausted to protest the language. She yawns and grimaces as I read, then, dropping her head back on the pillow, starts to snore lightly.

I tiptoe downstairs and find Darla alone in the lofty, elegant parlour. She has shooed out Saul, who claims an early-morning meeting; she still treats him like a little brother who doesn't know better. She greets me with a glass of wine and an eager little smile. Darla has intimated from the clues I have dropped all evening about traveling to Boulder and making a new friend in the poet Joseph Pasternak that there is intriguing new information to be learned from my life. Perhaps the first bit of information of use to her since we both worked at the same magazine in our twenties. She closes the tall door behind me and curls back up on the sofa, her blue eyes glittering.

"Is it Joseph?" she whispers. "Did he—break with Arlene to be with you?"

She has met Joseph in a previous time, as she used to be an editor at a Buddhist magazine in New York that publishes both Joseph and Arlene. They have been part of a small, significant, incestuous circle of engaged intellectuals—I suspect they have all slept with each other over the years. Joseph, for his part, remembers Darla warmly. The pretty, copper-headed young lady at the Buddhist magazine: he would certainly have remembered her. Is he surprised to hear that I, too, know Darla Worthington from a past life? Does he not suspect a setup when I tell him that I am coming to London? No, because these coincidences (and there are many to unfold in time) convince both Joseph and me that our coming together holds a mysterious fatefulness. Well, what is true love if not fate? I believe it—I have to. I am relieved to open my heart to my friend I have traveled this far to see.

Moreover, Darla is a Buddhist, and in her circle, Joseph and his companion Arlene Manhunter are—were—a highly visible couple.

"But he is . . ." she murmurs, truly pained.

"In trouble," I hasten to add. "Yes, it's going to be okay. You see, Darla, we met at a wedding. He sent me a book of translations he did," I explain, satisfied at last to hold her attention and speak freely to her. "No, it was the postcard he put inside the book that arrested my attention." I correct myself because Darla, like Joseph—and Arlene—understands the significance of portents. I begin to speak faster now, gesturing and stammering the way I do when I'm excited—the way I see my daughter imitate me. "The postcard showed a painting by Diego Rivera of the great Mexican hero Zapata leading a white horse in battle. There is a ragged army of peasants in sandals behind him. The peasants are clutching their iron tools and bows and arrows. Zapata is mustachioed and ruddy, a little like Joseph after he has been climbing his mountains. In one fist he's holding a sickle down by his side, while he grabs in his other outstretched hand the reins of a beautiful, slender-legged white horse. Its head is turned coyly to the side, showing one clear, almond eye. The horse is delicately stepping over a brown-suited warrior fallen at Zapata's heels. Zapata is standing on the blade of a sword the fallen soldier has evidently dropped, his hands curled submissively around Zapata's sandals. The painting is called *Agrarian Leader Zapata*," I tell Darla. "It spoke to me. Do you see it?"

She smiles beatifically, nods, and keeps her bluest eyes locked on mine. I marvel at how still she remains, how well she listens, and I think of her skillful training in psychotherapy. But I imagine she doesn't quite follow and I feel the need to be more forceful.

"Darla, it struck me," I say, "that I am the horse Joseph is leading in triumph, and the body slain at his heels is Harry—my husband."

Darla's eyebrows dance uncertainly. She looks momentarily pained, frightened, or surprised. She sighs and makes a noise of gentle understanding.

"I imagined that I saw the whole of our sublime connection unfold just then, foretold in that postcard, Darla. Joseph is going to be my liberator from the oppression of my marriage."

Now I have told her. I have come all this way to justify myself to Darla Worthington, my dear old friend, because she understands and will forgive me. She will not make a snap, superior judgment of me, because she is my *semblable*, and not above an act of human frailty herself. She will agree with the perspicuity of my interpretation; she is on my side. I feel instantly drained and very tired from the wine, and at the same moment it occurs to me that Darla, four months pregnant, must also be exhausted, having endured a long day in her office and being faced with an early morning's grueling schedule. Surely I am keeping her up. After a short while, during which no more revelations are exchanged, we kiss goodnight, and I ascend the narrow multi-stories to my room.

While bathing, I remember that I have left my notebook in the pocket of my raincoat, downstairs in the vestibule. Though I don't know where the big dog is, and if he'll bite a stranger wandering around his house at night, I tiptoe down the staircase. I hear Darla's voice coming from the parlour; the tall door to the elegant room is closed. I can't make out what she says, perhaps she's speaking on the phone—New York time is seven hours behind—and I don't need to listen. In the vestibule I rifle through the coats, find my notebook, and sneak back up to the top of the house.

I LOSE Cathy on a crowded street near Les Halles. It is raining persistently this afternoon and Cathy and I have been shopping in the underground mall. We have come from the Pompidou, hungry by mid-afternoon and demoralized that the museum's roof-top restaurant, prettily furnished with round nickel tables each holding a simple vase with one bright red rose, offers a prohibitively expensive menu. We watch business-suited men dining with young blondes in stiletto heels and sadly we turn to go. The area around Les Halles crawls with *riffraff*: a word Cathy pockets thoughtfully. She announces she wants to eat pizza, and in a café, though I tell her the neighborhood is a tourist trap and we should try elsewhere. She insists; we argue. This is a familiar sight, the two of us in an angry face-off, shouting over the other in the middle of the busy street. She knows my weakness when she complains of hunger or fatigue: what can I say? She's a child. She could be famished or ill and I am responsible. I steer her to a café. I hear only English spoken around us, German, and something else that must be a Scandinavian language, and I feel bullied and defeated.

"See," I hiss at her, when my salad arrives with wilted leaves and charred strips of chewy chicken, "this is awful. Why don't you listen to me? I've been here before."

"Here?" she demands. "At this restaurant?" She tucks into her scrawny pizza and won't admit a word against the quality of dough, tomato, or cheese. She drinks her Orangina in measured increments, glaring at me. "Don't argue with the waiters again," she huffs with great rolling eyes. I have been brought the wrong coffee—"I said *café au lait,* didn't I? I know I did"—I flag down the wily serveur.

"I ordered *un café au lait,*" I tell him in French, pointing to the demi-cup of sludge he has deposited on our table.

"You said *un café,*" he pulls himself up in English, sniffing.

"I said *un café au lait,*" I insist in French, ignoring his attempt to humiliate me in my own language, and as an afterthought, I add, "and I mean *un café crème,*" remembering then the precise words.

"You're confusing him," Cathy informs me, sucking noisily on her straw. "And you're giving him a bad idea of Americans."

"Be quiet! What do you know? You don't speak French."

"I understand *everything.*"

It's raining again as we pick our way miserably through the crowded narrow streets toward the métro station. We have purchased the rectangular tin with elegant French lettering that we will convey to Darla in London. Cathy won't take my hand as I plunge through the crowd, erratically, uncertainly, more than once stopping to ask directions of shoppers who seem to have no idea of the station I'm seeking; I consult my pocket map, which I have torn out of the guidebook so that I won't have to drag the heavy thing around, and also I'm too vain to be seen scanning a map in the middle of a busy Parisian street. At such moments I miss Harry's sense of direction, my husky, deliberative husband, and I recognize, resentfully, how I have come to rely on it when traveling. As an engineer Harry can splice any kind of space and rearrange it—elevations are what he draws, situations drawn from a dozen different angles as only God Himself can organize the universe. Harry consults a map upside down and knows where he is. Yet when he's wrong—and he has been wrong—I am enraged (just as my daughter huffs angrily next to me), kicking myself that I ever allowed myself to be duped by his so-called expertise. "Why am I listening to you?" I rail, when we are lost. I charge blindly ahead, in spite of the direction he gives. "I'm never listening to you again!"

"We're not going the right way," my daughter declares, unhelpfully. "We're just getting soaked." She draws back under her hood (protection from the elements I do not possess in my flimsy raincoat), and glowers.

"All right, Ms. Brilliance, which way then?"

I give up dragging her along. I stride forward and cease looking behind me. We pass under a Roman archway with three thick columns. I enter first; on a sudden, inexplicable impulse, a wicked, vengeful whim, I slip behind one of the columns to hide myself. She lurches through the archway several paces after me and I watch. Her head swivels, she is looking for me, but I am hidden; thinking that I am still in advance of her, she suddenly vaults forward, afraid to lose me, and passes through the archway and into the open, frighteningly crowded space ahead. She shoots frantic glances left and right. How long do I remain hidden? My eyes are glued to her rigid form. Some seconds, not many, but enough to scare her, enough to scare me. The street seethes with rushing pedestrians. A child can vanish in a matter of seconds. I shout her name: "Catherine!" and she turns quickly. I beckon wildly from where I stand at the column under the archway. She runs back to me, her face taut, her mouth lopsided with anguish and fear. Shaking, I grab the greasy fabric of her anorak and pull her along.

THE TUB is elevated and enormously deep, dominating the space in the small bathroom, and there are sturdy aluminum handles on either side of the tiled walls as if constructed for the aid of some hulking giant to lower and raise itself from the basin depths. We have procured this Olympian *salle de bain* only because I disputed the original room assigned to us on account of the deep-pile stench of cigarette smoke. The concierge, who is an Englishwoman, led us through a labyrinth of hallways to other rooms in the process of being cleaned, but after two hours threw up her hands, switching to English, and allowed us an upgrade at no extra cost. We don't mind, of course, and I instruct Cathy on the occasional necessity of pushing one's weight around. She rolls her eyes knowingly.

The hotel is located in the Marais; that is, the guidebook says it is. Actually, it sits on a long, fairly quiet street parallel to Boulevard

Beaumarchais and thus is closer to the Bastille. Only after hours do many of the storefronts open—bars and strange tattoo clubs. Still, we have found a friendly bistro on the main avenue: the food is well cooked, despite a meat-heavy menu, with excellent Bordeaux selections, and the clientele professional-class types and those who evidently live in the neighborhood. The men, who dine together, are alluring in a darkly handsome European way, hunched over the table intently as they castigate a caller over their cell phones, until you catch their eye and they suddenly smile with a glorious sexual energy; I imagine, momentarily, that I will encounter one of these men, find myself chatting over our glasses of wine, gesticulating charmingly as he inquires about my exceptional education—*tiens*, how well you speak French, how unusual for an American! But I recognize the impossibility of this, *moi*, a transient, a mother, a person of some baggage. Nonetheless, the place is never crowded, which I like, and Cathy has made herself acquainted among the smokers at the bar. They shoot dice, she plays with the mangy, slow-moving bar dog, and I drink wine and write in my notebook. I don't worry about her for a while.

Later, we soak together at night in the bathtub: she sits squat-legged near the spigots, so that I can stretch out my legs. Cathy experiments with spraying the mobile showerhead around the walls and onto the floor, and I have to hiss at her to stop. She likes the water as hot as I do, with lots of bubbles, and she no longer has to ease herself gradually in from the island of my belly. She heaps bubbles over her chest and makes shampoo horns, as she and her daddy like to call them, on top of her head. I've drunk numerous glasses of Bordeaux and finished her meal (*frites, poulet roti, tricouleur salade*), once I learn dolorously that *hareng* is herring and thus inedible to my palate; it's too late to be soaking in a hot tub. I could fall asleep for the rest of the night like this, Cathy splayed on my belly, in a relaxed and blissful limbo, before awakening cold and wrinkled as black oily *olives*.

"Are there any messages?" I ask, since she would know, being the one who can operate the television answering machine. It flicks on and off all night, like the beating heart of a lurking beastie, even if there are no messages. I drape a piece of clothing over the screen in order to sleep without distractions. Anyway, I can't sleep, the drape helps nothing.

"Yes," she intimates, "there is."

My eyes fly open and my heart beats a little faster.

"Really? Hmm. From whom?"

"There's two."

"There *are*. Uh-huh."

She hums one of her Suzuki tunes. She is teasing me, toying with my anticipation. We have not brought her violin—my concession to this so-called vacation, which is a kind of truce between us, a departure from the everyday. We have escaped the strictures of schedule. I tell her we are *on the lam*—she likes this expression, does she understand it? I think she does. She grasps that I am being pursued and have to look behind me. (*Who* is this message from? Has Arlene found me? Has Harry been indiscreet with our whereabouts?) And because we don't know how long we'll be gone, or even if we'll return to that other life containing Daddy and school, we both have begun to feel the absence of this sweetly rhythmic string instrument, her quarter-sized violin, with its rosin-coarsened wood, its miniature bow and Kun, which she attaches, then rests on her shoulder. We have begun to miss the kinship the instrument imparts, when we bend our heads over her music stand and study the notes yet to be memorized; I feed them to her, she plays and recognizes the tune from the tapes we are instructed to play regularly, until she learns to read the notes herself. As she matures, my function in her practice ritual grows obsolete. I can still tell her when she's not in tune, though she objects to my intrusion, and I can remind her to keep her fingers high—"tips, tips"—and I listen to her pieces and applaud. She bows; she still asks that I stay and listen to her practice, even if I don't need to be there. I take this as a vote of confidence in my mothering. The time is coming fast when she will want to do it all herself.

She hums Dvořák's "Humoresque," a piece she played in a concert last year. I remember wheezing with emotion as she played— what a lot of work learning that one was!—as the other mothers looked on askance. Harry couldn't make it, or he blew a tire on the way or missed the train that would have conveyed him to the school on time. Cathy hums the tune nostalgically, and I join her, a little drunkenly: maybe she's thinking of her father. Is she sad? Is she homesick? Have I ruptured her sense of security? Yet I only want to ask her about the phone calls.

We finish the song. I venture, "So who called?" attempting to lift myself out of the increasingly uncomfortable tepid water. The bubbles have vanished and our flesh is turning to putty. She grabs my thigh and pushes me back down.

"No! we're not done."

"It's not hot enough for me."

She yanks at the faucet and it spews out scalding water. She laughs her crazy, diabolical Abner-like laugh.

"Daddy," she says. And waits.

"Okay. Did he leave a message?"

"It says, 'Appelez immediatement.'"

"Oh boy. When did he call? Do you think Bernie is okay?"

"Fine, fine, have some wine." She furrows her brow, annoyed that I instantly think of Bernard—why don't I think of Harry?

"And Joseph," she adds.

"Joseph called?"

"Yes." She sighs. Ready now to exit the tub, she allows me to rub her down with a towel, blow-dry her short, wavy hair to a high fluff, brush her teeth (she can do it herself, but half-heartedly), exfoliate her crusty elbows, and rub lotion onto the backs of her fine, long hands. She won't tolerate more than this. Then she dives into bed and demands two stories, no three—

"Cathy," I beg, "it's nearly midnight. Even French children don't go to bed this late."

"When will I get to meet him finally?" she demands suddenly.

"Who?"

"You know: Joseph."

"Oh. You did meet him. At Douglas's wedding in Denver."

"That was years ago. I was so young."

"Yes, you were five. And I was two years younger, too. Cathy listen to this: Joseph had a dream in which you said exactly that: 'I was wondering when I would finally get to meet you.' That's what you said to him exactly."

She reaches back to plump her pillows, then leans against them comfortably, folding her arms behind her head. She is pondering, her mouth curled into a museful smile.

"Did he leave a message?" I ask, though it is strange to ask this of my daughter and I feel my face flush. I won't get any more information out of her.

"I don't know. Why don't you look?"

I do, when she falls asleep, which is instantly, still in the same pose, her arms crossed behind her; only her head is slightly altered, fallen to one side of the pillow, the eyes closed and the face relaxed into its fierce mask of incipient maturity.

There is no message from Joseph, or one that I can read. I won't be able to sleep. Since we've been in Paris I haven't been able to sleep soundly and without waking up a half-dozen times during the night, abruptly, wide awake as if I've heard a noise or detected movement in the room. I worry about Cathy, and though we sleep on single beds that are pushed together, I am acutely attuned to the slightest shifting of her supine body: the moany exhalations—connoting fever? pain? heartsickness?—the sudden sprightly flutterings of her eyelids. She gibbers and writhes and sometimes, when I fear she's feverish again, I stroke her cheek with the back of my hand, in the manner of my mother, the nurse. I've woken her up to give her a suppository, terrified of the swift, stealthful fevers that bring up the blood in her face and render her huge, nocturnal eyes liquid and glassy. She grows cool almost immediately, and sleeps so soundly that I hover over her, listening to her fitful breathing.

I must return these calls, but first I will sleep out the time difference. The tall windows to our room open onto a courtyard; the windows are hung with heavy, extravagant fabric and I thrust these aside to pull the casements open and let in the night air. Dank and swampy: an industrial vapor emanates from the Seine, and it doesn't smell salutary, but I let the coolness bathe my face nonetheless, while my knees press against the oven-hot metal of the aged radiator. I am shivery from my bath; I move away from the window and lie down next to my daughter. I watch her sleep, arrested in her idyllic pose, as if she has been lying on a grassy, sunny hill and grown drowsy watching her sheep. She has set aside her staff, or flute perhaps, propped her arms behind her head for a pillow, and fallen asleep under the benevolent, bluest sky. Such defenseless confidence in my girl! I doze, too, rigidly, and not for long, but I dream a vivid, delicious dream: Joseph and I are in a restaurant—it feels like Boston—nighttime, candlelight, maybe noisy, though I hear nothing, and we have been dining and drinking wine. We are seated side by side (as we once did in a Cambridge restaurant, early on) and suddenly Joseph pulls me to him, close to the skin of his neck so that I feel his whiskers on my cheek. He whispers suggestively, "Why don't we. . . ?" and I'm not sure what he means (make love? run away and get married?). I look at him questioningly: how to complete his sentence? Then he kisses me, a softly urgent, open-mouth kiss; a kiss of such exquisite, attentive feeling that it is like an offering to me, an offering of himself, and in this brief, distilled moment I sense I am finally holding my darling, all of him: I possess him at last. But then I jerk awake—why? Why can't this long-awaited oneiric communion with my beloved last? As I have always hoped to have this dream. But it comes too late, I see now, as I watch my daughter, who has rolled over onto her side; I see and I weep because it's too late to dream of possessing Joseph. He is lost to me. This is my last beautiful dream of my love.

I will call Joseph and he will lecture me. He is issued pajamas and regulation slippers; he sleeps in a dorm with the other men, who snore loudly away from the women they love. Joseph does not snore and he never wears pajamas. He sleeps always in a long-sleeved T-shirt and thick-cut boys' underwear to protect himself against the chill mountain air. He sleeps noiselessly on his side or on his stomach, his hands thrown up and over his head. He is not built for fighting or laboring. His dictionaries of ancient languages are ordered neatly on his bedside table. I imagine the other inmates respect his deep erudition and skills as a teacher. In any case, he can talk his way out of an argument. In Valhalla he is permitted one phone call every other night, and he does not have to use his phone card. He would call his daughter, of course, a teenager probably living now with her mother in California. Joseph has taught me the value of buying phone cards. He sleeps now as late, as long as he wants. I would never let my Joseph sleep, aware as I am of the latening of the day. I think this is the beginning of his turning away from me.

II

I didn't flee to Boulder, or to Boston, or even to Albuquerque, that Land of Enchantment. I came to Paris because it is a city that has always been good to me. In Paris I learned I could be someone other than the person I was expected to be: girl, student, wife. I have come again and again to this beguiling city.

First, I came as the companion of my high-school English teacher, who was the widow of a Frenchman. She had a *particule* in her surname, as an aristocratic remnant. I had attended a public high school in a suburb of Maryland, where my father at the time worked as a business executive in the capital. My teacher was a dour lady in her middle years, her long, dark hair not yet graying, and coiled in a messy bun at the back of her head. I had been the most dutiful student in her class and she believed me docile and sweet-tempered: once I recall her pointing out to the class how the morning sunlight streaming through the schoolroom windows reflected on my "golden hair." Usually she was severe and humorless. I tried hard to insert into my essays recondite vocabulary words that would impress her—words that I have since never actually heard used, such as *baleful*. In choosing me for her purposes she had checked out my family, though they suspected, I think, that she was a lesbian. Once *en voyage* my teacher kept to her solitary habits and was apt to be distracted by luggage and departure schedules. At night in our stately townhouse located in the tony Parisian suburb of Neuilly-sur-Seine—the apartment belonged to her in-laws owning the *particule*—she would ask me to comb her hair for her. She dressed in long, dark skirts and stockings that made her seem older than she probably was, perhaps forty. She had full lips lined in red lipstick and smooth, dusky skin; she read the novels of E. M. Forster on the train while I explored the work of the provincial Alphonse Daudet, recommended by my French teacher. Did she smoke cigarettes? The smell of her in my memory suggests now that she did, also the dun-colored skin and the pall of unhappiness that hovered always around her. She knew glamorous people in Paris, or so it seemed to a seventeen-year-old overeager young woman headed for college in New York in the fall: one evening we had dinner at a Vietnamese restaurant (I had never had such food!) in the company of a very grown-up man who might have been my teacher's brother-in-law. It was the Fourteenth of July, Bastille Day, and the city was festive and boisterous. They even listened to me, my teacher and this mature stranger, as I blushed and stammered in textbook French. I must have convinced them of my precocity, because they allowed me to take off by myself after our meal and explore the festivities at the Bastille, overrun by hordes of unruly, bloody-minded *citoyens*. But it grew late after the display of fireworks, and in my naïveté, I missed the last métro and had to persuade a Turkish taxi driver to take me back to Neuilly, at great expense. I had no idea in the scheme of Paris where Neuilly was located. Eventually, I arrived at the apartment building and knocked timidly on the in-laws' door. It must have been three o'clock in the morning; my teacher opened up in her long nightgown, her hair loose and silky in the streetlight. She did not speak to me or look me directly in the eye. After that night, she no longer asked me to comb her hair.

I returned to Paris as a college student and learned to smoke Stuyvesants—pronounced, that is, "Stewey-ves-SAHN." I hung out with my new friends at a café in Montparnasse that had some good pinball machines.

We attended classes at various state-organized universities across the city; they were dreary, concrete Roman-numbered bunkers with stark, graffitied exteriors—Université I, IV, VII, etc. Students were studying semiotics, Salvador Dali, and political constructs in post-World War II literature. I sat demurely in the back and let my more polished compatriots in leather pants gesticulate and contextualize. I smoked insurgently. We were of course in love with our teachers, such as the director of the institute that sponsored our foreign study, a lispy, dreamy-eyed lady who taught Surrealism and conducted a séance to conjure the actual Nadja from André Breton's seminal text; she instructed us in the meaning of the word *cuisse* by running her fingers along her thigh through the fabric of her batik skirt, to distinguish the *upper* thigh from the *lower*. We drank bottles of red wine daily and I discovered *bock panache*, a kind of crazy mixture of beer and lemonade that was the favorite beverage of my concierge.

Next (I won't say *finally*), I came to Paris as a bride—three years married. Paris was marvelous then, in the company of my professional husband, who could situate the various eras of building for me, and elucidate the grand modifications of Baron Georges Haussmann. We discussed art history over dinner. I could show off by speaking French with the service staff. I had arranged the accommodations, in my thrifty fashion, and secured a place for us near les Jardin des Plantes, on the Right Bank (imagining quiet and greenery), though there was an ongoing construction project nearby, and every morning we were awakened before sex to the incessant drone of a jack hammer. As a result, we were thrust out early, and visited every museum in the guidebook, drinking our way in the evening around the Périphérique. But even so, I'm fairly certain, or as certain as one can be in these matters, after numerous wine-soaked dinners and jack-hammered mornings, that I conceived our first-born there, Cathy my girl, my scourge. I am happy with Paris. I believe it still holds a charm for me.

Instead of calling Joseph, I call Harry. He answers sharply, on the second ring. To answer the phone in our home—and Bernard will be removing items from the lower cabinets, singing, banging with wooden spoons, twisting off tops and pouring out boxes of cereal and bags of rice—Harry has to vault up the stairs and into my room, where the phone is perched but where he is not allowed to penetrate. This takes a long while and many rings. As a result, he's taken to using his cell phone for making calls inside the house. When the land line rings this morning, however, he answers promptly. I only catch the hysterical last syllable, "'Lo?" and I sense he's removed the mobile head from its cradle and placed it somewhere conveniently in the kitchen. Probably on top of the refrigerator, where Bernie can't dismantle it. I hear sounds of pots clattering and my baby's singsongy voice.

"What are you doing?" I ask, an innocent question.

"What do you mean, what am I doing? I'm making dinner. It's dinnertime *here.*"

"What are you having?" I pursue, though I sense it's not a good idea.

He curses; there are squeaking sounds as the phone is passed to Bernie. Then great heaves of air ensue as my boy settles the receiver to his big head. He's a good baby, an affectionate, trusting darling, who is baffled by the absence of his mother and sister, though he accepts it with the fatal grace of a small child defenseless against the hard-shelled organization of the larger world.

"Momma, come home," he pleads.

I reassure him with a breaking heart. "I am, darling, don't worry. We're making our way home as soon as we can. We have things to do here in Paris," I tell him.

He describes the boo-boos he has suffered, friends he will play with, the menu for dinner. But the sudden, inexplicable proximity of my voice brings him back to the central ache of his life: we are gone and not with him. "Come home, Momma," he commands, and then begins to moan.

Harry takes over. "He misses you," he says sharply—an accusation.

"I know. We miss him unbearably."

"How is Cathy?" asks Harry.

"She's fine. She likes Paris," I reply, trying to sound upbeat. "She's sleeping now. It's two in the morning here," I add, more softly, glancing at my daughter's out-flung limbs as if taking flight next to me on the bed.

"How long are you going to keep this up?"

"I don't know, Harry. Have there been calls?"

"There are calls and no one there."

"You know I can't come back till this blows over."

"You should go and tell them—"

"They won't believe me!"

"Why not?" he demands, and after an echoey pause: "Why not?"

"I can't, Harry. It's too hot right now."

"Bring her back. She has no business being caught up in your affairs—"

"She's fine," I repeat. "This is a nice time together. We had always planned a trip to Paris together."

"Not like this!"

"Harry, just wait. Be good to Bernie."

"You're crazy."

"Be sweet to him. Reassure him. I'll call in a few days, okay?"

Harry hangs up. I ignore the clattering of the casements where the night air howls into the room, because I cannot move. I slide down next to my daughter and cradle her suspended form.

IT IS raining the morning we set out for the Rodin Museum in Montparnasse. We are not dressed properly for getting cold and wet, and I rush Cathy along the implausibly narrow sidewalks, dodging dog shit and speeding buglike vehicles and café chairs blocking our way. This is an area I knew once as a student, since I lived nearby, but I take no nostalgic pleasure in the day's prospects. Exasperated by my poking at her, Cathy runs ahead and twice disappears into the yawning entrance of an apartment building. I ignore her, and she reappears eventually. I curse the weather and the lateness of our arrival at the museum; we must wait unprotected in a long line and I am dancing in place and spitting with rage. I push Cathy under an awning and we watch each other warily.

There is a vast, pebbled courtyard at the front entrance and dripping gardens surrounding the house, which is encircled by high, thick walls. The museum occupies a grand old residence near the Invalides, chockfull of sculptural oddities and apocrypha, leaving little room to move around. It is a place I think Cathy will like to see and dutifully she brings along her notebook. She leaves me to argue with the *vestiaire*, who, illogically, won't take our wet coats on this wet day. I dump them on her counter and turn quickly away, inviting her to screech imprecations after me. Cathy parks herself on a marble bench in front of the strenuous human form of Jean-Baptiste emerging from his creamy constriction: "*La pensée de l'homme.*" She shakes out her wet hair and begins to draw.

I wander around the small rooms, hiking up my sodden pants, combing my straggly hair with my fingers. The room is airless and overfull, and I feel only annoyance at the other museum-goers: Why are there so many people here on a Thursday morning in mid-March? Whenever Cathy and I have been at each other, I feel out of sorts, strange to myself, ill at ease. I sense that I have been unduly harsh, but I am perplexed by her persistent intransigence. I can't concentrate on the beauty of Rodin's work for hearing still my exasperated goading of my daughter: "Blow your nose," I tell her, "take your fingers out of your mouth—stop pushing! And say, Excusez-moi." She eyes me from the bench she occupies and doesn't follow me.

In one room of glass cases displaying small plasters of ballerinas I have never seen before, I bend to read a description by a critic who has been greatly moved by Rodin's work. The phrase strikes me: *Je m'en roule.* It could mean something like "I am carried away," and I wonder that I never learned the phrase before, since it's exactly the expression I have frequently searched for. In my classes at the college where I teach Freshman Composition, I often try to impress upon my students the importance of learning new words, as they will suddenly recognize in the new word a thought they have always had and never knew how to express. *Shilly-shally* is another way of saying you don't know your own mind; *vertiginous* can be used to express the reader's feeling of losing one's sense of orientation while reading a particularly intriguing story in class. My students resist learning new words—what's wrong with the ones they already know? They use the word *thing* six times in a paragraph to describe concepts, notions, viewpoints, but they don't bother to find a more precise, specific synonym that expresses exactly what they want to say. Harry, my own husband, is overly fond of stock phrases, such as "in a time-honored fashion" and "it's all behind us now," by which he means that if his parents and teachers used these phrases, he needn't take the trouble to think up his own. I find his phrases unimaginative and laughable, especially when I hear the children mimic them: "That's neither here nor there," I've heard Bernie say, having no idea what it means but simply fond of the nonsense sound. But in this museum of stirring marmoreal silhouettes (shapes, to my mind, not unlike Joseph's), I have found just the right phrase for my feelings.

I am carried away. Rolling over myself, literally—and here I have to smile, imagining myself in a large hotel bed turning over to get at the slumbering achillean form lying next to me. It is morning: the room could be a bedroom in my grandmother's house in Cooperstown, with big red roses blasted across the chintz curtains and a white cotton-nubbed bedspread. Porcelain pitcher and wash basin set on the dresser top. My lover's arms are flung up and over his head, which is buried under a pillow, for it's too early for him to meet the day's light, too soon after late-night shenanigans to be disturbed in his precious sleep. The room reeks of beer from the glass knocked over on the bedside table by frenzied limbs. But I don't heed the hour, only my hunger to touch my bedfellow's slender, prostrate form. I cannot see his face; he doesn't turn and meet my burning gaze. His glance is shy and squinting upon waking in the early morning, his skin as ashen as his beard and thick, wild-ranging hair; his joints are creaky. Still I roll over him, my body warm, eagerly lubricious, my breath a desert wind in his ear. He doesn't move, though I know he's awake, and I whisper, "Am I too heavy on top of you?" since he is not a large man and I don't want to crush him. He murmurs no, a little groan. I roll and press and nuzzle, first with my head, bathing him with the strands of my hair, then with my mouth, my tongue. I cover him with little sucking kisses—I don't neglect his neck, creased from the sun, his armpits, where I swoon to meet his manly scent, the alluring furrows of his shoulders and back. His shapely, steel-hard climber's legs, and his feet, which are elegant and long. I return to nibble at his downy inner thighs, and engage at the center of him, his god-like buttocks, where I pause and hear myself now emitting short, breathless sighs that sound like pants. I am gasping as I part his buttocks and press my face there, between, to find his sweetest, softest place. I don't think he has moved.

Je m'en roule.

WE TAKE cover from the dripping gardens and duck into the café adjacent to the museum. I buy a few goodies for Cathy, who begs me—chocolate milk, a tuna baguette—even though I cart around our lunch box stuffed with items from the morning's breakfast table. I am stingy with our euros while Cathy, in contrast, is frivolous and greedy. She wants whatever she sees, surprise. When I do break down and buy her a candy or a sweet (an *extravagance*), she tends to carry it around in her hand, unwilling to consume it all and be finished with it until she accidentally drops the treat and has to throw it away anyway. With a sweet beverage, she won't actually drink, but insists on savoring it, until she spills it and watches it end up as waste. Are all children like this—savorers or gobblers? There are myriad delectable pastries displayed in the vitrines of any café, and for a moment I feel a pang of compunction—after all, I have brought my daughter to France to introduce her to the fine art of eating—but a quick check of our purse resolves me. Her eyes are bigger than her stomach, I decide—now where have I heard that phrase? I carefully order a *café crème*.

The café is mercifully quiet, mostly empty; the tables face a long bank of windows that overlook the wet, pearl-green gardens.

Cathy hops on the banquette at the sight of the chocolate milk carton I bring on a tray. She wags her head and pants with her tongue out, performing her antics from the school lunchroom. She reminds me of her ungainly pal Abner at such moments, and I growl at her to behave herself.

She stuffs her mouth with tuna and picks out the peppers with her fingers. Suddenly she points and says loudly, "That's the man we saw at the bar the other night."

I block her finger and look: indeed seated at a neighboring table is the well-dressed black man—the musician, the writer, the *rich man*—calmly reading a book. How very French, I note, as they read *books*, unlike Americans and their obsessive newspaper reading. And how curious to see the same person here. What are the chances of that? He does not look up or otherwise notice that Cathy has loudly pointed him out. He munches from a brioche, takes a sip from his coffee cup, rests his heavy forearms on the table. His raincoat is neatly folded on the banquette next to him; he wears a sweater and no tie. What is it about his studied casualness that tips me off? This Joseph-like training in nonchalance that sends a bristling chill down the back of my neck?

"It is the same man, isn't it."

"Who?" says Cathy, affected no doubt by my wary tone. Her voice is lower. "Who is it, Mother? Do you know him?"

We wait, and begin to talk quietly between us. The man doesn't look over at us and we lower our heads together and eat. I help Cathy compose postcards to Abner and to her second-grade teacher, Ms. Jeepers. The coffee is drunk, leaving a sweet ring of foam around the inside of the cup; I repack our lunch box. The rain has abated in a lead-white sky. I bundle Cathy first in her sweater, then her coat, but before I can stop her she is prancing near the man's table. I watch him look up, his open expression in a solid, middle-aged face, kindly, interested. He says something to her, not sternly, before glancing at me—is there a flash of dark suspicion there? Then he resumes reading in his book.

I wait until we are outside and well out of sight of the café before I chide her.

"What did he say?" I ask, knowing I won't get a straight answer unless I go step by step. I venture, more gently, "What did you say to him?"

"I asked what he was doing."

"What he was doing? Oh Cathy—in English?"

"He speaks English!"

"All right. What did he say?"

"He said he was digging for the truth."

I drag her along, jostled by the pedestrian traffic along the narrow sidewalks. My knees weaken and I feel myself short of breath.

"And then what, baby?"

"What's the matter? I asked him how you dig for the truth."

She waits, dancing along next to me. I see her smiling: a sneaky smile she tries to suppress. I resist the urge to slap her face. I have to stop and rest against the front of a boutique. It's started to rain again. I pull her anorak against me, so we are out of the way of traffic.

"And what did he say?"

"He said, 'I dig for the truth by asking lots of smart questions, just like you do.'"

"He did not."

"He did," she replies, and sighs at my cluelessness.

We are descending rue Vaneau, near métro Duroc. I stop abruptly at an imposing, elegant apartment house behind a high ironwork grille. My heart is racing and I feel little electric sparks at my ears. Through the iron gate can be seen a wide gravel driveway encircling a garden of resplendent daffodils. The first signs of spring: I must take a picture of Cathy next to them, if I haven't forgotten the camera. I shake the metal bars of the grille in both hands and yank at the door. But I remember that I'll need a key to get in.

"Look, Cathy—see those tiny rooms along the top of the building? Those are called *chambres de bonne*, the maids' quarters, and I lived in one of them, seven flights up, no elevator. I had a tiny room with a doll-sized kitchen, a single bed, and a bathtub, and there was a shared toilet down the hall. All the students lived like that—like artists."

Does she believe me? She grips the gate and sticks her face between the bars. "Were you an artist?" she asks, considering me with new interest.

"A college student."

She sighs, then seems to give up. "Well," she breathes, not really a question, and abruptly collapses on her rump right onto the wet pavement. Her attitude of utter resignation unknots the last vestige of stamina in me, and I slide my hands down the bars of the gate and fall next to her. The rain settles over us in a fine, cold mist.

"Well?" I echo, weakly.

"Now what?" she wonders.

"What?" I ask, stupidly.

"What do we do now?"

I have no clue what we should be doing. There's no dinner to prepare, or groceries to buy, for that matter; no kids to retrieve from practice, or bottoms to wipe. No papers to grade or books to review, laundry to stuff into the washing machine, or haul out with a breaking back; and not one dish to wash or remove from the dishwasher. I don't have to clean the house or cut the grass, although by now it must be as high as Joseph's skinny tibia. The thought of having nothing to do enlists a strangely disorienting but not unpleasant feeling of weightlessness.

"Why, I have no idea. Can't we just sit here for a while?"

We watch elderly Frenchmen walking small dogs on leashes. We observe the navigation of absurdly small cars driven by grown men and girls in skirts riding astride speeding mopeds with their hair streaming behind them. We note laborers in blue coveralls blustering over their midday glasses of calvados in the café across the street.

Cathy considers the sky. "Let's go to a movie," she suggests.

"A movie? Do you know how long it's been since I've—*hey*! That's an idea. Help me up, will you?"

Wet, not unhappy, we trot along, and do not consider again that we are being followed.

III

I am a naïf, the Beat poets might say. I come from the East Coast and wear straight black skirts that graze my knees, navy slingbacks and heavy-framed glasses when I teach at the college across the county. I don't wear jeans; I don't remember if I own a pair. I possess, with Harry, a house in the New York suburbs, modest but still worth more than when we bought it. I know something about literature but not poetry, not really, although when Joseph reads to me I respond—I feel my soul amplify. (*Soul* is not a word he uses, too Christian.) I am not acquainted with psychotropic drugs; I've never, for example, dropped acid. I am a little wary of savage, untamed nature: I don't know the names of many wildflowers and trees, but mostly stuff you can plant in your garden, and eat. The thought of encountering a bear or a bobcat while hiking astounds me. I have agreed, by getting married, to abide by certain conventions of my well-ordered society. I am sheltered by this society. Why did I marry? Because my parents are still married and it was expected of me. (*Not* to marry, indeed, would have been a kind of defeat in everyone's eyes.) Was I in love? I was: there are pictures, even if I can't find them anymore. I would never have acted in such a mercenary fashion to marry without love. So what changed? The light, the resiliency of my skin, my tolerance for close smells and cramped quarters in safe houses. An unexpected yearning for the homeland of the West, where I was conceived and lived the first four or five years of my life. And then I meet Joseph. I am not prepared to re-encounter the West, the rocky, outlaw, make-your-own-rules Wild West, except that I fall in love with this man and resolve to travel wherever he is. I have much to learn.

IT BEGINS at a wedding, of course. A wedding in Denver. I do not want to attend this wedding of an old college friend of mine and Harry's; I attend *under duress*. Douglas is an old beau, an oddball New Yorker I met my freshman year at Barnard, when he attended Columbia; he was a poet who went on, rather improbably, to law school. Everyone was going on to law school, after sampling the punk life as writers and artists and actors for a spell. We were a group riven by contradiction. Douglas once said to me, when we were dating—and this was after we had all graduated and were in our mid-twenties already, enjoying joyless upscale bar rendezvous and well-behaved parties with the same college scene-makers who were completing degrees in architecture or medicine or law—Doug says, "When people know you want something so badly they're not going to let you have it." I ponder this bit of cautionary advice. We sit in a midtown bar and wait for his friends to arrive. He always had more interesting friends than I did. I wear an expertly tailored navy jacket borrowed from a girlfriend and at my wrists a smear of odiferous perfume offered in samples from the glossy pages of the magazine where I work as a copy editor. My job is pretty cool, but I'm not sure what I'm doing in my life, and perhaps I have hinted too coarsely about wanting a steady relationship. Douglas refers no doubt to my directness of manner, which tends to put people off. I must learn that a certain obliqueness is more effective in gaining what one wants, especially for women. Douglas is right, but I don't think I will ever forgive him for teaching me this life's lesson.

His father is a psychiatrist and Douglas fancies himself a brilliant psychological mind. He gleans that I want to get married—maybe I do, but not to him. For women, I think, getting married has more to do with not getting left behind than the actual getting married part: no one wants to be the last one chosen for the basketball team. I like Douglas okay, but he is critical in a lawyerly fashion and possesses fastidious, elderly habits, such as the injunction against touching his face. I like Doug's best friend better, who is a quiet, bespectacled, soft-spoken engineer with a lovely phone voice. He calls at the magazine where I work and impresses my girlfriends with his gentlemanly phone manner. A repressed man, but not unattractive, Harry is on the rebound, and we end up together on a sad and empty Christmas Eve when there is no one left in the city but other sad and lonely types. We don't mind; we commiserate. Douglas is skiing with his family, out in the cold. Eventually he moves to Denver with another woman, an architect (not the woman he will marry), and there he practices law and also starts a poetry review.

Eventually I marry Harry because he has a lovely phone voice and is shy and wears thick glasses like coke bottles.

Because I don't want to attend Douglas's wedding in Denver, I insist on bringing our children, the two of them, Cathy and Bernard, five and nearly two, respectively. No one else carts their kids along, not our glamorous New York friends, Gloria and Markus and Nikki and Samuel—the men, a banker and architect; their wives designers. They leave their kids at home with costly babysitters in order to fly-fish in the Rocky Mountains for this auspicious September weekend. And to be alone together as couples. But we haul our kids to torment us. We bring them because we claim we don't have the money for a weekend babysitter, but mostly because Harry and I don't want to be alone together in a hotel room. They do a good job of tormenting us: at the hotel swimming pool, in restaurants, in the rented car hopping around without seatbelts, and so on. At the rehearsal dinner the night before the wedding, Bernard climbs into my lap where I am seated at Douglas's table of honor and the child fusses and fumes in full view of all the guests before he falls crashingly to sleep. Cathy is a gadfly, flitting from table to table, while Douglas watches her, charmed. He has his eye on my little sprite, and this is part of his oddballness, I decide. I miss the actual ceremony in the country club because Douglas's mother, Lucille, casts me a bristling look when Bernie begins to act up and I have no choice but to take him out. Lucille adores Harry because after a boisterous college party he and Douglas threw at Lucille's apartment on the Upper West Side, Harry offered to repaint the soiled walls, and he did. Lucille will retell this story about my husband to whomever will listen. I wander with Bernie through the empty clubrooms.

I resist attending Douglas's wedding because college was already a long time ago and I've put away the old crowd. I haven't bought anything new to wear but dig out a long, sparkly silver dress that I wore to a Christmas party when pregnant with Bernie; I tie it in the back. Nikki wears a black little spaghetti-strapped dress—she has ready for the evening a closetful of slinky black numbers—striking against her platinum head, while Gloria displays her Roman medallion across her bony chest. She's a sexless general of a person with a raspy voice and forbidding Connecticut ancestry. My friends have prosperous husbands and live in the city; their children attend private schools. We drink a lot of wine and we gossip. Harry runs after Bernie and I keep Cathy from breaking dishes and dropping forks. Since Douglas (or is it Lucille?) has not made room for the children at our table, I place Cathy at a flimsy side table to eat her dinner, but she presses into it with her elbows and the dishes go flying anyway. Everyone dances except for me and the poet Joseph Pasternak, who has appeared at my table, crouching at my feet.

He wears a small gold ring in each earlobe like a pirate. His hair is thick, wavy, and graying; his expression intelligent and attentive. He is lean, fit; not an old man, but not young, either, and exudes a manly vitality—the salt-and-pepper beard, the blood in the cheeks, the earrings—and is clad in jeans and a sports jacket. He is in conversation with my table mate, a publisher from upstate New York. As he crouches on his heels, we are introduced—he mentions his name several times as if unsure I will remember it—Joseph. They speak about Mexican villages I have never visited. In fact, I've never been to Mexico, but only to Europe, a cultural blindsidedness that I am ashamed to admit and that I will eagerly want to correct once I know Joseph. I observe this man with interest: I recall noticing him at the rehearsal dinner the night before, next to his companion, Arlene Manhunter, whom I learn is a famous poet; Joseph is erect and regal, moving through our chatty college cluster with a little bemused, if somewhat superior smile, on his way to more edifying conversation. A man cultivated in the arts of Aphrodite. He and his crowd of poets are older than our suit-and-tie group of former Columbia cronies, and as if to underscore our differences (in ages, length of hair, style of clothing), Douglas has seated us on opposite sides of the reception room. I have been placed among the money people, apparently. The publisher, sensing an upset, gets up to leave the table. Joseph remains, having penetrated enemy territory; he remains kneeling and I thrust out my hand.

"Frances," I say, and for some reason the sound of this word makes us laugh.

The other guests dance. We talk at length, I don't remember about what, strangely. Joseph stares at my bare feet in sandals. Bernie wanders around, tugging at my arm; Harry taps at his wristwatch in annoyance. But Joseph attends only to me, and eventually the others give up and distract themselves elsewhere.

When we part from the Cruise Room in downtown Denver, where the wedding party mingles over last drinks, his companion who is not his wife, Arlene, takes his hand as I stand before them to say good-bye. She is more handsome than her pictures convey, wearing a riot of native jewelry and iridescent silks the color of exotic fishes. She holds his hand in a tenderly protective gesture, I see it now, though I ignore the warning. I will pursue Joseph until he becomes my lover.

SOME WEEKS later I receive from him a book of love poems that are his own translations from the Sanskrit. He inscribes the slender volume both to me and to Harry. Joseph has mentioned at the wedding that he teaches Sanskrit and poetry at a small arts institute in Boulder, though I get the name wrong when I look for it later on the Internet—that's how little I understand about the rarefied life of the mind that Joseph leads. The Diamond-cutter Institute of Unformed Conceptions is the singularly formal name, after the Diamond Sutra, I assume, revered in Buddhism, or a reference in Jack Kerouac's *Dharma Bums*. The school, I read, is a stronghold of the "outrider" tradition in American poetry, a Platonic *akademi* or oak grove where peripatetic philosophers and rhapsodists gather, swap ideas and songs, and test out theories.

A kind of *vihara*, or "house of the muses," such as the ones that sprang up in North India between the fifth and eleventh centuries, I learn, part monastery, part college, part convention hall or alchemist's lab where contemplatives, wizards, hermits, and yogins congregated. Joseph descends from these ancient troubadours and scholars. He is an impoverished nomadic seeker; I have never met anyone like him.

I read the translations and I am stunned: they are ephemeral confections of the rarest beauty couched in simple, sensuous language. They describe petals of roses scattered in the folds of bedsheets after lovemaking; a single wisp of hair stroked beneath the naval like a line of poetry; the tell-tale love scratch on the thigh, exposed as the wind whips at the girl's thin skirt. The ancient poems strike me as so fresh and erotically charged that my eyes blur with tears after reading a few of them and I let the book fall open in my lap. The sensations they evoke reach me from a very long distance—from beneath the accumulated strata of innumerable geological time periods. Have I ever experienced such passion as these poems describe? I fall across my bed, which is now my possession and no longer Harry's, as he sleeps on the sofa downstairs. I learn from the back cover that the book of translations has won for Joseph a major translation award. I read in his biography that he was educated in Berkeley, worked as a baker, truck driver, warehouser, and bookseller. A man of the people. I study Joseph's picture and try to match it with the man I met at the wedding: he stands serious and unsmiling against a tree whose gnarled bark holds the similar black-white striations as his beard. The shot is credited to Arlene Manhunter.

I ache and I weep; I throw myself across the bed. I slip my hand inside the waistband of my pants and touch myself to climax. And then I write to Joseph, setting him straight on the shared inscription to the volume he has sent: "My husband and I have grown estranged. A man who will not claim his wife sexually does not value her, and deserves to lose her, it seems to me. Harry is a decent man, a devoted father, but I have grown cold and unfeeling next to him and sometimes I don't recognize myself."

But I'm not dead, it seems. I'm going to live. In a few weeks I make my first trek to visit Joseph Pasternak.

I T IS freezing in Boulder. An icy wind slices through the town huddled at the base of the snow-capped peaks. I can't see the mountains well at night, I'm partly night-blind, but I sense the violet brooding power of them just outside the window of my hotel. I bathe, I pace nervously. Joseph has written that he will pick me up in his Subaru at my hotel, which stands next to the Diamond-cutter campus. He has suggested this hotel because I write that I need only a "modest" place to stay. And I don't want him to think of me as bourgeois—a suburban housewife, after all. Then he appears, tall in boots and jeans and a black leather jacket, handsome in his ruddy, vital way and surefooted as a goat on the ice as we dash through parking lots. Joseph is slim and agile and has the build of a swimmer—a climber, he corrects me. He tells me to take his arm so that I won't fall in my city boots. I ask him: did he really memorize my address from the night in the Cruise Room? He nods gravely. At a bar he orders a Scotch and I ask the waitress to recite the list of beers in order to give me a moment to think: I pour it, slanting the glass in a manner I think expert. I feel Joseph watching my hands with the same serious attention as he stared at my bare feet in sandals at the wedding reception.

"You're so pretty," he says, as if he has never encountered a pretty woman before, and I have to laugh. There are plenty, don't I know, at the University of Colorado and all over this Western town there are pretty girls. But he is quite serious, considering me: what kind of woman would sacrifice herself as I am doing? My left hand rests lightly on the table and Joseph lifts it and kisses the place where my gold band would be. I have taken off my ring and left it in the hotel room. The skin underneath is pale pink and moist; I watch the puckering of his lips and wish the skin of my entire body were as unscathed as the skin of my ring finger. I have never actually *not* worn my wedding ring, but something has been decided by my coming all the way across the country to meet a man I hardly know, and the thought of the ring being stolen by a maid at my hotel does not occur to me.

We have driven to a restaurant located in a mall. One must drive vast distances to arrive in the West. Coming from New York, I am unused to the car-mad sprawl of the place. We order a bottle of wine; that is, Joseph orders the wine. I wonder about this capitulation with the wine list, as I have taught myself a goodly bit about wine because I like to drink it and under usual circumstances I always buy my own. But no doubt I allow Joseph to choose because he is older than I am, and as a good girl I defer to the man in these matters. (Driving as well, but we will get to that.) Ever since this night he has chosen our wine, and he is also the one who cooks for us, puzzlingly perhaps; but he is a stylish cook, adding olive oil and a pinch of hot pepper to an omelet mixture in a manner I would not do. I'm an expedient cook, and habitually resentful about it: I scramble up eggs and throw them on the table and my kids hum over their plates happily.

This night we are watching each other over the simple, delightful ritual of dining. We are a little nervous, gauging the other, wondering each of us whether my coming all this way has been a sound judgment. A whim, yes, but is she crazy? Joseph quickly suggests we share a chèvre walnut salad, and I agree, flushing with embarrassment. The place is rather posh, with close-set tables of diners in pairs: is he so poor, a poet who writes to me exquisite letters but works as a teacher for a pittance? And if so, should we have ordered a bottle of wine? I don't know what to think. But he's moved on, propounding on some of the works he teaches in his Asian literature classes, such as Sei Shōnagon's *Pillow Book*. I grapple for my notebook and write it down. He is a teacher possessed of a polished delivery, convincing and wonderfully articulate. I give him my Lady Murasaki smile while trying not to spill my wine. I watch how he holds his wineglass, lightly by two fingers around the stem; in contrast, I cradle mine at the belly of the glass, as if warming a cognac. I know this is wrong: it's silly to hold a wineglass in this fashion because you don't want to warm the liquid; it is ignorant and pretentious the way people will say "between you and I," convinced it sounds more educated. I think of how my husky, deliberative husband would hold his wineglass, pinky extended from his thick fingers with exaggerated affectation, when guests come to dinner. I put down the glass helplessly. The place empties out and we are the last to pay our bill.

I have never been so cold as I have been in Boulder, at night, with Joseph. I am a thin person, and the high-altitude shock is eviscerating. I cannot get warm in Joseph's car; he doesn't bother with the heat because he doesn't feel the temperature. He is at home in this rarefied air. I will learn that he hikes up mountains in Irish walking shoes (not boots) and writes what he calls tundra poetics. Yet when he kisses me this first night, leaning in from the driver's seat, he is trembling. Despite the blast of dry ice, I sense he is trembling because the experience of being out on a date with a woman is new and deeply troubling. Am I wrong? Have I even asked about Arlene Manhunter? I have not. Later I will wonder in my notebook.

Nimbly he moves around my hotel room, opening the bottle of New York state wine I have brought with a corkscrew he keeps always in his rucksack for camping. The wine is called Black Dirt Red, made in a small winery across the Hudson River. "Foxy" is how the clerk in the wine store described it, as I shyly lowered my gaze—not a bottle Joseph would likely find in stores in Boulder. Joseph is pleased by my original gift. He lights small votive candles that have appeared from the mysterious rucksack and places them on the nightstand between the two double beds. We sit, smiling crazily, perched at the edge of one of the beds. Then we kiss and slowly undress each other. We have known since the beginning of the evening—since our first letter exchanged—that we would be alone together in my hotel room, making love. I take his earrings in my mouth, first one earlobe, then the other, just as I have written that I aim to do. He shudders. And when he comes inside of me, suddenly, precipitously, he does not ask if I am protected. I am not protected. "But you can't," I say, tears squeezing out of my eyes and down into my ears. I imagine the consequences of this night: having already two children and then another by a man I've only met twice! Will I ever see him again? He is abashed, deeply pained. I hold his slender form as he collapses into me. Then I understand. Who has not loved this man? Dearly, I want to.

I awake in a dark, stifling room. I have turned up the heat before sleeping and now I kick off the blankets, craving air and water. What time is it—still night? I grope for Joseph next to me in the bed. But he is not there. A gust of sharp, cold air rakes my skin and I turn toward its source: the emergency exit door to the room has been thrown open and there is Joseph, my lover, standing in the threshold, wearing only his underwear, which is thick-cut, boys' underwear much like the kind my little son wears. Joseph stands nobly in the threshold, illuminated by the moon off the mountains, his head thrown back as he gulps the cold night air. His head and beard are shaggy, his limbs long and supplely proportioned, his skin tawny and unbearably smooth in places I am only beginning to know. He doesn't see that I watch him. I blink and rub at my eyes; I try to sit up but feel too weak from thirst and my arms have lost their resiliency. I am never sure again whether I did see him standing there (beast or god?), or whether the vision besieged me in fever. Later he sleeps. I reach for my notebook.

ONCE, ON my journey from the Denver airport into Boulder at night, I share a cab with a woman who reveals to me her plans about her new life in the West. She is coming from California with small children after her divorce. She speaks about alternative schools she has found, healing strategies, networks of displaced, bipolar parents (does she mean antipodean or merely nuts?), most fleeing "broken" marriages (a word Joseph doesn't like to use, as it stigmatizes divorced parents like himself) or other dubious, ill-begotten earlier lives—drugs? jail? Escaping bad karma. There is an intensity about this woman, a kind of ferocious gleam to her eyes that I cannot forget. A haunted look that bespeaks of coastal grief and soured dreams. She is venomously hard knocked. The West will suit her. I tell Joseph about the woman who shares my cab: is she recounting to me a cautionary tale? Joseph nods sagely, replies quietly: "All Jan's friends have divorced parents."

But the parents of Cathy's friends are not divorced. People stay together around here for the sake of the children. People shove their grief under the Iranian carpets and put on a brave face for Back to School night. We carry on. Which way am I going? I bathe, pack, and kiss my babies good-bye on the living room floor where they are engrossed in the construction of Legos. I write down the number of the hotel where I will be staying in Boulder and place it under a magnet on the refrigerator. And for weekends over many seasons I fly to join him.

AFTER OUR first tender nights at the Boulder Quality Inn next door to the Institute, he takes me back to his house—technically Arlene's house—for breakfast. It's Sunday, dazzlingly sunny and starting to snow, and Arlene is traveling for the month of December, giving lectures on new poetic paradigms and teaching chant seminars around the world. Like Joseph, she teaches at the Diamondcutter Institute; in fact, she co-founded it. Her work is selfless and creates universally good karma. I remember her from the wedding (indeed, how can you forget ever meeting Arlene Manhunter?): a heavy-moving mature lady adorned in colorful native silks and much jewelry that enchanted my small son; a beautiful face in which the large, dark, piercing eyes form the riveting centerpiece, framed by long raven tresses. She reads from her poetry at the reception, but I only catch her briefly before I have to take Bernie out. In a room in which she is present you are always aware of where she is. Here, in her house, in a low-lying bungalow on the outskirts of Boulder, she is perhaps hiding behind the Japanese screen we unfurl over the broad front window.

Joseph concocts his omelet with olive oil and red peppers, and toasts oatmeal bread to serve plain, no butter, only jam, as if we are in the war. I sample damson plum jam at his table for the first time. We listen to jazz—fifties bebop. He manages to make coffee for me, though he has no coffee machine; he is a tea drinker. I sit on his lap. Out the broad front window we watch the snow settle softly over the level neighborhood of one-story bungalows, covering, too, Arlene's twilight-blue sedan parked at the curb. It must give him the chills, watching that car with me in the house. I have learned that despite their happy arrangement of mutually agreeable artistic pursuits, this stellar convergence of karmic fortuities, all is not well at home, and Joseph is as lonely in his partnership as I am in my marriage. We knew this at first glance at the wedding.

But we don't discuss her. We talk about another woman in his life. He has mentioned his ex-wife, indiscreetly, and we are talking about that one, something new lovers should never do.

"Why does she hate you so much?" I ask, in my rather direct fashion. For I have heard about Belinda, the mother of their teenaged daughter, and her troublesome force in all of their lives. She is from California and has not had a lasting relationship since Joseph left her for another woman—Arlene—ten years before. Belinda does not speak to Joseph, and though they work in the same building, she as an administrator at Diamondcutter, he as a teacher of Sanskrit and poetry, she covers her eyes when he happens to walk by, in the manner of a Sephardic man who blocks from view an attractive Gentile woman strolling the streets of Greenpoint, Brooklyn. The former couple shares custody of their daughter (it's written in the divorce contract) and communicate only by e-mail.

What I really want to ask is, How could you work in the same building as your venomous ex-wife? But I'm learning to respect the incestuous nature of these outrider types.

"We could never have stayed together," Joseph states flatly, in the sad, defeated manner with which he speaks about his past lives. "Jan even said once—long after the divorce—that she was glad we didn't live together because of the fights we used to have." Belinda is a jealous woman, and the move they make from Berkeley to Boulder (magical names!), where Joseph can finally pursue his poetry and become published, only stokes her rage. Jan is three, and Joseph, his mangy seventies' beard newly trimmed and just showing a touch of gray (he shows me pictures of his transformation from this time—truly irresistible!), can sense the exciting beginning to his career. What won't he do to ascend among the exalted circle of Olympian poets? Belinda drinks, provokes scenes, accuses him of not loving her, threatens to have an affair with someone who will appreciate her. Her instincts are dead-on, absolutely, as Joseph has grown estranged from her and is pursuing someone else. Belinda hurls a wineglass at him across the dance floor at his brother's wedding. Joseph has to admit that when she behaves in this appalling manner he does not love her. Then he leaves her for the Queen Bee herself, Arlene Manhunter. I've learned too much already and don't ask about this part of the story.

"But why," I persist, unwisely, "would a woman who loved you so much once—you, the father of her only child—hate you so bitterly now?"

It is incomprehensible, really; he shakes his head sadly.

"You wouldn't," I wonder in a careless tone, moving off his lap, "still be sleeping with her?" For the gyrations of this passionate, murderous woman sound familiar to me, and I can imagine her as a heroine in one of the novels I read.

I am teasing, but there is a soupçon of truth in my accusation, as my feminine instincts are also very good.

Joseph stands at the counter, wearing plastic gloves to rinse each glistening leaf of organic spinach. He looks up sharply. He will serve a spinach salad with a selection of aromatic cheeses he keeps in his refrigerator. He is nobly thoughtful; he waits always two beats before he speaks, as the gentle sage he is. He pierces me with a long, steely look I take to mean I am digging where it is none of my business.

"Sorry," I say, backing down. I look away. I watch the drifting snow through the front window and wonder if my plane will possibly be cancelled and we can make love in his bed under the topographical maps of Colorado. I have promised not to pry into his sacred inner places—I have written this to him.

IV

We leave Cathy's book in the room when we check out of the hotel near Boulevard Beaumarchais. It is C. S. Lewis's *The Lion, the Witch and the Wardrobe* and we have only gotten to the part when the four siblings finally believe the youngest sister Lucy's claims that there is a world behind the wardrobe and they have emerged from it for the first time together. I complain to the English concierge, who wears large glasses and speaks English and French with equal chirpy fluency, despite the fact that we are checking out a week earlier than stated on my reservation. Cathy loves the book and is crushed that we can't find it. She sits glumly in the hotel café, disemboweling a croissant and smearing each clump with gobs of jam. I don't bother to restrain her. The concierge is mystified.

"I'm sure the cleaners will find the book this morning," she assures me. "Is there something wrong with the room? It's a larger room than you had reserved in the first place—"

"The room is fine," I tell her. "We simply must go."

"I see. *C'est ça*," she sings, handing me the bill to sign. "Will you be needing transportation to the airport?" She is careful to enunciate every word.

"No, thank you."

"We hope you think of us again when you are visiting Paris."

"Oh, we're not leaving Paris," I say, then add quickly, "that is, metaphorically."

"I see." Her glasses flash. "*C'est ça.*"

I beckon to Cathy, who is sticky up to her elbows and down the front of her "2" sweater. I take her downstairs to the toilet and wash her off, vigorously. She glares at me in the mirror, moaning, and won't stop asking questions: "Where are we going now? What are we going to do? Why can't we stay in this hotel?" I shush her and hurry her out and up to the boulevard, dragging our bags. I study the métro map for a while. The day is gray and raw, another inhospitable start. We detest these dark moods in each other; we mirror each other's bad humor and end up not being able to tolerate the sight or proximity of the other. Yes, that is being a mother and daughter. Cathy will needle me until I slap her, and I nag at her until she resists by whining or doing a disappearing trick. Now she senses that I'm on the edge and unsure of what to do next. I trace the underground journey to the Luxembourg, aware of the curious glances from men who sit leisurely in an open café. It is Monday or Tuesday; we are laden with baggage and I've only got a few euros left. I consider stepping into the café and ordering a *pichet* of wine, even if it's well before lunchtime, but Cathy tugs at my arm. Wouldn't you know, it starts to rain.

"Can't we take a taxi?" Cathy whines.

"I have to find a bank."

"Where are we going?" she demands again.

"Ask me again and I'll tell you the same."

We take a near-empty train to the Luxembourg, always a safe bet in my book. I pull Cathy along, though she complains incessantly of the cumbersome rolling bag she is in charge of. Her teddy bear, Mike, named after a cherished cousin, is stuffed into the side pocket of her bag and dragging his head along the pavement as if in deep shame and lamentation. We must stop every few paces to readjust him. He is filthy and bedraggled, his limbs hanging by strings of loose fabric. I am scanning the storefronts, heading aimlessly. Along the rue Vavin there are glamorous shoe stores, still shuttered. Ahead of me on the narrow sidewalk, a well-dressed man, perhaps in his fifties, with a graying, neatly trimmed beard, wild hair, and sharp eyes, pulls a much-younger woman to him and she kisses him hard on the mouth. She is laughing, looking a little frightened and bold, and he is roguish and daring. The scene rivets me: as I step around their comic love drama I can't take my eyes off them. Who is he? I wonder. A professor flirting with his young student? A married man who has seduced a neighbor living in his apartment building? Finding them together at this early hour suggests intimacy. Certainly she'll sleep with him for his wisdom and experience, while he will yearn immodestly for her fulsome, impressionable gazes. She'll do anything for him, and he will ask. I can't stop staring at them, but they don't interrupt their naughty prankishness; I turn back continually to keep them in sight, hoping to learn more about them. Cathy marshals blindly ahead, dragging Mike along the sidewalk.

Finally I come to a hotel on Montparnasse that suits me. I remember the hotel from when I stayed in Paris as a student. It delivers breakfast on trays to your door, I tell Cathy, and pots and pots of jam. She sighs and sinks into a threadbare armchair in the lobby. The hotel, like many things in Paris, has seen grander days. I hand over my credit card and we are ushered to a small room with two single beds and a tiny bathroom with a bidet, which sends Cathy into raptures. I pull open the tall windows and let in the din of the breakneck traffic on the boulevard below. It will be too loud for me to sleep. I don't examine the sheets.

"We'll wash Mike," I tell her. "We'll buy shoes. We'll find another book for you to read."

"In English?" she insists.

"Yes, all right."

I can't stop thinking about the smooching professor and his girl. His foxy, ardent gaze, her willing, wide-eyed acquiescence. Why does the sight of them so rattle me? I contemplate lying down on one of the beds, but I know if I sit now I won't get up. I'll have to let Cathy watch French TV all afternoon. I'll order wine from the proprietress or even, desperately, send Cathy downstairs for some.

"Let's go have lunch, okay?"

"Already?"

"Sweetheart . . ."

"What's the matter?"

"I miss . . . I miss . . ."

"Look at this, Momma," she exclaims, fiddling with the bidet gears, "if we have to get up in the middle of the night we can *pee* in this and see how it flushes—"

"No, listen. I miss . . . the smell of your room, remember? It smells like chamomile shampoo and green-apple soap, glue and markers and construction paper, stuffed animals hauled around and squashed against your sweaty skin, all those plastic book covers handled by sticky, jammy fingers, clothes washed, stained, and washed again, dust and asphalt from the playground, and neglected flowers you would pick for me . . ."

She stands and stares at me, her hands on her hips. Then she frowns.

"Oh I miss him, too, Momma," she says, and flies into my arms.

SHE IS asleep. I sneak out and sit in the café I have noted from our windows across the boulevard. I have plotted this maneuver over several nights, and only now have summoned the courage to leave the room, deserting my daughter, who sleeps defenselessly and alone. I have imagined every scenario in her waking up and not finding me: I have even written a note in bold non-cursive letters and left it on the bed so that she'll cast her eyes immediately over it and be able to decipher my message before panicking at my absence. She claims she can't read my handwriting; she's a bright kid and will surely recognize the important words: *café*, *minutes, stay, please, love, Momma*. I can't sleep. I must have been dreaming of bears, as I was reading Isabella Bird's *Adventures in the Rocky Mountains* before bed and wake up trembling as if I've just encountered a grizzly during the ride to Lake Tahoe, as Bird and her horse did in 1873. She writes that the horse ran in one direction, the bear in the other, and she had to walk for miles, dragging the saddle blanket and bag, before catching the horse. Later, in Cheyenne, a local horse trader will tell this intrepid Victorian lady trekking through the wilderness alone: "There's nothing Western folk admire so much as pluck in a woman." Pluck aside, I'm antsy and restless, and if I'd possessed a pistol I'd have strapped it on. My anxiety overrules any sense of guilt.

The café is a bit shabby and not terrifically heated, but it's open. The serveur, macabre in a long stained bib apron like a butcher, brings me some wine, and no one bothers any more with me. I've brought my notebook and feel impelled to write a list: to organize imparts control, and in a recent novel I've read the protagonist embarks on a "break-up list" as a form of healing from her ruptured romance. This is what fourteen-year-olds do. Still, it's a direct activity that requires concentration, such as a crossword puzzle, which I don't have handy. So I delve into my own break-up list, glancing up from time to time at the darkened windows of our room across the boulevard, three flights up.

It occurs to me I should write in French. But Joseph never learned French. Just as well, I think, to write in a mixture of both French and English (*franglais*) and give the waiter—who doesn't come by anyway—something to puzzle over:

Qualités facheuses in the Man Who Got Away:

Perfidieux and Turncoat (a Patriot no less!)
Tends to dissemble when trapped (*comme un renard*)
Likes football (*comme le mari*) *mais ne joue pas au sport*
    (never saw him *run*, curiously)
Trop maigre—skinny! prominent tibia, neck, not a manly
    quality—men should possess *du boeuf* (*comme le mari!*)
Un pauvre poète (also goes in the plus column), truly
    penniless so that *J'avais souvent payé le conte*—not a
    manly quality
Never wears anything but jeans (denotes insecurity)
L'opportuniste—a climber, no less
Picks his nose, has gray hair—is not *un jeune amant*—ages me
Sleeps in his undies—never nude! Afraid of being *piqué*
Wino—drinks a lot
Ne parle pas français, ni espanol, ni chinois, ni . . . OK, knows
    Sanskrit
Replaces the women in his life as effortlessly as changing
    espèce de fromages
Lacks endurance—in the love bed! OK, he could lick me on
    the slopes, etc.

I am tempted to make a pro list, in juxtaposition, and contrast the items one by one, maybe even ascribing each a number value, thus neutralizing each as I go in order to ascertain, in the end, whether I have more pros than cons, and thus feel especially vindicated when all is said and done. But I feel confident, after perusing my anti-list, that I have destroyed the man I adore and don't need to second-guess myself or rehabilitate him. I feel better after three wines. Men enter the bistro, smoke, drink, and leave, and no one has spied me out. I congratulate myself. I watch the hotel windows across the street for a light and none turns on. Elated, smiling, I pay my bill and meander back across the slick pavement—crossing carefully—as if I have gotten away with a great crime. What I recall of my list in days to come is that I write in the present tense.

UPON RETURNING I don't dream about Joseph, but about Arlene:

I see her coming at me from across the room. Charging across the reception room, her walk heavy, unevenly weighted. She wears a sea-green iridescent pantsuit and metallic tangles of exotic jewelry. Her glossy raven tresses are blown about her face. She tosses them back with a quick, impatient gesture. The guests are spilling out through the wide double doors to the antechamber—toward cars and last embraces. The party and dancing are over. Joseph and I stand alone, somewhat startled by the room's desertion. We watch her coming, rooted to the spot, as if a great anchor is keeping us from moving elsewhere. I turn to him: "Is that. . . ?" I ask. He nods with a small, assured smile. "It is she." I greet her warmly. I am a wife and a guest at this wedding and she has seen me with my children. What am I to make of this couple? A man who chats up a strange woman the whole evening while his companion who is not his wife works another part of the room. Is this the way they usually operate, the two of them? Does he think she won't notice, a public figure monopolized as she is by other people's attention? Or does he want to make sure she does notice, then present me as his prize? He has caught me in his gaze; I receive the ardent beam of his attention. He stares at my mouth, my feet, my hands as if he wants to devour them in kisses, and listens to my speech like music. He is practiced in the ancient arts of seduction, a very good cocksman, as they used to say. I love this attention; I have missed it over a decade of married life! A decade spent smashing dishes in my kitchen. But now his attention is mine and not hers; his adoring gaze is trained on me. Later she takes his hand at the after-hours bar and we bid good-bye: "Good luck," she says in her crisp, direct fashion, as if sending me off, free of me. *Pretty girl*, she beams at me, with scornful, deadly psychic rays. What are you but a pretty girl, and next to me? She holds his hand but knows already that she's lost him. Don't you think a woman knows when a man loves her? And when he does not.

I KNOW when Arlene will call me because of the hang-up calls that come first: the air grows static as if before a lightning storm and I roam through the house, cross and restless. I am already shaking before I answer the phone on an early morning when I have to run out to teach at the college across the county. I hesitate to pick up the receiver. But on the last ring I snatch up the phone, hoping it is Joseph. "Is that Frances?" comes a voice bold and thick and surprisingly youthful. "This is Arlene Manhunter." She sighs thunderously.

I've expected her. "Arlene," I say, caught pulling up my stockings, helpless now, since there's no way to move around the force of this lady. I say her name, testing its power.

"I've known about you for more than two years," she says.

"But I only met Joseph a year and a half ago," I correct her.

"I mean, metaphorically."

First mistake: she has supernatural powers. Second, she's a poet. Metaphorically, she means—how stupid of me. She harnesses the eternal fluctuating feminine energy from ancient goddesses and unleashes it in her poetry. She chants, she wails, she constructs long categories of dizzying repetition: I am a thorn, I am a tear, I am a stag. Her poetry performances are famous: her *cri de coeur*, Everywoman's cry. They enact age-honored rites of sacrifice for the propitiation of the gods. I wouldn't be surprised if she's a witch, a sorceress, a sticker of voodoo dolls, and I bet she's got one of me. She reads her tarot cards regularly with her lesbian friends and would have long ago seen the Queen of Cups hovering tenaciously over her lover. If she knew about me—sensed Joseph's emotional absence, the cooling of his passion, his *blankness*—why wasn't she more prepared when Joseph finally revealed that I exist?

"Who was the aggressor?" she asks pointblank. "I have to wonder what kind of person you are."

All's fair in love and war, lady, I think, but don't say. Instead I manage to be polite: "Arlene, it's our essential loneliness that brought us together."

"Speak for yourself."

"And we began to write each other letters."

"I once tried to maintain a long-distance relationship," she reflects, letting down her guard for a moment. She draws me in with her folksy tangents. "Over two continents. We wrote letters."

Which famous poet was that? I wonder. "Well, Arlene, what happened?"

"It can't work out, you know," she resumes, not hearing me. "He tells me it's all a terrible mistake." She regains her murderous momentum. She means that I am the mistake. "He tells me he's not in love with you anymore."

She says "he's not in love with you," rather than "he doesn't love you," which is a rather romantic distinction, I think, and winning in my book.

"Well, when you twist his arm . . ."

"I do not!"

This formidable teacher of writing, one of the founders of the Diamondcutter Institute, an original subterranean: she still sounds like a cool cat from the sixties. When she performs her poem at Douglas's wedding, a pastiche about marriage which is a kooky incantation that makes the assembled married couples titter and glance sideways at each other, she stabs the air, "Wedlock, wedlock, wedlock!" bending from the waist, and speaks fast and forcefully. She chants, she cries out like a possessed person, and she is marvelously convincing. When I shake her hand, I am surprised she is not taller. Her husky voice, the trunkload of native jewelry she dons like a vaudeville performer, her satin, slimming pantsuit, her long black snake coils, and deep vibrant eyes with the dramatic bags underneath as if the skin has been painfully scored: I find her sexy in a big-momma, bosomy way. But Arlene does not inspire a maternal kind of solace, but rather terror. I think she was already trying to hex me at the rehearsal dinner, where I sat in the festive Provençal room at a long table with a baby thrashing in my lap; she threw me a hypnotic stare and I had to look away. I hadn't even met Joseph yet, who must have been seated beside her, inclined pleasantly toward his neighbor in his gallant fashion, hands folded in his lap, to regale with the tale of the vituperative Mooks and Gripes from *Finnegans Wake*.

"I have one question," she asserts over the phone, after long, breathy pauses that are strangely reassuring for me to hear. In fact, now that I have her on the phone I don't want her to ring off. There are sharp exchanges between us, then quiet, and I listen hard to what she needs to know. Have we slept in her bed? Have I been to her house? She doesn't ask.

"I have to know one thing," she says. "Did he take you to visit our land?"

I feel suddenly terribly weary and sit down at the edge of the bed. I let my half-stockinged leg hang down. I can't remember which land she's talking about. I detect exasperation in her voice because I am not catching on fast enough. How early must it be in Boulder—seven A.M.?

"In Western Colorado," she persists. "Shad Creek. You heard about it, when we battled the corporation that wanted to install a communications tower there."

"He mentioned it. I didn't know it was your land. I thought it belonged to Joseph."

"It's sacred land," she cries. "It's my land!" She is offended that Joseph has misrepresented the ownership of the land, perhaps more than she would have resented my visiting it, though I have

not. Not yet. Joseph occasionally drives there to record the infestation of mountain beetles and to take his daughter and her friends
camping; the summer before, I remember how he describes the
great victory in court over the communications company—David
over Goliath—without mentioning that Arlene might have factored
in the triumph. Indeed, he has neglected to tell me many details
about their past and Arlene has no restraint in disclosing them.
This is her purpose.

Why would I listen to such nonsense?

"I have to know. He's been leading a double life. He's sick, he
needs therapy . . ."

"Arlene, I love him. It's true love we've found." It comes out
before I realize that I will hurt her—*true love*, as if her feeling for
Joseph was not true.

"Don't patronize me."

"He'll see a therapist. What else can he do?"

"There will be a reckoning," she snarls. I know what she wants.
"You don't belong out here," she warns, low and steady.

"It's not over," I reply.

And it's not until Arlene decides it is. She gives her final performance: she disappears. Vanishes, simply, into the thin mountain
air. What about Joseph? He is hauled in on suspicion of murder.

"Get up," says Cathy, sitting heavily near my head. "I'm hungry."

I can't. I turn my head and am bludgeoned by the light infil-
trating the cracks in the stiff, waxy curtains. "I'm sick," I tell her.

"Oh, for heaven's sake." She mimics me. She wants breakfast,
fun, running with dogs.

"A glass of water?" I utter, thick-tongued.

She brings it to me, sloshing and wet, from the bathroom.

"What are we going to do?" she asks impatiently, as I drink.

"Be kind," I whisper. "Be patient, be quiet . . ."

She has gotten up and is pacing the room like her father might
do. "There is so much to do. It's already late. Where are we going?
Who will we see?"

I blink at her. "Isn't there a croissant left from yesterday? And cornflakes?"

She rummages in the bags.

"Chocolate," she replies, munching.

"Cornflakes, please," I sigh. "Give me a minute, will you?"

I manage to roll into clothes, wash my face, and rake my hair with a brush but give up from the ache in my scalp. Cathy frowns at the sight of me and hands me one of her hats. We put on our coats and head down the feebly lit stairwell, trying to calculate through the dingy windows what kind of day it is. Incredibly, she's in a prancing mood, and I decide that over breakfast we will make resolutions and write out lists and make all sorts of plans and stick to them. I let her run ahead, and she flings open the outside door, where the noise and traffic hit us full in the face.

Across the street, right in front of my café, stands the man. The well-dressed man, the dark-skinned man, the selfsame from the museum café. We must spot him at the same time because we both rear back: Cathy clasps her hood, I my hat, and we take off running down the street together.

PRETTY GIRL, she beams at me.

I have aspirations; Joseph reminds me to attend to these. He writes to me long, elegant letters on coarse vellum paper in tones of dark earth and moss. The pen is a fine felt tip; his hand is small and neat. Sometimes he tucks a sprig of juniper from the mountains he climbs inside the letters and it falls into my lap when I open to read. I bring the sprig to my nose and sniff it, detecting the sharp, herbal aroma such as you encounter when first opening a bottle of bath oil. Or there is a perfectly flattened, dried wildflower—a purple lily, a pink nasturtium—and I smell this, too, hungrily, but discern no odor that conjures my love.

I stand at my lookout, which is the back bay window in my kitchen. It is late afternoon, early evening, when the intense slanting light through the still naked trees reflects brilliantly off the narrow stream that separates our yard from the elderly sisters' below us. The grass is a tender, vivid green, the shade of the earliest spring; the daffodils are already drooping a bit but the hot pink azaleas haven't emerged yet from their buds. Once in a while a couple of deer amble through our conjoining backyards, plucking at weeds, on their way across suburban highways and through linking woods. It must be mid-March and I hold a letter in my trembling hands. I wear my apron and pour myself a glass of wine—a buttery Vouvray, because the winter is over and I remember drinking this wine with Joseph. The words from his letter make me pause; I can scarcely believe such words are meant for me:

"Already I miss your
Long shapely ivory legs
& the bright petals
of your cunt."

He has been walking in the mountains, climbing Bear Peak. The sun blazes across meadows and he spots just-emerged purplish, paper-frail lilies amid the tiny prickly pear cacti. He glimpses amorous, edgy mule deer scuffling uphill to avoid his downhill trajectory in the piedmont, or a coyote, its luxuriously bushy tail the color of mud and brittle grass, loping along the meadow, pausing, looking back at Joseph, its gorgeous tail billowing behind. Its tail reminds him of another delicious pelt—we witness it together—a red fox, or *vulpes vulpes*, as we discover the name later in his naturalist dictionary. We are descending a plateau on a hike together. It is late afternoon and we have walked for hours under a strong sun; the sweat has darkened the furrow between Joseph's shoulder blades where he carries our rucksack. We have spotted hawk and many deer and Joseph has pointed out to me the flutey trill of a meadowlark. The fox has ambled before us down the slope, her impossibly lustrous tail undulating behind her like the grasses. We freeze in our descent, and Joseph unhitches his field glasses and hands them to me. The fox has planted herself in front of a critter's den, and crouches there to wait for dinner in the clear, still light of the late afternoon. Joseph, propelled by his feral instincts, begins to move closer to the animal, while I stand as still as I can, drawing in my breath. I shake my head—why does he have to move closer? I step carefully, quietly down the hill, which opens to a vista stretching from the town of Boulder all the way to Kansas, or so Joseph has told me. Still he moves closer to the fox, who waits patiently, motionlessly, in front of her hole, unafraid of Joseph's stealthy approach. Only the sound of dogs unleashed and barking wildly, the companions of young hikers, seems to agitate our fox, tail twitching, as she crouches low. Joseph ceases to draw nearer only when he is a mere several yards from her, then stays and observes her reverently. I am far below him now, looking up, fearful of his proximity to this wild, unpredictable beast, though I, too, am intrigued and excited. Then he places his palms together in front of his face and bows his head solemnly. He turns finally, and makes his way slowly down the slope to join me.

Later, back at his house, which is Arlene's house, though she is traveling, we will take a bath together, our first.

JOSEPH WRITES of birdsong. In early spring he notes the arrival of the tiny chickadee, with his dominant voice, the first and loudest each morning. After hearing him day after day outside of his bedroom window, Joseph decides to get up early one morning and take his field glasses and go out to discover who this interminably cheerful singer is with his two-note love cry. Joseph is not an early riser, and I have to marvel at the power of this modest bird to get him up and out of bed when even I could not do so. Then he laughs to locate such a wee creature lording it over the neighborhood. "The songs of birds have a single burden," Joseph writes to me: "'Where is my beloved?' sung in a thousand different melodies. Sweet melancholy and brisk optimism. Behind them the great ache of wanting and enormous desire."

After a slightly overcast day, when all the foliage is richly green, and massive pewter and white clouds bulk in the sky, with a few breaks where dry sunlight comes through, and a steady wind tosses the trees, Joseph is sometimes sad. Alongside Arlene, his longtime companion, who toils in a massive display of energy and wisdom, filling their house with guests and paper and much noise, Joseph feels neglected. He has his own projects, to be sure, collaborations and translations and readying manuscripts for publication in small, erudite presses. He fashions tundra poetics, reads accounts of the explorer Zebulon Pike, studies anthropology and *The Birder's Handbook*. He dearly loves his birds. He tends to keep his distance from Arlene's explosive metabolism, her large presence in every conversation and event at the Diamondcutter Institute they both care deeply about. Her mission—and his, too, as he is dragged along in her formidable wake—is toward negotiation of the global arms race, cessation of logging and offshore drilling, maintenance of the Clean Air Act, abrogation of the Mining Law of 1872, and endorsement of organic farming bills, waste, cleanup, and recycling programs, protection of biodiversity, and a moratorium on the killing of whales. I have read the school's manifesto, also the writing slogans: "First thought, best thought" (Chogyam Trungpa, Rinpoche); "Do I contradict myself? Very well, I contradict myself" (Walt Whitman). And so forth. To Arlene, the government (run by men) is a great Machiavellian force bent on the destruction of the benevolent and useful: she has been called shrill (that old chestnut lobbed at feminists!) and unable to make political distinctions. While she boxes and harangues on the battlefield of Mars, Joseph feels smothered. He withdraws to create small pockets of quiet: reading (he admits he is a slow reader), walking in his mountains, lingering over a newspaper or a friend's letter—mine, always mine. "She is clipped to a wheel of endless, grinding work," Joseph writes of Arlene, "and sometimes seems twenty years older than me"—a startling statement since Arlene is already an older woman by eight or nine years. "Sometimes I wish she could turn it off," he tells me sadly.

When he writes of loneliness, I can smell him again, that is, the smell of his house, when I first step inside. A stale, slightly acrid odor of dusty, unloved flesh. Maybe it is the odor of Arlene, after all, who resides upstairs, in an overstuffed lair, crammed with books spilling out of shelves, clothing draped over furniture, and videos stacked haphazardly. She watches old detective movies late at night because she cannot sleep. I peek upstairs once or twice, though Joseph does not take me by the hand and lead me upward. She seems always to be traveling or on retreat (by design, no doubt), and our paths never cross, Joseph makes sure of that. She is not a presence is his letters, neither in his calls, and it is easy to forget that her existence looms over his. Except when a detail emerges—for example, they are throwing a going-away party for Arlene, to send her off to Italy to write for six weeks—and Joseph requests, discreetly, that I do not call his home during the evening. "Now I have hurt you," he murmurs when I grow quiet.

"DEAR LIFTER of Spirits," he writes, "carriage of desire! Somehow you seem more like one of those supernatural creatures, too lovely & wise for the touch of a human, that crop up in Asian stories. In India they are *apsaras*—in China maybe rainbow maidens. I must have met you along a creek in the redwood forest once, when near a little falls I found a wild purple iris in the spray. Was that you?" His letters arrive every other day, sometimes two in one day. I retrieve them in the early afternoon, after I have put down Bernie for his nap. I tiptoe out the front door and find awaiting me a crimson envelope, the most exciting kind, thickly spongy from its contents of several folded pages covered in his fine, elegant hand. Or there is a pale oyster or lichen shade, thinner by weight and containing one postcard of a Japanese print he has chosen for me from a museum—a scene from the *Tale of Genji*. These postcards I display over the shelves of my room which is my domain now, not Harry's, and I don't upset them unless I dust or vacuum. Cathy has remarked on this eclectic selection of postcards: "Who sent you these?" And I respond: "My friend Joseph, from Boulder." She doesn't bother to decipher the writing: what would these passionate jottings of shy, interminable longings mean to her? She is baffled, a little troubled, too. The epithet "my friend from Boulder" signifies simply the temperamental shifts her mother assumes from day to day, from manic and energetic, to cloudy and despairing. She has gleaned the connection between these daily missives and her mother's moods. "Do you have a headache?" she asks, when I am frowning and irascible, and by this she senses I have not received assurance from these letters. "Didn't you sleep well last night?" she wonders, when I can't get out of bed because of receiving Joseph's call at three in the morning. Boulder is two hours behind New York. He is calling to amend or correct a letter he has sent; he finds me in bed, docile and sleepy, the way he prefers me. He has put the dinner dishes away and is wandering like a stray dog under the starry mountain moon. Or he sits in a bar, elated, scribbling a note to me on the back of a flier he finds. He needs to hear that my womb is dreaming of him.

His letters return to the details of our last visit, in Boulder or New York, or, later, Albuquerque; they sift through every nuance of word and gesture and touch. We are creating our own mythology. We sit together in the greenish dusk of the Japanese garden at the Metropolitan Museum of Art one Friday evening in spring. "I think you put your hand in my hair," he writes, "we were nearly whispering and even that seemed frighteningly loud in the calm of gray rocks, patient greenery, little rills of water. Whatever we communicated was deeper than the words we spoke—like making love but in cool twilight with no heat or ferocity." He is coming to love me wildly, he writes, and I have come to need these letters. Can I deny it? I begin to live for them, feed on each until the next one arrives, grow greedy to hold another crimson envelope in my hand like a beating heart. The details of our mythology become more real, more necessary than my life at home, with my children. As long as I hold Joseph's letter in my hand, standing at my lookout in the kitchen, the repetitive tasks of my day fall away. I am not Frances, harried mother of two. I am Joseph's "shadow of delight." I am a rainbow maiden.

SHE ALLOWS me to bathe alone. She is bored, flicking on and off the television radio. I ask her to work on a few chapters in her math notebook while I'm in the bath, but she doesn't mind me. I can't make her mind me, less and less the older she grows. She calls my bluff, but I have lost my terrifying edge and seem merely ridiculous to her. I am slow moving, often lost in thought, perplexed by the simplest activities. I prefer that Cathy bathe with me because I am often afraid of my own thoughts: afraid in reflective moments that I'll conjure the image of Arlene Manhunter and not be able to rid her from my mind. It's happened in sleep, in those awful naked hours of the morning when I wake suddenly as if I've heard a sound in the room and all thoughts of sleep are banished. Then I'll see her, the raven-headed poet, bleeding from the side, enraged and vengeful, before the vision will vanish to the strains of sitar music.

Songs inspired by wine and love. I remember how Joseph likes to lecture me, possessed of unbearable (to me) pep at the oddest hours. "Each piece of music," Joseph notes, sitting upright in bed as we listen to classical Indian sitar strains, "embodies one of the nine *rasa* or moods that the poetry calls forth—though in the Sanskrit poetry it's clear the erotic modes are central." We have returned late, not yet made love. I am bone tired, lying fully clothed next to him in his spare room at his new place. He had to rent his own saltbox once Arlene threw him out. The flight earlier from New York has whipped me, and the wine, the dizzying height of these regions, and his ardent, windy lectures. The candles flicker. "The erotic divides into two themes," he continues energetically, "love enjoyed and lovers separated. Yearning, longing, desire, expectation, anguish. Who does this sound like?" He cranes his neck down at me to flash his foxy look. He maintains that Western music is devoid of this richness and complexity, though I cannot agree, thinking of the classical music my daughter is learning for violin.

"Not true, can't be," I murmur, and feebly offer Romanian pastoral folk tunes adapted by Bartók. "Or how about the innovations of the bop 4/4 beat, Lee Konitz and Charlie Parker and those dudes?" I suggest, only because Joseph has read me an article on Kerouac and the influence of bebop on the rhythm of his prose. "And don't you ever watch old Fred Astaire musicals?"

Will the man stop talking and look into my eyes?

But Joseph is perusing new avenues. "We're *earning* something Frances, dear," he asserts, hopping out of bed to retrieve his photo album of pictures of his daughter at age two. "Her first Grateful Dead concert," he says, pointing to his carrot-headed lassie in her pjs rocked by Joseph, *sans* shirt or gray hair in his shaggy beard. And there is Belinda, the first wife: a moon-faced young woman of ample figure in peasant skirt and blouse. She is veritably beaming—a round, sunny face a little like mine, if the full figure is nothing like mine. We pore over these photos of his first life, when the young family lived in the woods outside of Santa Cruz, growing a forest of tea. The marriage ceremony held outside, simple and spiritual, among friends and family: Boston-rigid mother, four brothers of various grades of hirsute posing roguishly like the Musketeers, and Joseph himself, achingly boylike in an unkempt beard (he doesn't trim it until he meets Arlene) and yellow silk shirt with his signature Indian scarf tied around his thin neck. My arm goes to sleep propped up politely pointing.

Why is he showing me these? Why now? We have been sighted at the sandwich shop, in line for the movies the night before, and having drinks at the bar of the Boulderado Hotel. *Turn to me,* I whisper in his ear. *Joseph, touch me, before it's too late.*

But I am interrupted in my reverie by noises coming from the other room—clicking, rattling, rustling sounds that might be the television set being flipped on. I sigh, drawn reluctantly out of my bath. What is she up to now? I wrap a towel around me and pad with wet feet into the bedroom. And then I scream.

My suitcase has been ransacked. Cathy stands in the center of the room. She turns to me, outfitted in a headdress with red-tipped feathers, riotous beads strung around her slender neck, a native-woven poncho that hangs absurdly from her narrow shoulders to the floor. She laughs, her wild Abner laugh, lurches, and starts a dance around the room.

I lunge at her. The towel around me falls to the hideous carpet. I am shrieking at her: "Take them off, take them off—they'll burn you!" I tackle her and strip the ceremonial garments from my daughter's slim body.

V

After a few queries in a café we frequent on rue Boissonade near our hotel, I find work as an artist's model. I know it's work I can do; I've posed before for a photographer in New York, who was my friend, and I used to sit for Harry, when he took classes at the Art Students League and needed to practice. Then I was still encouraging him in his artistic pursuits, and he was very good—his mother was a painter, trained at the Beaux Arts in Paris, and her paintings remain all over the walls of the house— though he was a little shy about drawing from life, and perhaps believed it antithetical to his work as an engineer, to which he was devoted. I encouraged him but he didn't continue; there was always something else to be done, site visits for his work projects, the train to catch, evening coach meetings for the sports league, and he never pursued what I believed was his true artistic pen- chant. At a certain point one stops looking up from the track one has trod.

In Paris I meet a grizzled American painter named Abelard. Not his real name, which is something like Arthur Smedley, as I learn from snooping among the papers from his agent on his desk. Abelard lives in a basic two-room walk-up off rue Mouffetard and I bring Cathy there the first time. The painter must be near sev- enty, vigorous of build, with a white beard and wearing patched- up, paint-stained work clothes; he stinks of oil paint and layers of unwashed body sweat and black tobacco, though I don't find it en toto a bad odor. He has painted in Paris for years and years, mostly portraits, and before that, in Greenwich Village, where he would regularly empty his pockets of change for the bums at every corner. He places Cathy at a small table with paper and paints while we work; she becomes absorbed in her mess and doesn't bother to wonder at me posing in the altogether. Abelard smokes his black-tobacco cigarettes incessantly and peals in soft, lilting laughter when he's amused by something Cathy does, such as fall off her chair without the least provocation. He stands me next to the window, contraposition, with one arm akimbo at the hip, the other hanging straight down; he asks me to look sideways and frown fiercely, the way I do when scolding my daughter, and he gives his high, happy giggle.

His rooms are very cold and untidy and as I pose he sets a small, ineffectual heater at my feet. Abelard wants to hear about New York, which has altered radically since he lived there; I try to give him something funny and fresh but I tell him I've been stranded out in the suburbs so long and only visit museums anymore. But Abelard knows my town on the Hudson, for he has traveled a great deal in the world. "Now there's a pretty village," he says, with a little giggle. "The Hudson River painters worked out of a colony there. Hills and rocks, with tugboats going by, and the view of the Palisades across the river. What's not to like about it?"

"What brought you to my neck of the woods?" I ask him, shaking my head, because we are in Paris talking about my small town which is hardly on the map.

"A woman, of course," returns Abelard. "It's always a woman who takes us places, isn't it?"

After the first time at Abelard's studio Cathy doesn't want to come again to the sitting; I hire the teenaged daughter of the concierge at our hotel to take her to the park. Cathy is excited about a young new friend until she learns that she'll have to speak French for the afternoon. Then she pouts and won't let go of me when we say good-bye.

When Abelard finishes his portrait—he calls it *Frances debout*—I decide the figure needs only a helmet and a spear and I am pleased: Joseph would like it hanging in the bedroom of his saltbox.

I READ while Abelard paints me, standing naked and freezing in his dusty studio. I turn sideways and hold the book to the window's light. I am reading Diane Di Prima's *Memoirs of a Beatnik*. I read it because it's on my list of Joseph's recommended titles, but also because Abelard relates to me his own curious turn of career writing porn novels for Olympia Press in the sixties: Abelard is actually his nom de plume, as if I didn't guess. Unlike Di Prima, Abelard did not have to ask friends to demonstrate possible physical positions that might occur during sex, he informs me with an impish wink. He gives his rollicking whinny at the expression on my face—why do I have to react in such a bourgeois fashion? I nod and shrug with annoyance, since I don't like to imagine this sweet old man writing porn novels while he paints me naked. He is stewing a hefty tomato sauce on the stove at full flame; the robust aroma of ripe fruit billows thickly through the small rooms of his flat and from time to time we hear a zapping noise when the splashing sauce bubbles over the iron skillet and into the fire. Abelard doesn't care; he hasn't cleaned the stove since he was married to a Frenchwoman, and that was two decades ago. He doesn't mind the vermin I catch sight of, out of the corner of my eye, or the dust, or the many odd smells; he paints, he cooks, he smokes, and he giggles at the joy of it all.

When I leave the studio in the late afternoon, I sense the presence hovering nearby, and I catch sight of him: the powerfully built black man, broad in the shoulders, though not tall, mid-fifties perhaps (I've lost the ability to distinguish ages), well dressed in a raincoat and dark, creased trousers. So he has found me. He seems infinitely calm reading a book, leaning against the Morris column at Place Monge. My heart gives a little lurch: my heart murmur, which tends to the skipping of beats at moments when I am least aware, and not necessarily at times of physical exertion. My breathing nags at me, heavy and ragged, and a blazing bulb throbs at the base of my skull. I hightail it to the métro, only a few paces away: the man has placed himself in direct view of the underground mouth. He will look up once I reach it, and if I turn to meet his gaze we will establish the fatal intimacy of strangers. But I don't deviate from my path. Cathy is jumping on the trampolines at the Jardin des Tuileries and I have to hurry to relieve the exhausted babysitter.

Instead, I sneak up on him. He rattles the book he's reading, then closes it and puts it away.

He calls himself Lewis. Not Loo-eee, in the French fashion, because he's American, or was, and it's cooler anyway to be Lewis among the innumerable Louises, which in Paris no doubt amounts to being a Tom, Dick, or Harry. Lewis: after Joe Louis, Louis Armstrong, or Louis-Ferdinand Céline, perhaps. He takes me to our café off rue Boissonade for a drink, like it's his place not mine. It's late afternoon and the teenagers are newly sprung from school, filling the place with great bombs of cigarette smoke as they bang on video and pinball machines. We order from the churlish waiter: a cognac for Lewis (a gentleman!), a cassis for me, though I haven't actually ordered one since I was dating in my twenties. The color: Crimson. Scarlet. Ruby. Vermilion. The glorious colors of red Joseph names for me that a poet has at his disposal. A sensuous, complex color, deeper than the wanton petals of the first rose I sent him from my garden, richer even than the walls of the Tuscan restaurant in Boulder where he might have proposed marriage—a color much like the brick of my home or the shade of my winter lipstick. I stare at the fiery liquid in my glass, hold it up to the wan afternoon light from the street, watch its elusive facets dart like jewel tones. But similes are dead, really, and can't be taken seriously anymore in poetry.

"What are you reading?" I ask the man, Lewis, when he doesn't move to cross-examine me or even ask my name. Of course, he knows my name. I motion to the book he has gently set on the marble tabletop.

He shows me the book: Apollinaire's *Alcools*. Well, what a relief! I imagine he's reading a contemporary novel, the kind the Parisian bookstores are full of—slender, sexy, first-person narratives written by impossibly soignée intellectual Frenchwomen who also look good on TV. "It's very stressful to be a stylish

Frenchwoman," I remember one lady was quoted in the paper as saying.

But I assume the book he's carrying is a ruse, a decoy. "How enchanting. You're reading poetry. Just for fun?" I ask, narrowing my gaze with a frown. I wonder how terribly rude I must sound. "Won't you kindly recite us a line?"

But he's not offended; he's amused. "Voici le temps où l'on connaîtra l'avenir sans mourir de connaissance," he recites with a lovely accent, smiling with his teeth.

"Oh, not fair," I say. "I know that line. That's the epigraph quoted in Allen Ginsberg's poem about visiting Apollinaire's grave. He and Peter Orlovsky are walking around Père Lachaise cemetery holding hands and looking for the grave. Ginsberg is envisioning his own death and takes poetic inspiration from the light *bleeding* from Apollinaire's grave. Do you know it?"

I am excited to learn that Lewis is reading something that Joseph might pick up, though Joseph, disappointingly, does not read French. My love is not good at learning foreign languages— his tone-deaf ear, perhaps? An imperfectly applied high-school education botched by too many drugs? I make a note to find this volume among the *bouquinists* along the Seine and send it to Joseph at Valhalla.

"Do you mean the poem or the grave?" asks Lewis. "No, I haven't . . ."

"The grave at Père Lachaise."

"Maybe you'd like to come with me and help me find it."

Lewis sips at his cognac. I like his face; I am partial to open faces that appear as if they might break into a receptive grin at a slight provocation. I think of Abelard's face, whose lines offer a kind of world map of his humane generosity; or Joseph's sly visage grooved by his selective wisdom and disciplined concealment. My own Cathy's dear face that moves from precipitous joy to stormy petulance to sprightly mischief. Lewis's face is attentive (I like to hold the gaze), however immobilized by a watchful patience, and does not give anything away.

"Have you lived in Paris a long time?" I ask.

"Twenty-five years. I grew up in Newark, New Jersey, but came to Paris like everyone else, to be a writer. I never made it as a writer," he adds quietly.

"You fled your home?"

"A hot time, Newark in the sixties, seventies. I knew Amiri Baraka when he was LeRoi Jones. I worked with him at this Spirit House Movers Congress of African People and Jihad. I got involved in the violent dismantling of the racist state." Lewis speaks without emphasis, matter-of-factly, or perhaps he is simply modest. If he is trying to impress me, he is certainly succeeding.

"You were committed to the political struggle. *Engaged*."

"I was stupid."

I don't laugh, if I'm supposed to find that funny. "Why?" I shoot back. "Why so unforgiving of that time in your life? Your youth? Do you repudiate the person you were, and what you believed in?"

"Not exactly," he replies, steadily. "There were lies everywhere, monstrous lies. It was wartime. But there are other ways to accomplish your goals: nonviolent demonstration, for example, and lawsuits and writing books."

"Yes, but the spark of the moment. What could be a more powerful argument for change than a sudden, swift action—a spontaneous, albeit rash, but purely motivated gesture?"

"It kills, Frances. I can't condone violence," he replies, quietly inserting my name for the first time.

"And that limp you have—a battle scar?"

He smiles, humbled, surely, or touched that I have noticed the slight hobble in his walk.

"An old hip injury. I tried to blow up a bank, but we didn't know shit about explosives. Now I need hip replacement surgery but they say I'm still too young."

"Now you're working for the other side, is that it?"

He smiles, sips at his amber drink. We listen to the crashing of pinball machines, slammed by hard teenaged bodies.

He asks: "Would you like to smoke some tea?"

WE DO not find Apollinaire's grave. The weather is fine, almost like the first soft spring day in New York when you feel the wind at last has lost its bite and winter is finally over. Lewis remembers such a day, too. We have shrugged off our coats—first Cathy, instantly upon being released among the radiating avenues of the ancient, overgrown cemetery, tosses me her anorak to carry around for the afternoon. I will use it for our blanket when we stop to eat the sandwiches we have bought at a café. She whistles and prances, stopping briefly in front of a somber marker to wonder aloud: "Why are we walking around in a *graveyard*?" I have to agree. I'm not sure of the wisdom in poking around among dead souls when the spirit of Arlene Manhunter is at large, free range—stalking me.

Cathy runs ahead, then drops behind a fruit tree heavy with imminently flowering petals, until we catch up and she leaps out at us. "Ma!" she shouts, the way I do when chasing Bernie around the house on my hands and knees, turning corners abruptly to provoke his trill of laughter. (I will go to great lengths to see his big, laughing tomato face and tiny even teeth.) Then Cathy takes Lewis's hand, curiously, pleased to enjoy the attention of someone other than her mother—and a man, no less. The child is learning quickly. Lewis drapes his coat over his forearm and keeps to a steady pace, looking straight ahead; he's on duty. He catches her antics out of the corner of his eye and smirks.

Mausoleums of Proust, Wilde, Chopin, Balzac, La Fontaine: we explain these names to Cathy in turn. How in a lifetime will I introduce my daughter to these legends, their work, their lasting beauty? To stand where she is, a blank slate, with an entire world of exploration ahead of her! If shown the mountain of our ignorance, would we have the strength, or will, to climb it? A teacher once asked me whether I had visited Rome—or read *The Cantos* or climbed the Matterhorn, for that matter—and when I said that I hadn't, she replied, "Then you have that to look forward to." It *was* an exciting thought, to know that a lifetime is full of such discoveries, richnesses still to be unsealed—but now I wonder, gazing at these sad tombs containing decayed relics of time and place, whether I have lost the desire to know more. At what point in one's life does this happen? The names begin to oppress me, and I have lost the certain someone with whom I most want to share those cherished discoveries.

Cathy ducks behind an elaborate sarcophagus: Molière. She is picking flowers—weeds—chestnuts.

"Are you married?" I ask Lewis, who takes the question in stride.

"I was married when I was young, stayed as long as I could, once we grew apart. She got into drugs and a bad scene. We have a daughter, and when she grew up and went off to school, I finally moved out. They live in the States now."

"Well, are you of the opinion that people should stay together for the sake of the children—as you seem to have done—or move apart and enjoy happiness and satisfaction in a new relationship?"

"The children's consideration is important. My generation tended to make pretty facile justifications for their actions."

"Meaning they put personal happiness above duty."

He ponders silently for a while. "I don't think anyone has the right to make the other feel diminished," he says finally.

I wave to Cathy, who is turning cartwheels over someone's final resting place: the grave of Sarah Bernhardt? Some slouching youths pass us, on their way to find Jim Morrison.

"Diminished. That's an interesting choice of words. Love, I have read, probably in a novel, is the craving for identity, the urge to lose oneself and be validated in the eyes of the other. Do you think?"

"Pascal said that all men's miseries derive from not being able to sit in a quiet room alone."

"We need the assurance that we are worthy," I continue, hardly listening to his words, which I understand too well, for aren't we somewhat alike: two lonely characters with deviant histories, in short, outcasts? "And in love we are allowed to be greater than we are, to renew our courage."

"That's true," he considers. "But love—the name of love—can also be a tool for destroying the other, for obliterating identity, for making the other feel small and—"

"Diminished."

"Yes."

"You must be talking about marriage," I murmur, laughing.

"Yes, some marriages . . . Would you like to tell me about your marriage, Frances?" Lewis asks me suddenly, with a subtle but unmistakable solicitude I find tremendously moving.

"Is that where I've been going?" I ask. Then sigh and kick at the ground. Cathy is trotting toward us, a bouquet of pretty weeds in her hand.

"Oh sweetie!"

She looks from Lewis to me, flushed and smiling suspiciously. She offers the bouquet finally to Lewis. Stiffly, he bows.

"What are you talking about?" she asks.

"You. Let's eat."

I THINK Lewis likes my stories. He's a wonderful listener, like a therapist, and he doesn't interrupt, as girlfriends do, and give his own opinion, or lift his eyebrow and grimace at a part he doesn't approve of, then jab at you and tell you pointblank what you should or shouldn't have done. Even if he's getting paid to listen, like a therapist, and extract those stories from me, I am happy to sit with him in the sun, eating our sandwiches on Cathy's spread anorak as she darts among the grave markers, and drinking wine straight from the bottle, by turns, as we have forgotten to buy cups. I don't mind doing all the talking, though frankly I'd rather be speaking in French.

"Harry sleeps in a hut in the backyard," I tell Lewis, which seems suddenly terribly hilarious and it takes a few moments before I am able to continue.

HARRY HAS taken to hissing a name under his breath: Lunatic. It refers to me and also to his Hungarian mother, whose husband drove her to an early grave by substance abuse and his chronic philandering. I can tell by the vehemence with which Harry spews the word at me that his father, the tall, elegant Southerner (nothing like his son, who favors the grounded Slavic build), must have used it repeatedly to humiliate his wife. I call my husband Fatso. It hurts: Harry was the fat boy as a child, coddled by his fragile mother and left in front of the TV to snack on salted peanuts dropped into bottles of coke. The children hear me once and I am ashamed. Really, name calling! I do apologize. I have scratches on my face from trying to claw at him but Harry is built like a pro wrestler and I can't make a dent in him. Harry does not apologize for calling me Lunatic, however, so I throw him out of the house.

He is going to construct a hut in the backyard and there he will reside. But not just any hut. He is a master builder and designs the hut over many evenings of watching television alone downstairs in the living room. He rents films to view late at night, movies punctuated by bloody violence and rough language: I can hear it all from my bedroom upstairs. In the middle of the night he puts down the shades and watches the Playboy channel. "I had to see if I still had it in me," he sputters, ashen-faced, when I find the bill. The actual construction of the hut takes countless weekends and trips to the hardware store. We tell the neighbors that we need a shed for storage space and not to be alarmed. The elderly sisters across the stream worry that the noise from the building will scare away their cherished pair of mallards who migrate here every year and roost on the banks of their lawn. We don't have an answer there: the mallards aren't reproducing because the muskrats are stealing their eggs, but we don't mention this. The other neighbors are never home or rarely emerge from their houses.

Finally the hut is completed and it is beautiful. The children help paint it the color of Tuscan brick, like the house. Harry moves his things into the hut over the first spring of my love for Joseph and sets up house. There is enough room for a single bed and some bookshelves, and Harry could even install a drafting table if he tackles the boxes that have been stored in the basement since we moved into the house. He and the children spend hours puttering in the hut, and when items begin disappearing from the house—certain favored toys they know I don't approve of such as plastic guns and slimy putty that sticks to furniture, swords and shields and Bernie's stash of summer shorts I won't let him wear yet—it occurs to me that Harry's hut will become their secret hide-away from me and they are delighted. Harry removes from the living room shelves many volumes of art and architecture, leaving room for sprightly titles of literature overflowing from my own shelves upstairs. The children run breathlessly into the house to tell me sporadic news of the moving process, ecstatically holding aloft some wondrous lost plaything they have regained from recent excavations. Their daddy's little hut out back is their secret treehouse and his removal there the season's big adventure, or so I imagine they feel, though I watch Cathy from the kitchen bay window and detect her pensive sadness.

Where is this all going to lead? she seems to say, with her roving, dark eyes. She appears suddenly behind me in the kitchen, standing so close I don't see her; she nudges into me, her head hanging, her arms snaking around my middle. I clutch her to me and sigh helplessly, beating her on the back.

Harry taps on the door when it's dinnertime, bellowing, "I'm here!" just in case I'm on the phone with Joseph. Harry is allowed to cook, and in the mornings when we're all still sleeping I hear him clattering and banging pots in the kitchen to get the pan-cakes started. He's big and clumsy and the house is dainty; he still takes up too much space around here. Has this arrangement not been a compromise to keep Joseph from leaving me? Yet still he won't come and stay with me, even when Harry and the children are away at the beach, which happens once a year. I recognize that nothing has changed, and as I stand at the back bay window, which is my lookout, my perch, where I drink a glass of wine in the early evening and read Joseph's letter, I sense the familiar, creeping despair making its way from my calf muscles to the back of my neck. Why have I agreed to this? I am the one who needs to leave. I only want to get out of the house.

I HAD written to Joseph that a man who does not claim his wife sexually does not value her. This is where it all begins, in bed with my husband.

If we want to have sex in the morning, when we are still sharing the same bed and having sex, we have to awaken well before the ululations of the clock radio and rouse the slumbering, reluctant other and perform intercourse noiselessly without letting Cathy know what we are up to. If she hears that we're awake, she will come into our bedroom. She climbs onto our bed and I cannot persuade her to go back to her room even when I give her a stern order. She is a stubborn, defiant child, and very intuitive. She asks a thousand questions: Why aren't we wearing any underpants? So we are discouraged from having sex in the morning.

In the evening, if we attempt to have sex at bedtime (and we have to agree in advance to go to bed at the same time and at a reasonably early hour), we turn off the lights and remove our clothing in separate corners of the bedroom and get under the covers, all the while wondering, a little anxiously, who will do what first. Harry might try to kiss my lips, but I no longer like him to kiss me. I taste on him our dinner, the chicken carbonara or the beef stew I have made (recipes from my mother), and I don't want to return to the toil and exasperation that went into the making of our dinner. Or he might taste of toothpaste, since we have just brushed our teeth in preparation for bed, and the minty taste reminds me of the nightly struggle to get Cathy into the bath and then to sleep. I turn my head to one side and we try something else.

He might touch my breasts, if they aren't tenderly premenstrual and I don't block his hand. Or he stimulates my vulva, valiantly massaging with his fingers, and I try to think of something sexy—something written by the poet I am reading at the moment, "My only regret is not having been my own mistress"—and open my legs, but I find myself listening to Cathy snoring softly in the next room. I hear the barking of the dog down the street from our house and I make a mental note to go chew out the owner in the morning for allowing such a racket. I move Harry's hand. With a sigh he positions himself on his back. I scoot down and take his penis in my mouth.

I give him a tug for encouragement but he never likes it when I'm rough; I slow down and try to be gentle. Soon I become aware of the crick in my neck and the uncomfortable position of my limbs. I do not feel relaxed, he does not feel relaxed, but nonetheless, with some effort and alacrity he ejaculates in my mouth and that's that. He makes the requisite groan, and flops back and tries not to fall asleep. He wonders about my pleasure—he does ask—and attempts cunnilingus, as I nudge a pillow under his head or maneuver him to a position we can manage comfortably. I push him this way and that for maximum pleasure ("Harder," I cheer him quietly, "harder, faster, *stronger*"). We move awkwardly to keep the bed from squeaking. Or I have given up. "It's okay," I concede, and we close down and go to sleep.

Harry is a heavy man (*husky* is the word his Hungarian mother had insisted on, because that's how they're built): when he lies on top of me he exerts himself and the droplets of his sweat shower my face. We are half-listening for Cathy, trying not to let the bedsprings rattle. He doesn't prefer this position. He likes me to mount him so that he can lie back and fondle my breasts and the place where my hips swell over his thighs. I can see the blood color suffuse his broad neck as I move up and down, though I find myself distracted by the blinking of the digital numbers on the clock radio next to the bed. I feel the petrifying of my facial muscles. It is a kind of perverseness on my part, because I see that he is experiencing pleasure—the dark whiskered skin around his nose and mouth slacken and his eyelids partially shudder—and yet I resent his pleasure. I recognize that I am looking on his pleasure with coldness, experiencing none of my own.

In fact, I am harboring animosity. I feel hateful: toward my husband and myself for feeling this way about him. Somehow we have lost the taste for sex (or I should say I have), like the taste of a certain food you once craved because it made you feel more productive and happy—those little amber sesame candies I used to buy in bulk at the health-food store and peel them open one by one and chew incessantly while writing or studying. But I find them sticky and insipid now. I don't remember why I liked the taste so much. Harry would say he doesn't know what candy I'm talking about; he's never eaten such things in his life.

We have grown anxious about when to have sex and how we should start, whether Cathy can hear us, and who will do what first. Is the other experiencing pleasure or just being courteous? Because our marriage is a courteous one. Is pleasure the end result, after all? Or is it rather duty? I begin to think that having sex is a duty and it no longer holds any pleasure. It holds anxiety. It is an obligation, among a hundred obligations endured over the course of our marriage and child-rearing years, such as pro-curing the proper car seat for Cathy, sending out Christmas cards, or having Harry risk falling to his death from the ladder when he cleans out the leaf-choked gutters in the spring. The obligation to have sex (because that's what married people are supposed to do) is like having to remember to cut your runaway toenails. Harry does not cut his toenails—*bat claws* is what I call them, in dis-gust. I cease to want to have sex with my husband because he does not cut his toenails. Having to remember to have sex bites into my freedom, or so it seems to me, since marriage assumes for me the gradual constriction of my liberty. I think it is all about that—*liberty*—and toenails—or maybe I have been reading too much French literature.

It doesn't happen so efficiently. We hold hands in the beginning; I sleep holding onto him—clasping his wrist or throwing my arm over his furry vault—until he makes it known to me that he isn't comfortable sleeping this way. I take his arm when strolling down Broadway, near his apartment at the time we are graduate students, except that he keeps trying to extract his sweating, limp paw from my grip. We kiss in public, glancingly, on the lips, then he looks around, embarrassed; he is not a physically demonstrative man. He is modest, that is, before his modesty turns to shame—shame for a body that has grown onerous to him, undesired and betrayed. But I find this modesty exciting, in the beginning, when we are groping for one another in the darkness of his bachelor bedroom. Then he touches me and he spins into a kind of trance, his face contorted with what seems like pain, and I ask, "Harry, are you all right?"

breaking his spell. He is instantly alert, his eyes wide open, and he nods rapidly.

When Cathy is around four, or possibly it happened much sooner, on our honeymoon in Greece, I become aware that sex between me and my husband is not a pleasure but an obligation, and I am disturbed and unhappy. I imagine this is the great humiliation of marriage. I begin to wonder at Harry's abashed and admiring look and it seems to me that it holds something grudging, something shamed. His look asks something of me that I cannot give. I begin to resent being asked to give this, which is no longer a pleasure but an obligation. So we are relieved to give up sex by the time Cathy is four or so—I am. As a result I regain to some extent my *liberty*, which is popularly known as personal space, or breathing room, and we can live like this. We can get up in the morning without having to begrudge our daughter for intruding into our bedroom and disturbing us in our lovemaking; and, similarly, in the evening, we give each other a kiss goodnight freed from the pressure of thinking what to do next (does he want it, does she want it, how to proceed?). We turn over and sleep with an easy conscience.

Eventually, it's easier and more convenient that Harry sleep downstairs where he passes out in the evenings after drinking a beer with dinner and watching violent rented movies. These feature plenty of guns, gore, and cursing, and there is the occasional Playboy show in the middle of the night, maybe Monday after football. Only once or twice do I tiptoe down the stairs and peek into the living room where he sleeps on the sofa. He doesn't bother to remove his workaday clothes, except his tie; one of his legs is dangling down because there isn't much room for him. I creep down to refill my glass of wine in the kitchen. I barely scrape the bottle across the counter; the cork is soundlessly dislodged, the crimson liquid gurgles, and there is the barest brittle clinking of the bottleneck as it grazes the crystal glass rim. Harry's voice is low and mumbly, and if you're not standing next to him watching his lips move you can't understand a word he says. I have to move closer to hear him. He's talking about his movie, or the black flies that have hatched in our house, making a nuisance at our windows, because it's early spring. My voice is high, sometimes so high and shrill that Cathy wakes up and wanders downstairs.

She wonders if we're arguing. But we're not arguing. After a while talking and drinking my glass of wine, I climb on top of Harry and we make other noises, sounds of the upholstery being gripped by forceful hands and some huffing and groaning. These are the sounds she must detect. We hear her coming by the wincing of the banister. I dismount my husband and creep back up the stairs as cat-quiet as I came.

This is how Bernard comes to be, because I want him so badly. I name him after my grandfather—BURN-erd—though the child is affectionate and silly and nothing like his forbidding Yankee namesake. Cathy needs a sibling and an ally against me, her mother, and I need a sire. I imagine that this child will save our marriage. Once Bernie exists I no longer have to come downstairs at night again.

HARRY AND I spend the afternoon chopping side by side in the small kitchen, bumping into each other to open and close the refrigerator. We snipe over the menu (a pasta pesto salad he will concoct or my warm potato salad with dill? Marinade for the barbecue chicken or meat cut up on skewers? A green salad that will require the tiresome washing of leaves or a couscous salad with peas and parsley—and who neglected to wrap up the frozen peas in plastic so they won't taste like freezer burn?). I'm not yet dressed, though it's twenty minutes to the hour. We will entertain the Broadmans, whose youngest girl is in Cathy's class, or the Calamaris from church, or the Riles, since Harry keeps running into Sandy Rile on the commuter train and can't deflect her persistent summons for a get-together. They invited us once for Thanksgiving, after all, and we were blessedly relieved of the cheerless task of having to face the holidays ourselves. The stressful joined effort to bring out a pleasant familial face frays our habitual courteousness. Our public face. The children have already laid waste to the arrangement of cheeses on the dining room table; I catch sight of the little savages out the window as I dash up the stairs to bathe: they are digging their dirty hands into the bowl of potato chips displayed like goose down in elegant bowls on the patio table. They cram and scatter the gossamer flakes across the newly spread tablecloth, spot me through the glass, then shriek like devils and run away. Soon our guests appear at the house: it is late afternoon and still mild enough to sit out on the patio for a barbecue. I am clipping up my hair and mashing the color over my lips when I hear the doorbell, while Harry, glasses fogged from sink condensation and oven fumes, hasn't managed to change his clothes or—come on!—trim his nose hairs. We all float in and out of one another's embrace in greeting: I propel myself into outstretched arms and seize the bottle they have brought.

"What a charming house!" our friends cry, as surely they will, if they haven't been here before. They clump around in heavy shoes, admiring the paintings on the walls, which are family renderings by Harry's deceased mother, trained in the Beaux Arts. They examine the pea-green walls (Harry's idea, not mine) and declare the color most original. "I would never have imagined this color on dining room *walls*," Sandy Rile is sure to interject, and I hurry to add, "The house wanted to be green," as I always do, because Harry said it once and it's a good line. She exclaims, "How cute!"—or *adorable* or *sweet*—while marveling at the cottage details: wooden beams, stone fireplace, kitchen bay window. She wonders, "Did you just fall in love with this house at first sight?" meaning that it's way too quaint for her taste. I concur quietly, politely, though I add, "It's a perfect place for an older couple whose kids have left home"—because it's truly small, and too cramped to contain the energy of two boisterous children. I don't mention that it's a cold house, with chilly bare floors and unfriendly plaster walls that keep me in deep-freeze from October till April—and that if she looked closer, Sandy Rile, who has a cunning look, would note how everything is broken, chipped, or frayed. Discolored plaster on the dining room ceiling from a nagging, undetectable leak; furniture legs tied up with hemp; Persian rugs hastily repaired with tape. I choose not to see these fissures: why wear glasses in my own home? But maybe she does notice and the look she pierces me with is not in fact envy (*her* house is so unmanageable! though spacious and light), but possibly, probably pity.

"Let's go outside and eat," I urge our friends, after they have pounded up and down the stairs. They peer into the master bedroom, which features only artifacts of the mistress of the house (do they detect Harry's absence?), and gaze critically at the green-and-white tiled bathroom whose small rectangle window, still curtainless after nearly a decade of our habitation, invites occasional luggage defenestration. (The children make an excursion of gathering these tossed items the day after an argument with Harry, and I don't have to worry about excavating my rolling airline bag while pruning.) I lead our genial friends to the Tuileries chairs set up outside, and we sit and drink wine while Harry tends to the grill. The children have formed gangs and are galloping across neighboring lawns; they carry sticks and other heavy objects as weapons. I'm always surprised—when I actually sit and listen (once a year?)—at how loud the whirring of the traffic is past the barrier of trees along the Saw Mill Parkway. And how sorry the state of the lawn: the season of drought, and I haven't had the gumption to water, not since Joseph came into my life and alarmed me with dire words about letting the children waste precious water in the sprinklers. I used to admire my house—we exchange pictures of my friends' recent Burgundy vacation—and relish the cultivation of quirky details, though it has remained intractable and frosty (a little like my husband), in spite of my efforts to inculcate in the place a warmer *human dimension.* After years of this waiting and watching, to see what *goes* next, I notice how the upkeep hardly matters in nature's relentless thrust toward gravitational doom and collapse: everything seems to fall apart at the same rate. I have grown more interested in watching its decomposition.

"Harry, the *lights*," I mutter, or remind him of the condiments or beer or onion slices, and I wonder at the sharpness of my tone: when did it first enter my voice as I addressed my husband? Was it over the long exhausting nights of baby feeding, when Cathy would be wailing from her room and one of us—it's *his* turn, damn it, I mutter, and I kick him out of his infernal snoring—had to get up and attend to her? Or was it before then, on our wedding day, when he stepped on my flowing tulle train at the church and I snapped at him—the big oaf!—to move off? What did I imagine I was getting, a prince or this man of clay?

The torches flicker from the corners of the lawn. Sam Broadman—or Marvin Rile or Dave Calamari—hulks over the buffet table and shovels onto his paper plate a heap of ghoulish pasta. He murmurs, "I am a cautious person, which can be a good or bad thing," and I exclaim, "But I am impulsive," and behind us, watching us, Harry brandishes his Father's Day barbecue implements. It's that look he has behind his glasses, which creep down his nose so that you can never tell exactly what he is looking at— that coolly appraising look, though essentially impassive and non-committal, that reminds me to hate him.

"But I don't hate him," I assure Lewis, on a sudden afterthought, as if it's Harry's body that is missing, instead of Arlene's. "I don't hate my husband at all."

"I believe you," Lewis replies, simply. He rests his heavy forearms on the table, making it buckle and knock. He turns from me to gaze abstractedly into the elaborate café mirror, not in admiration of himself but to view the mutable contents of the busy establishment at midday. We have met at this café for lunch near Abelard's studio, as it's perfectly clear Lewis knows where I go and what I do. His face, upon closer inspection, seems somewhat bloated with age, or ill diet, I can't be sure—perhaps he's been ill, and he drinks coffee constantly—and there is about him a heaviness like resignation, as if he has recognized the foolishness of grasping after something that he knows will come to him eventually, and without the wasted effort. He orders a creamy, hot meal, and I order mussels and Meursault, feeling like Ernest Hemingway at La Closerie des Lilas. I wonder if my woeful tale of marriage saddens Lewis, though he's probably heard it all before and I'm boring him. I wish I had a better, more hopeful story for him; it occurs to me that maybe I should lie.

"Joseph says that he knows only unhappily married people," I venture, shucking my shells merrily.

Lewis gives a quiet laugh. "Is that so," he says, not quite a question, and adds, thoughtfully, "That's probably right."

"Shall I continue?" I ask, feeling bolstered by the wine. Lewis glances up from his casserole warily. "You know, when I first talked to him, to Joseph, in the bar at the Cruise Room in downtown Denver," I recount, "and we were speaking to another friend of mine from college, Ted, who wasn't exactly a boyfriend at college but we were all in the same circles, and Ted, who's a lawyer in California and kind of shy, for some reason mentioned that he and his fiancée liked to have sex in the morning. Well, I don't know what we were talking about—whatever adults talk about late at night in bars. And Joseph asked me, right there, sitting all three at the bar, when *I* liked to have sex, which is a curious question, don't you think, for a man to ask a woman he knows nothing about? But I told him, by way of answer, that married people *don't* have sex, and I remember making a slashing motion across my throat, and the men laughed."

"How did that strike you, what Joseph asked you at the bar?"

"Sleazy. It struck me as in rather bad taste."

"Though you gave him your address?"

"I did. I couldn't wait to have him alone."

"Even with Arlene there?"

"Oh, especially with Arlene there."

I'm wrong. Lewis raises an eyebrow.

"And you know, this Ted," I resume quickly, "the friend from college? He was staying at the same hotel as Harry and me, as all the wedding party were, and he even drove me home from the bar, because Harry had stayed with the children. As we went up in the elevator to our respective rooms in the hotel, kind of tipsy and laughing, Ted, this old friend from college, kissed me good-bye—he tried to stick his tongue in my mouth."

Lewis chokes on his coffee. He coughs violently and I have to reach my arms around him and whack him on the back.

VI

Joseph is a Buddhist. To me this means he is a being of infinite gentleness. Besides, there are three Marks of Existence to keep in mind: that existence contains suffering; that our condition is transitory; and that there is no permanent self. Once you recognize that suffering is not a permanent condition, you can be liberated by waking to your true nature and resist clinging and grasping and feeling insulted by your existence. Waking up in the morning screaming mad, as Allen Ginsberg says: he is a favorite writer at Diamondcutter and Joseph quotes him off-the-cuff. "Buddha" means the Awakened One. A Buddhist vows to embark on a path to enlightenment from suffering, and from causing suffering to other sentient beings. In his room, next to his meditation mat, Joseph hangs a little Tibetan "adept" that he is supposed to recite during the course of the day:

Everything is illusion, and I am confident that all is well.

Joseph works to create good karma—or the greater consequences of one's actions—in the universe, although Joseph's karma is not good. It's rotten, in fact. Joseph is a sage, but in certain ways he's not smart, and especially not smart about women. His compassion for all sentient beings translates into his not being able to be cruel to the women who love him—that is, honest. For a man who holds Henry David Thoreau as his model, and the dictum "Simplify, simplify" the first order by which to live, Joseph has created for himself some serious complications. Namely, an ex-wife named Belinda who still holds out that he will return to her, and when he doesn't, she aims to avenge herself for his betrayal. Also, a lethal ex-companion who will ruin his professional reputation and boot him out of his school once she finds out that he is sleeping with a younger married woman he meets at Douglas's wedding. Third, a now-teenaged daughter from his marriage to Belinda who has a sweet voice, long honey-blond hair, and a womanly figure like her mother: Jan gets nose bleeds and is often seized by panic attacks that send her to the emergency room. She complains that her erratic behavior has chased away her friends from high school. Her father is chagrined. Even though Belinda has done her best over the years at making her daughter hate Joseph, Jan adores her father and protects him—screens his phone calls—though Arlene has intimated that theirs is an "unhealthy closeness."

I tell Joseph, one evening in our hotel room when he visits me in New York—it's at 34th and Lex, I choose this time—that he keeps women spinning around him so that he won't have to feel. That he lets them embroil themselves and he is excused from feeling. This seems to me a momentous insight and I tell him so. "They writhe and churn around you so that you don't have to," I tell him, bitterly, and leap off the bed and shut myself in the bathroom. The small bedroom is elegant and spare, the walls painted the color of Scarlet Ibis that I like so much. I have sent Joseph imperial roses in this color upon the occasion of his moving out of Arlene's house, the color of Thai iced tea, or the saffron robes of Buddhist monks. It is January, a troubled weekend, shortly after Joseph's breakup with Arlene—she threw him out when she realized who was calling him over the last year: me. Joseph has a poetry reading in New York, at which he does not want me to appear, so soon after the breakup, though he cannot keep from seeing me, either. "How can I come to New York and not see you?" he laments, when I offer magnanimously to stay away. He is conflicted, tormented, though my offer is a bluff, as I am determined to appear at his side.

"Arlene used to tell me that I was attracted to angry women," Joseph remarks sadly from the bed. His torso is bared, slenderly muscular, and brushed by soft, golden down.

"Now, why is that?" I ask coldly. I wash my face in the bathroom, rinse out the venom from my mouth, and emerge determined to resolve this crisis so we can resume our lovemaking. I am angry: perhaps I am the angriest woman of all. He does not witness the rage I demonstrate at home. He imagines me a docile creature; he has never heard from my lips the blood-coagulating shrieks that trill the ribcage and rattle the pea-green walls of our adorable little Tudor in the suburbs. It is a half-hour train ride into the city, but I have arrived late at the hotel because Harry has come home early, unaccountably, and seized the picnic basket that I am preparing with loving care to bring to Joseph's room. Wine, cheese, elegant crackers, grapes, cloth napkins from my dining room. My husband and I exchange murderous words and I storm from the house. Words from the mouth of a fishwife I swore I never would be. Only my family knows intimately, daily, the anger that seethes from my pores. They flinch and hang onto their hair. Yet Joseph believes in my sweetness. My sweetness is my sex. And though he has been chastised by my temper, more than once, usually in moments of swift, cutting jealousy, it is deemed part of my irate Gypsy makeup—the "black Irish" in me—that intrigues him. How can you enlighten a man who is pussy-whipped? As he has called himself several times. ("Frances," he scolds me in a restaurant in Albuquerque, "if you won't let me order what I want the waiter will think I'm *pussy-whipped*"—"But, Joseph, aren't you?") He is not ashamed to say so. He loves me.

Calmer, I approach the bed and stroke him. "Darling," I breathe. There are moments when I can't believe the desire I feel for this man. I can't remove my clothes fast enough and scoot underneath the fragrant warmth of him. But something has seeped through and we can't get past it now. Our eyes are almost an identical shade of leonine hazel—but he's not hunting the savannah, he's wounded. Guarded. I say, "Darling, she's demented by having lost you," and he nods again, so sadly. "She thinks you don't know your own mind," I pursue, quietly. I am revealing my own thoughts, not only hers. I imagine that once he breaks with Arlene and moves out of her house, she will dissolve from the picture, from his life, and Joseph will be mine—finally my own. Do I think so truly? Do I underestimate the power of her? She has been calling me at my home. She frightens me and I fear for my children. "Back off," she growls. We have not banked on her fury.

"You must tell her in no uncertain terms. You must tell her," I plead, "or . . . or . . . you'll have to kill her."

I say it: I have even envisioned a fatal fall from these stairs in her house. I imagine it so precisely (as I have imagined Harry's slipping in the soap-slickened shower stall and cracking his head open) that it has become very real. The fantasy becomes essentially the same as making it happen.

Joseph coughs and bolts forward, spilling his wine over the sheets. It is red wine, the sheets peach cotton. I can't tell if he's laughing or exclaiming in horror. "Frances, come on!" he cries. "What are you saying?"

But he agrees. To what? That's it's over between them, and he must cease being her caretaker, or that he will do her in? He doesn't specify, and if I press him he replies, "Do you mind if I don't answer right away?"

At Abelard's opening, I restrain Cathy from immersing her face in the iced punch bowl and licking out the floating cubes of champagne. The loft, located on the Île de la Cité, is unlike any SoHo space I have ever seen: a commodious room with heavenly ceilings and garlands painted gaily about the moldings in the style of the ancien régime and views from the tall French windows that open out with startling clarity on the flying buttresses of Notre Dame. The Seine, as you gaze, courses beneath you on its inexorable journey through history. I have never seen Paris from this angle and I can't get over it. I try to keep Cathy from gobbling treats served from clear plastic trays. She brings her face so close to one of the hanging canvases that I feel Abelard's agent shoot a glance in our direction from the other side of the room. Friendly, but nonetheless. I sigh, grabbing the child.

She is wearing a simple garment my mother gave her: a brown corduroy jumper printed with discreet red flowers, and she wears wine-colored tights, little French flats, and a shiny barrette in her short dark hair. I find the whole effect very charming. I watch my daughter and wonder why I never wore my hair short: what is it with girls and long hair? The other mothers think short hair on girls is somehow ungirlish, unfeminine—boys won't like them. Yet we want girls to be athletic, and they have to pull their hair back in heavy ponytails in order to run around a field, kicking balls and yanking at sticks. They'd jump a lot higher without all that hair, it seems to me. When ladies age, they cut their hair short as if to signal, by their cropped, no-nonsense look, that the lure of sexuality is over and they are looking toward more *serious* pursuits. Mothers think short hair on their daughters denotes lesbianism, perhaps. Cathy has always been a tomboy, and loves her short hair, and running with the boys. I like to think that her short hair has allowed her to do away with the frivolity of girlieness, the uselessness of it. She has already cut to the seriousness of life.

Anyway, I think she's more amusing than anyone who comes up to talk to me. With her next to me I become a different woman than I would be alone. I am fuller, not exactly respectable (*sans* wedding ring), but alluring, more approachable. People feel comfortable accosting a woman with a lively, prancing child in tow: they smile at me and ask directions, or give us a benevolent nod when they hear us quarreling in English.

Abelard thinks her short hair is the bomb. He has shaved off his beard for the occasion, which is slightly alarming. I think he wants to look younger. He hasn't had a show in many years; his portraits demonstrate an impeccable, masterly technique: he is truly of the "old school," but the paintings are throwbacks, not quite edgy or brazen enough. He is unsure how to proceed in this new world, and I want to tell him just to be himself, quirky, giggling, and stinking of leathery black tobacco. Tonight he even smells strange to me. Without his beard he appears as a newly shorn lamb. He catches my eye and winks: he is having his picture taken in front of the portrait *Frances debout*. I hide behind my daughter and whisper in her ear, "Your *manners*, you urchin."

We are fancy-free tonight. Anything could happen at this opening. That is, in theory. I could pick up one of these oily Frenchmen roaming the room with their slim hips in creased trousers. I think they wouldn't mind; they might gladly return the favor. I cast my eyes over the crowd and speculate on some sort of kindred collision we romantics dream of but which rarely happens. We want romance because it will change our lives and we want desperately to change our lives. We leave our homes in Topeka or New York and come to Paris and we will be transformed. Anything, as long as it isn't what we have at the moment.

A man walks up to the drinks table. He is middling handsome, bespectacled, dressed in the understated professional fashion of the European bourgeoisie. He is smiling tentatively, a bit unsure, and I know if I look away he will veer and avoid me, but if I hold his gaze for just a second longer he will attempt to engage me in conversation. It's a fraught moment, this: which way will it go? Will we find sufficient sympathy to exchange pleasantries, or will I find myself in the tiresome position of deflecting personal comments and turn our attention to Abelard's sense of composition? The weather? It's decided in an instant, more or less: I size him up, he sizes me up, or maybe he has already been appraising me from elsewhere in the room before approaching. So he has the advantage of surprise, which isn't quite fair, and I have an instant to make the cut. But there is nothing recognizable about this man (or rather, he is too familiar to me), slightly graying and tired, neither thin nor fat, dressed for work in an office somewhere; perhaps he is an account manager or an actuary. He is neither predatory nor timid, but merely available, and it isn't me he wants, but anyone like me will do. He is not objectionable and there is nothing wrong with him, but I know in that instant that I could never love him, and I feel sorry about this even as we speak: what is he doing here? Who has he loved? I will not pursue this man, or give him my number, or take his. A kind of sadness holds me apart, resignation, an emotional paralysis, and the knowledge that I have loved elsewhere, another man, and it is enough.

"JOSEPH, HAVE you been well?"

"As well as can be expected. My spirits seem to have their own autonomous powers—tenuously connected to the phenomenal world—but have me on a wild ride yet. At least I've managed to pull out all the tatters and threads of duplicity and lies."

"Are you working?"

"Excavating, Frances, from the tough old languages. Hoping always to make a well-made song. I don't know . . ."

"You *will*."

"And Cathy? How is she? I dream about her. I dreamed that we met."

"I know, Joseph. She's fine. She won't take off the '2' sweater you gave her." I lie, I don't have the heart to tell him that she has left it on the seat of a subway car. "She wants a pet."

He laughs. "Which one?"

"Oh, a cat. A dog. Someone to play with."

"I had a dog. His name was Diego."

"I remember. I mean, you told me," I add quickly. "He nipped you once on your lip." My love doesn't remember telling me this story: is he really growing elderly? Having what he jokes as a "senior moment"? I feel a spasm of alarm at his forgetfulness.

He laughs his sweet laugh again. "That's right. I buried him in the redwood forest."

"Dogs love you. Remember you told me how you would play catch with Jan when she was a kid and the ball would go over the fence where the two big dogs lived in back of your house? And you actually climbed over the fence to fetch the ball and the dogs never cared or bothered you? They recognized one of their own."

"That's because I'm part dog."

I smell again his wild animal hair.

"Darling, I would never have ventured over the fence!"

"Frances, you can't be afraid of dogs?" He ribs me, though he knows I am. We laugh a while and are glad. Then I ask seriously, for I have a reason to call:

"Joseph, have you told them . . . I mean, do they know that I was there . . . and that we saw each other?"

"Frances, I don't want you and your children mixed up in my mess. I have to face this alone."

Alone, he says. Sadly, I remember his words from before, *I have to do this alone,* and other words, too: *Wait for me.* I have also read that single men (divorcés, widowers) of a certain age are snatched up within a year or so of their freedom. And by someone who will take care of them.

"But if you tell them," I pursue cautiously, "and if *she* tells them, they'll let you go."

"No," he says quickly. "I don't know. Anyway, I don't remember what I've told them. There're so many people asking questions, Frances, and I'm tired of the sound of my voice."

"Well, Joseph, that's a first."

"Oh, sweetheart."

CATHY BLOWS bubbles in her glass of milk. Hard to get, a glass of milk in a Paris restaurant. I try to pay for our lunch with a credit card, but am politely rebuffed and directed to a bank across the street. The waiter lectures me on something that sounds like a retail tax. I nod and nod, draining the last of my wine.

"What's he saying?" she asks.

"I have no idea," I reply, smiling.

Outside, we pick our way along the crowded Quai de la Mégisscrie so that Cathy can dart in and out of pet stores. She delights in watching the exotic birds in cages, proud colored parrots and pastel cockatiels. Tiny furry creatures that must be guinea pigs (I dislike them since one named Petunia bit Bernie at his nursery school) and numerous litters of sweetly tumbling kittens and blubbery puppies. Now I shall hear her whine the rest of the evening about getting a pet. I steer her toward the fish tanks and we watch the silk-tailed goldfish meander seductively. I indicate the beauty in their diffident self-sufficiency, but Cathy grows bored at my obvious attempt to distract her.

"You can't *play* with them," she brays.

"A turtle?" I suggest.

"Can I put him in our luggage?"

"No. Nothing that moves."

We lose ourselves for hours in La Samaritaine. I need to find the right tablecloth for Joseph's kitchen table and I sift through what must be dozens of fabrics and sizes. We are sent to one floor, then up the central steel-trestled staircase to the next. I remember the table is oval, of goodly size, long enough for the two of us to sit comfortably at breakfast. Here Joseph places himself to write mid-morning, as the sun dapples the grassy yard just beyond the sliding glass door. In his notebook he toils over his translations and etymologies (*pashu:* domestic animal, also wealth = relating to cattle, sexual intercourse), then pauses to write a letter to me. His soft, sharpened pencils and fine-tipped felt pens are ordered to each side, his dictionaries and notebooks in which the spindly Sanskrit letters dangle from the ledgered pages like wet clothes flapping from a wash line. He has made himself a cup of black tea in his peculiar fashion, loose tea rinsed first in the boiling water, then the water discarded and the pot refilled. "To weaken the caffeine," he informs me (showing his age). Then he begins to write, in neat, elegant script:

"Dearest Frances, you've flooded my life with possibilities I was afraid had been lost long ago! When we make love the world does right itself: nothing seems more right. Don't you see that in my 'cosmos' I want at the center of my domicile, not the kitchen (though kids need that), not the work desk—certainly not the tv!—but the love bed should be the center—with all the sweet fragrances, flickering candles, ecstasy juice, pungent sweat, knees, ankles, moist hair, whispered words, shared squeals, commands, surprises, greediness, sacrifice, trickles of ecstasies, abasements, proud eyebrows, glint in the eye, lingering kisses, vanished hours, excruciating minutes, dear flesh fruit, pulses quickening, convulsive pleasures . . . The 'soft rites of Aphrodite' are the civilized part of me. Oh Frances, you give me the sweetest raptures! I go nearly mad tossing in bed at night, missing you so acutely."

He puts down his pen, stretches his back, then scribbles a quick note to Jan: "Gone to take a swim. I'll be out and about for a few hours. Call the cell if you need me. Yours, Daddy-O."

I've seen these notes on his kitchen table, and I've been tempted to snatch one and put it in my pocket. Instead, I pilfer one of his pencils and use it to write in my notebook on the airport bus out of town. I can't recall the colors of his kitchen—I know he prefers greens and blues, the hues of the mountains, but I choose oranges and reds. My colors. The color of the Scarlet Ibis hotel room. The color of the mandarin roses I sent him as a housewarming for his new saltbox. The colors of sunrise, when he is never awake, though I lay still, next to him, obsessively counting the hours we have left together before I have to return to my laundry life. The colors of my lipstick, Prune Brûlée, left at the corners of his mouth, the tips of his fingers, along his Grecian thighs. I select a tablecloth called Darjeeling, rectangular and far too expensive, then ask Cathy, who is swinging from the store's balcony railings, what she thinks.

"Who's it for?" she asks suspiciously. "Daddy?"

"No, I'll get him something else. Maybe a sweater, but the French sizes are too dainty for him." She frowns; she knows what *dainty* means, and it's the opposite of *large*.

"You're buying a tablecloth for Abelard? He shaved off his beard for you."

"For me? No, I don't think so." I think of Abelard, standing clean-shaven before *Frances debout,* to have his picture taken. "It's a woman who takes us places, isn't it?" he has said, giggling.

"Then who?"

"My friend Joseph in Boulder."

"Him again? Why not that nice brown man we met? I like him."

"What? Why would Lewis need a tablecloth? He only eats in restaurants."

"Why would Joseph need one? Isn't he in prison?"

I drop the box. We stare at each other. "I beg your pardon? What did you say?"

"I said, Joseph's in prison, isn't he?"

"Did Lewis tell you that?"

"No. But I figured he's somewhere he can't get out, locked up, and isn't that prison?"

I turn away from her. Later, as I purchase the tablecloth, despite the cost, she ferrets her moist little fingers inside my glove. "Do you love Daddy?" she squeaks.

"For the record, I do."

She stands with her head slightly lowered, considering what she will ask next.

"Look, missy," I tell her preemptively, "do you think I could have married a man I didn't love? I think Harry is a fine person, a wonderful father. I knew he would be, and that's why I chose him. And he's loyal, the most loyal man I ever met."

The force of this startling revelation stings my eyes. Cathy wonders what *loyal* is.

"Like dogs are supposed to be—devoted and faithful."

"But why don't you love him *now*?" she insists.

"I love him in a different way. Our love changed. Because he drives like an old man. Because he sucks his teeth after dinner. Because his socks stink up the house. I don't know! Because—because—" I almost shout, and stop before I tell her the rest: the strain of child rearing wrecked our sex life.

"Look, it's not your fault," I murmur.

Glumly, we move into the hair salon, for I have promised Cathy a Frenchified do.

"Ah, qu'elle est mignonne!" cries the young hairdresser, fussing around her small wet head. He elevates her high in the chair and she grins devilishly at me from the mirror. I sink into a chair opposite, letting my arms fall heavily at my sides so that the bags I hold kerplunk noisily to the floor. The warm vapors of chemical botanicals make me instantly sleepy. Young Monsieur asks me many questions and can't believe how well an American speaks French. He fingers and fluffs Cathy's hair, all the while chatting and gesticulating. His brother lives in Miami, though he himself has never been to New York; he hears it's very expensive. Why go anywhere more expensive than Paris? He brings out the gel and mattes Cathy's hair for a windstorm, then steps back triumphantly. "They say they've never had a better cut!" he exclaims, inviting my praise.

His eyebrows hitch at the sight of my own brown mane, clipped up expediently in tortoise-shell claws.

"You, Madame, next?"

"Ah no," I tell him, "I prefer the Simone de Beauvoir look. You know, in a turban?"

He stares blankly and shrugs.

I tip him largely, nonetheless. I am happy to have an adult to talk to. Cathy waves gallantly, tossing her new sleek head, too preoccupied with her own reflection to ask another question, for an hour at least.

I KEEP assiduous records. In that way I'm a little like Cathy, who's afraid of missing anything if she naps, who slips the receipt inside the pocket of her anorak because she wants to make sure that nothing is lost on her. I'm old school that way. When Joseph alludes to a book of poetry or nonfiction (he does not read fiction), I write it down in my notebook. I will find the truth in the books Joseph suggests I read. I have aspirations; Joseph is impressed by the avidity with which I read. He lies still, preternaturally still, in my arms at the modest hotel in Boulder and he describes for me his first encounter with a wolf—the eyes. "A fierce green fire dying in her eyes," he cites an earlier encounter by Aldo Leopold in his book *A Sand County Almanac,* in which the hunter author has shot the animal and watches her die. "I was young then, and full of trigger-itch," Leopold writes, but after watching the green fire die, he learns something new, "something known only to her and to the mountain." Joseph once happens upon a mountain lion (a cougar, a catamount), or rather climbs into the animal's territory, because Joseph's own hair stands on end as he senses the danger. "It was then I dropped into a fern and wildflower gulch, fantastically pungent with the odor of mammal. I knew who to watch for," he says. He keeps climbing, however. I couldn't have told you what a catamount is, or what juniper looks like, or imitate the sound of a meadowlark, for that matter. I listen to Joseph's cowboy stories: he spreads his arms eagle-like in demonstration of a buffalo dance he has witnessed on a New Mexico Indian pueblo. I bite his animal hair, mold my fingers claylike into the furrows of his form so that I won't forget an inch of him.

There is an abrupt knock at the door, the sound of the bolt turning, and then the head of a hotel worker, a janitor, pokes into our room. I cry, "Excuse us!" and pull the sheet over our naked bodies. When the door quickly shuts, I leap out of bed and run to bolt it. I return to Joseph, who laughs at this untoward intrusion, delighted at the indignant alacrity of my response.

When I am preparing to leave this room, it is afternoon already and I fold up the few black garments I have brought and stuff them back into my duffel bag, which has become heavier, no doubt from the books and kites I have purchased for my children. Joseph stands at the far end of the room by the window and watches me. He takes out a parcel from his rucksack: a book he has carefully wrapped in white tissue, tied with a slender hemp cord, and knotted with a sprig of juniper. He hands the parcel to me and tells me I mustn't open it until I get home. A sprig of juniper freshly plucked from its parent tree and still moistly redolent of the mountains. I am nonplussed, overcome, and also mortified that I haven't thought to bring a present, too. Here begins our Japanese courtly ritual, inspired by the gracious eleventh-century lady writers Joseph incorporates into his teaching. He urges me to read Sei Shōnagon's *Pillow Book*—the title alone fills me with nightly raptures. Like me, and Joseph, she is a scribbler: an intelligent, most exacting well-born lady-in-waiting to Empress Sadako who gathers her personal notes of court life over ten-odd years into a "pillow." She writes (in a translation by Ivan Morris): "I set about filling the notebooks with odd facts, stories from the past, and all sorts of other things, often including the most trivial material. On the whole I concentrated on things and people that I found charming and splendid; my notes are also full of poems and observations on trees and plants, birds and insects." Sei Shōnagon has marked likes and dislikes: for example, she delights in a stormy wind that suddenly blows into the room and stings her face; she loves donning a carefully scented robe she has forgotten about, then wearing it again to assimilate its delicious odor; she is pleased to receive a visitor she hasn't seen for many weeks but who is inspired by the moonlight to remember their previous encounters. "And then, if it is at all possible, I will keep him with me for the night." She is also a snob, and vents her displeasure at breaches of protocol, ugly faces, ill-bred children, a shameful man's heart—because when he finds the woman he has been with tiresome and distasteful, he continues to treat her in such a way that she cannot imagine his feelings are anything but sincere.

These are tender discoveries, and I pocket them secretly.

Together Joseph and I visit museum exhibits of Japanese prints, which we find in Boston or New York. The Asian wing of the Met is the least visited part of the museum, an abandoned appendage, and even on a Saturday afternoon we have the softly lighted, carpeted rooms mostly to ourselves. We peer closely at ukiyo-e prints—depicting the "floating world," fleeting scenes, a world of gauze. These are often highly stylized colored ink drawings of lovers in private quarters, not necessarily at erotic play, though we find these, too, at private galleries in New York. The figures in ukiyo-e are theatrical—kabuki players—kissing, beseeching, bidding farewell. Or a young woman is seated simply, adorably, at her toilette. There are also prints depicting scenes from Lady Murasaki's *Tale of Genji*, Joseph's absolute favorite; he even has a print in his bedroom, purchased many years before, showing Prince Niou spiriting the lovely Ukifune to the Islet of Oranges on a boat during a snowstorm. He must have bought it from a friendly Berkeley bookseller who was forced to close his shop, since Joseph would never have been able to afford a costly print. (He attempts several times to mention the teaching salary he makes, but I won't hear it.) We stand side by side for hours gazing at these intricate, fragile works. Joseph crouches low to read a label and absently strokes my black-stockinged leg.

He has translated Mirabai, a popular Indian singer of religious songs who lived in the sixteenth century, and these violent, passionate lyrics pierce me acutely. "Come to my bedroom, I've scattered fresh buds on the couch, perfumed my body," she lures.

A princess who renounced her exalted lineage, and an arranged marriage to a lord of a neighboring clan, Mirabai took up the way of the *sadhu*, or wandering holy man, to sing songs to Krishna, her beloved, mysterious Dark One. Her songs are endowed with sacred devotion, suffused with ardent erotic love: "Listen, friend, the Dark One laughs and scours my body with ravenous eyes." She is persecuted throughout her life by her in-laws, but remains a fearless, defiant, ecstatic seeker: Whom do I think of when I read her? Of Arlene Manhunter, of course, shaking her terrifying aegis, forsaking all but her vow to poetry. Joseph has dedicated the book to her.

When I go West, Joseph introduces me to writers who are important in his desert mythology. On the plane coming to meet him in Albuquerque I read Wallace Stegner's *Beyond the Hundredth Meridian* and attract mild interest from my fellow passengers. They speak with open, lazy vowels, colloquial and youthful the way Arlene speaks over the phone, and sometimes I catch the same accent in Joseph's words, although he grew up in the East. He picks me up at the airport and we drive to the foothills of the Flatirons; I change my shoes so that I can walk along a trail. He has packed everything we need for a picnic, cheese and bread and a bottle of Vouvray, a blanket and real wineglasses, and we perch on a craggy lookout high above the town. There are occasional hikers along the trail, mostly descending, since it is near sundown; the air is ripe-spring and fresh. We neck and fondle; he brings me to orgasm with his fingers. He reads to me from William Clark's diaries of his Western exploration of June 30, 1804: "A very large wolf came to the back and looked at us this morning," reads Joseph, withholding more wine because he is afraid I will turn over and pitch down into the ravine. He kisses me. "That's how I must feel when I look at you after love." Do I believe him? I do, I've seen it: I believe every word he tells me.

Hungrily I list in my notebook works that must be devoured: Edward Abbey's trenchant, seventies' *Desert Solitaire,* Mary Austin's *Land of Little Rain,* and, since we have visited Santa Fe together, Willa Cather's *Death Comes to the Archbishop.* I learn from Abbey, who lived alone in a wind-ravaged trailer in Moab, Utah, where he spent several stints as a park ranger, how to get rid of rattlesnakes sleeping under your porch steps. (Get a gopher snake.) From Austin's book I carry away the excellent phrase "high truce at noon" to describe the unrelenting midday sun that nearly kills me, hiking without a hat on as we peer at petroglyphs in New Mexico. I borrow the kerchief Joseph wears around his neck like a bandito to catch the sweat. I vow to filch one of these kerchiefs before I leave him so that I may carry his scent always with me. (He thinks his neck is long, as mine is long, though for a man it is deemed a flaw. I cannot agree, and I am sorry he even points it out because I believe him perfect.) From Cather I glean the topography of the desert country, and the fierce single-mindedness of the initial settlers: French missionaries who introduced the concept of growing garden vegetables.

I read poetry and essays by Gary Snyder, a mountain man like Joseph turned Beat poet and Eastern seeker. Snyder writes in the essay "Ancient Forests of the Far West" about his experience as a chokersetter for the lumber industry in the Pacific Northwest in the early fifties, when men relished "the skills of our hands and our well-made tools," even though the work they did—felling massive old growth—"is no longer quite right." Later, when Joseph teaches his fall course on Ezra Pound, there are *The Cantos* to read, though I falter a quarter of the way into them and cannot go on. I buck and snarl and sense that I have encountered an imposter, and I say as much to Joseph. He sympathizes, because he believes that one needs a guide through these stormy waters, and I am too far away for him to offer the proper assistance. The gap of thousands of miles between us has begun to torment us endlessly. I feel I have failed him by not tackling this book.

By the time I get to Jack Kerouac, Joseph has left to take Jan to visit prep schools in Boston. I have urged him to look into schools that will challenge her, and his family lives in Boston, besides; secretly, I am hoping this is a way to bring him East. I immerse myself in Kerouac's love-glutted, heartbreaking prose the week Joseph is away; I read *On the Road, The Subterraneans, Tristessa,* and *Visions of Cody*, because Joseph suggests I start with these. But I have not gone to Boston with Joseph, although he asks me (Bernie has an ear infection and Cathy must perform in a school concert), and when he returns a week later, Arlene and ex-wife Belinda are after him like two knives sharpened to dagger-points. (This must be a metaphor I remember from *Madame Bovary*.) Belinda reveals to Arlene, after these many years of hostile silence between the two women, that he slept with his ex-wife again. "We made love in your bed," she tells Arlene. "He said that if I ever told you he would never speak to me again." Is she triumphant? Or relieving a heavy conscience? The double, triple, betrayal leaves Joseph reeling, and there are days, nights, when he does not call me at all.

We speak of Kerouac only once, and that is when I rebuke Joseph for his coldness toward me:

"These harridans have iced your heart."

"Ah, you've been reading Kerouac," he replies.

In *Tristessa*, Kerouac's narrator agonizes intoxicatedly over a bony skid-row junkie in Mexico City, whom he might or might not have slept with, since she ends up marrying the sinister, independently wealthy William Burroughs character for a ready morphine supply. Old Bull Gaines, as described, with his "thin, emaciated, long nosed, strangely handsome worlding ('student of souls and cities,' he calls himself) decapitated and bombed out by morphine frame." Over breakfast at our Albuquerque hotel Joseph describes this book to me as a beautiful love story. I write it down in my notebook. Later when I find *Tristessa* in the library and read about the poor lost girl and her rooster and her complicated Mexican poverty, I heed Kerouac's words, "the beauty of things must be that they end." On this trip to Albuquerque I have begged Joseph to tell Arlene about our liaison; I have warned him that if he does not come clean, she will hate him forever. It is sound advice and he will try to follow it, he says, but he does not.

I WAS born in Albuquerque, I tell Joseph, and it's the truth. He can't believe it. A city girl like me? Afraid of dogs? We are lying half-dressed on the big hotel bed, stalling over our wine because Joseph ejaculates precipitously when we haven't seen each other for a while and he requires time to recharge. Sometimes we are simply fondling each other; he touches my naked breasts ("I have dreamed of your breasts") and he comes in his cotton underpants. It is an adorable quality, boylike, guileless, and I remember the sweet confusion of our first night together when he came inside me unannounced and unprotected. (Is he a scoundrel, I wondered? Can he be so clueless? Or had he and Arlene ceased conjugal relations altogether?) Sometimes I do mind when he comes too quickly, and I curl up on the bed in frustration, as it's been weeks since I've seen him; but this weekend we have three days ahead of us, and long splendid nights when he will bite my neck and rough-ride me from behind.

"Placidas is where we lived," I tell him. "We moved around a lot when I was a kid. We moved steadily east, as American families did, in search of better jobs. We lived in a small adobe house in the middle of the desert then. I don't remember much. The Sandia Mountains, the tarantulas out back and centipedes in the bathtub, the rattlesnakes on the front porch that drove our dog into a frenzy. My mother would lock us kids in the car and go after the snake with a garden hoe. And once my uncle brought a wild pony for us to ride—a wild pony! As if we could ride it."

Joseph, intrigued, toys with the hem of my skirt, nibbles underneath. I don't often speak of myself and my family. Or maybe my love does not ask? He wonders:

"You wouldn't want to move back out here?"

"I would, darling. I never wanted to end up living in New York. I don't know how it happened, except that I simply stayed after college and then got married and my husband would never consider leaving. I wanted always to live in Paris, too."

"I would love that, Frances," he says with warm conviction.

"If I moved out here?"

"Yes."

"I would live next door to you," I tell him, slipping out of my skirt and guiding him gently toward me. "And I would never bother you."

We meet in Albuquerque the first and only friend we make together: a sad-eyed middle-aged lady waiting in the café at the tram stop on Sandia Peak. She makes room for us at her table, and we fall into conversation. She is a teacher from Minneapolis visiting some friends who live out West, though they have not come sightseeing with her. She adores Georgia O'Keeffe and likes to gamble at the big new casino that has just opened in one of the nearby reservations. We tell our stories and laugh together and she does not look at us disapprovingly, wondering at the connection between us. When the tram arrives, we all pile in and descend together. It is twilight: the beady, distant lights of the extended city blink open like the startled eyes of owls. Joseph and I stand in the center of the tram, squeezed on all sides by other folk buoyed by the liquor imbibed at the café. Everyone is laughing and singing, exclaiming at the godly view of the blood-bathed mountains rising before us. Joseph and I kiss, a deep, tongue-winding kiss, while our neighbors hoot and slur, and it feels like our honeymoon.

WHAT HAPPENS when you've been loved grandly, then discarded, is that you combat the urge to bury yourself. To let others bury you. The shame (of loss, of failure) is debilitating, and wears away your fighting spirit—the will to defend yourself. It happened, didn't it? He loved me, didn't he? You're left with a sense of unreality: it was all a dream. You no longer *exist*. Arlene's mission, once she learns that the woman who is calling Joseph is the same woman she met at Douglas's wedding, is to annihilate me. She will undermine Joseph's love for me. She procures my number from Douglas, and particulars of my living situation. She calls in the evening when I am fixing dinner for the kids or trying to shepherd them to bed. She calls when Bernie has insisted I put on the Jan and Dean CD that he loves to listen to. She calls on Saturday afternoon, when my baby is asleep, and I am rocking in Granny's chair, watching the phone. I am hoping for a call from Joseph, though he has been strange, distant, preoccupied with school duties. And it is not my love I hear after grabbing up the receiver at the first ring, but Arlene. She is violently troubled.

Do I hang up the phone? No, I do not. I listen, the blood pounding in my ears.

"You don't belong here," she insists, in her low growl.

"What do you mean?" I ask, though I know what she means: I've spent the weekend in Boulder and she has spotted me, or rather her spies have, since she knows everyone in town. I am not of her *tribe*, not an ex-husband, ex-lover, child from this marriage or that, not a Buddhist, contemplative, or poet, for that matter, who buzz around her like drones and preen and flatter her particular brand of queenly radiance. "Joseph invites me to come, and why shouldn't I?"

"These are my establishments," she retorts, "the hiking trails Joseph and I walked together, the movie theaters I frequent with my friends. This is a small town."

Yes, we hike in the hills. We sit for hours on the vast, open meadow, under a mild blue sky, watching the solitary hawks soar above us. I'm wearing one of his leather jackets even though it's not terrifically cold for a March afternoon; I can't get warm in this altitude. I inch off my boulder to encircle him in my arms. He has sat upon a cactus and had to extract needles from the seat of his jeans. We don't laugh; it's not funny, and we're not in the mood, feeling hungover and gloomy after a stormy weekend (I'm not aware it's my last in Boulder), before he has to shuttle me to the bus station for a ride to the airport. Joseph recites for me poetry he has memorized years before while baking bread in the wee hours of the morning; he used to work at a bakery in Berkeley. He remembers mostly Yeats, "Crazy Jane Talks with the Bishop": "A woman can be proud and stiff/When on love intent;/But Love has pitched his mansion in/The place of excrement." I laugh; I rock him tenderly in my arms. Such a treasure is he!

"You spy on us," I tell her.

I recall what Joseph has affirmed, slightly sinisterly, when I admonish him on his extravagant tip or his servile exchange with an oily maître d': *"I have to live in this town."*

"I don't need to," she replies. "I have a lot of friends. They've seen you."

She's in Florida, always traveling, always on the move to spread her benevolent karma. She mentions that it's very beautiful there, but I don't ask more than that.

"He slept with Belinda again, did you know that? He brought her to our bed and slept with her over several weeks when I was away in Indonesia."

She thinks she's got me here: but don't I already know? Didn't I already guess that first morning in the kitchen of their house, when I sat on his lap? Hasn't Joseph already unloaded his accumulated grief on me? I don't express surprise. Arlene is irksomely quiet and tries another tactic.

"Good, so he told you."

"Of course. He told me early on."

"There have been others."

Again she thinks she has me, but Joseph has confessed to minor adulteries over the years of living with Arlene. A couple of his "dear students," one who renamed herself Sunflower, an orphan, unstable and on medication, with a history of seducing her professors. I have been jealous of Sunflower, especially since the game graduate student is now teaching in his Buddhist studies department and there have been communal dinners at her house in Denver. Sometimes he fails to mention at whose house the dinner has been held, and I have hit the roof. Still, I have been apprised of these inconsequential encounters during Arlene's prolonged absences from their house, when Joseph, starved for affection and tenderness, took comfort in other arms. He did not fall in love. The problem, of course, is that the university holds strict guidelines forbidding the untoward fraternization of a professor and his student, to the extent that a teacher cannot even hire a student to mow his lawn.

"Sunflower, yeah."

"And others."

My friends have asked me—that is, the church ladies to whom I have opened my heart, Claire and Prudence—why would I let

Arlene even speak to me? Why not hang up? Why allow her to pour her venomous words about my cherished one into my ear? A complicated question. Arlene is a famous poet, an intelligent and sensitive woman, and I have been complicit in wronging her. I feel much like Joseph when she calls him in the morning, his most vulnerable time, and screams for several minutes, simply screams, releasing an elemental fury, and Joseph cannot hang up on her. He sets the phone on the bed while he takes a shower, possibly, or tidies up the books on his bedside table. "But you can hang up on me, why can't you on her?" I demand, petulantly, reminding him of a hissing argument we have over the phone one night when he admits, belatedly, that he has not called me back because he is out drinking with "dear friends." What writhing I endure over the hours of his revelry! "Oh that's rotten," I chastise, and curse, which I never do, because it is not ladylike and Joseph will intone, "This is not a dignified discussion we are having." Then he hangs up on me, leaving me speechless on my knees in my bed as my two children slumber innocently in the rooms next to me. It is the first time he hangs up on me, perhaps the only; nonetheless, he will not hang up on Arlene. She is entitled to her fury, and she has braved it out among Beatnik male poets in sixties' Greenwich Village. She has sat under the Bodhi Tree with Allen Ginsberg. She is interesting, historic. The truth is that both of us are terrified of her.

What do Prudence and Claire think of my pusillanimity? They are appalled. "Why do you have to listen to this woman? Tell her to go to hell!" they cry indignantly. They are both married to good men, who love them and still regard them as beautiful. My friends wouldn't hesitate to bang the phone down righteously on Arlene's fury. Yet I find about these ladies an inflexibility, a quality that rears up at moments as unforgiving, rigid, or blinkered, and perhaps results from not reading much literary fiction. Prudence, for example, tells of an earlier boyfriend who cheated on her, then confessed contritely. He wanted to marry her, but Prudence moved out immediately and never forgave him. She did not send birthday cards, as his other girlfriends would; she did not call him. Once he strayed it was clear to Prudence, who had adored him, that she was not his *beshert*. Well, I agree, yes, but also: it's not quite the way the heart works, is it? I sense that if my friends knew the extent of Joseph's history they certainly wouldn't love him.

When I ask Arlene why she took Joseph back after learning about his adulteries early on—for he had his affair with Sunflower three years into their relationship—she answers, simply, "I love him."

And adds quickly: "I don't fall for Lotharios."

I have to laugh. Who is she kidding? (Who am I?)

She intimates that there are "others."

"Hasn't he had to find new friends because your shared friends deserted him?" I demand. "He is isolated, a pariah. He has had to *reinvent* himself," I tell her, feeling slightly foolish using the expression Joseph has written to me.

I let her ramble, but I don't hear her tumbleweed opinions about his "sickness" and need for therapy.

"Arlene, I have to go. The children need me."

"And your husband? How is he?"

"Harry is fine. He's, he's . . . sad, grim, smarting, but he's grasping the inevitable."

Harry is sullen most mornings when he appears from his hut. He unloads the dishwasher with an infernal clatter, tossing the breakfast dishes on the table so that we all wake up in a sour mood. These mornings we do not speak to or look at one another.

"I saw Douglas yesterday," Arlene purrs, apropos.

"Douglas loves Harry. Douglas doesn't know anything," I add with quiet resolution.

She backs off. But the harm is done. The mistrust sown like a poisonous weed. Isn't this why I have let her talk—don't I need to know about Joseph and his secret arts? But then, I already know.

SHE PAYS her seven euros to the surly fellow in the ticket shed and finds an empty trampoline at the Tuileries playground. It's a cool, overcast day: still a stubborn, lingering winter that won't let me forget that I may not see springtime in Paris. Lewis appears, in a snazzy leather jacket, not the cracked, worn kind that Joseph wears, but buttery-smooth, flawless; whenever he appears I can't actually remember telling him when and where we've agreed to meet. I note to myself that I won't mention our whereabouts the next time. I'll test him. Yet he is very kind; today he brings pastries in a little white sack for Cathy. She waves from the trampoline, her short, dark hair bowling around her face as she jumps. She has discarded her jacket and shoes. She is intent and competitive, using fully her time on the low, ground-level trampoline, having learned from her last experience here that the shed keeper will shout at the children when their paltry ten minutes are up, and make them hastily vacate the equipment unless their parents have paid for a second jump. She is oblivious to the beauty around her: the seventeenth-century galleries of the Louvre within a stone's throw, the stately symmetry of the tidy French gardens. Lewis and I stand and sip at coffees we buy at the little outdoor café, deserted during this interregnum between winter and spring. We watch Cathy jump and we speak about this and that; specifically, I find my opportunity to ask him questions.

"What is it you do for a living?" I put it to him directly, scowling across the eyes.

"I'm a private investigator."

"How interesting! What stories you must learn."

"Not really. My work involves a lot of waiting around and tedious follow-up. It's not glamorous work, actually."

"You mean it's not very amusing having to watch a kid jumping on a trampoline when what you're really getting at . . . is. . . ?" I turn to him severely, daring him to answer me truly.

"Frances," he says. He looks around, the tip of his nose reddening slightly from the nipping cold. "Can we sit down a minute?" He thrusts his cup into my hand, then trots to the ticket shed and offers the glowering attendant another bill so that Cathy can continue to jump for a while. I feel a little awkward, wondering where all of this is going to lead. Should I grab Cathy and run? Has the moment of truth arrived? Am I ready for this? Lewis returns and I shrug. We repair to the café chairs, a few feet away, and put down our now empty cups. We watch my daughter jump and I wave from time to time. Besides a couple of other families, there is no one around: the sky is nearly white, the trees bare and valiantly shivering.

"How long," Lewis begins, with a pained look, "are you planning to stay in Paris?"

"I don't know. Till the money runs out."

"But school for Cathy?"

"I'm home-schooling her."

"I see. You know, you'll need to go back and answer questions."

"How's that?"

"Arlene Manhunter has disappeared."

We shift on our hard Tuileries café chairs.

"I had heard that."

"You could help us find her."

"Lewis, come on. She went underground. Leave her be."

"You could help us find her," he repeats, sternly.

"Why do you think she wants to be found?"

"*Quoi?*"

"Lewis, haven't you ever wanted to run away?"

"Frances, I suppose so." He sighs.

"Why can't Joseph tell you where she is?"

"He says he doesn't know."

"Then let him go."

"He doesn't have an alibi on the night of her disappearance."

Lewis watches me closely. I'm not sure what to do with this new information.

"Time's up," I say, indicating my daughter, bounding toward us without her coat. My little bird dog has spied the white bag of pastries.

I KNOCK at the door of Harry's hut. The night is raw and damp, the grass still brown and hard from a savage winter. I can't find the moon anywhere overhead, through the shutters of the towering pines. Cathy sleeps in the room that opens to the backyard, and so soundly I know she won't wake. I carry a box of Harry's favorite cookies, delicately layered wafers called gaufrettes. I see through the window glass that he's listening on his earphones, probably to the punk rock music he's crazy about, which appeals in a curious way to an unrestrained Harry he rarely allows anyone to see, and maybe I have seen once or twice, or even brought out in him: the New York Dolls and Iggy Pop. Harry doesn't answer my knock, so I wave my arms around at him through the window. Behind fogged spectacles he blinks at me for a moment, then removes the unwieldy black earphones from his head and opens the door in his work shirtsleeves—a starched white shirt he'll also sleep in. If he's been out in the sun a bit, a white shirt sets off the olive in his skin handsomely, though this night he is darkly unshaven, his skin sallow in the pale moonless winter's light.

"Here's a snack for you," I say and hand him the gaufrettes. He mutters thanks, his head sunk low and glasses so opaque I can't read his eyes. I ask, "Do you mind if I come in and talk to you for a minute? I—" The sound of an approaching emergency landing by a frantically wing-batting duck makes us turn and look at the same time: one of the mallards, the emerald-headed male, dive-bombs flat-footed into the creek. He has arrived from warmer climes to join his mate of numerous past springtimes, who bobs patiently in his glimmering wake. Reunited with some clapping and splashing, they settle down and together they paddle noisefully downstream. The spectacle does not strike us as comic, but rather sad, and I resume quietly, "I can't talk to you out here."

We glance instinctively up at Cathy's second-story window. Harry steps back inside and returns to his drafting table, illuminated by a stork-legged lamp. He traces lines for a Palladian façade with his sliding parallel rule. I ask, "What project is this?" with exquisite formality, since I used to know in detail all the projects my husband worked on. He mentions the Manhattan address, which means nothing to me, and I glance around: the place is cozy, lined with shelves housing Harry's (and his deceased mother's) extensive collection of art books. Also manly bric-à-brac such as his father's silver flask and beaten-leather shaving kit and a small, rippled photograph of his tanned young mother skeet shooting back in Transylvania. What does my husband think about in this hut at night? I perch at the edge of his single cot, to keep out of his way as he works, and imagine, briefly, making love in this place where there is barely enough room to turn around (it's cozier than our bedroom ever was). But I can't imagine, since we haven't made love since Bernie was conceived, and along with the memory of passion vanishes the curiosity even to see the other naked.

"Listen, Harry, I want to get away for a while"—*whoosh!* he stresses a long, deep line with his parallel rule—"and I thought I'd go to Paris, after all"—*whoosh!* the outline for the Corinthian column—"and I want to take the kids with me, if that's okay with you."

He moves his ruler an inch to the left, "No way," says he. "It's the middle of the school year, Frances."

"I know. But Harry," I murmur, lowering my voice, "there's trouble. The police are going to come around."

"Ha," he says, shaking his head.

"Harry, they suspect Joseph. What if they arrest *me?* Who's going to take care of the children so you can work? You'll have to feed them, give baths, and wash the dishes every night by yourself. Make lunches in the morning and catch the bus on time. And what will you tell our neighbors when the Feds drive up in trucks to take me away?"

Harry spins around and glares at me. He curses silently, shakes his head, but he doesn't ask. My husband does not ask. He returns to stroke his lines vehemently with rule and pen, and I can tell by the truculent slouch of his rounded shoulders that I've caught his attention.

"Harry, do you remember when we went to Turin"—*whoosh! whoosh!* goes the parallel rule—"and we stood in front of the Church of San Lorenzo where you were trying to explain to me Guarini's Baroque aesthetic? You despaired of my inability to grasp the subtleties, or rather extravagances, of it all, but I did—and do, by the way, and think you're really extremely good at what you do—but maybe I was just distracted, or full from lunch, or simply overwhelmed by the beauty of everything and not deserving of your scorn, Harry?"

"Let sleeping dogs lie," replies Harry, coldly.

"Yes, but I think our brains just work differently"—*whoosh!* he sighs—"I mean, you have to *draw* everything and set it out on grids, while I need to *describe* it in words: your brain is analytical and mine is intuitive, and how can two people be so different?"

He puts down his pen and turns to face me, elbows working.

"All right, Fran," he says finally. He is the only one who calls me Fran.

"All right?"

"Take Cathy. And when do you plan to come back?"

"Harry, I can't say."

"Ha," he says, and returns to his drafting.

THE FRENCH expression goes: to be uneasy in one's skin. And that is Joseph when he visits me in New York. When I see him again after many weeks spent apart I am struck by how small his face is, how delicate his frame. He wears his jeans and rough-hewn, long-sleeved shirt that protect him like a carapace from the bewildering traffic and the city din. I am eager to remove these harsh, heavy fabrics from his skin, eager to unshell the man and get at the wild Western smell that still clings to him. I wear something extravagant and black, brought out from the back of my closet because I rarely dress up in my life as a mother of two, and he is delighted. "I knew you would have shoes like that," he might remark. Or, "I imagined you in just that coat," and he turns me around to gaze at the cut in the back. Is he in love with me, or the ideal of me, the Platonic table that is me? I never know. He brings always his soft felt cowboy hat, though he wears it only once before a fierce January gust from the urban canyons sweeps it up and off his head. He scrambles back to pick it up from under the scaffolding and brushes it off. Then holds it firmly in his hand as if he is afraid it will act up mischievously on its own.

I take his hand. I walk quickly and make him keep up. I lead him across the street against the traffic signals. We descend into the subway so that he will learn how to maneuver the trains, and I make him ride with me all the way uptown to Columbia—116th Street. We stand in the center of campus, the proudly tarnished alma mater seated on her throne to one side of us, her arms raised in welcome, though dappled by bird shit, with the descending monumental swath to Butler Library on the other. Joseph indicates he will sift through some Sanskrit archives. I am skipping along-side him, breathless with excitement, though I don't know how it will go: Joseph seems at sea, overwhelmed amid this teeming urban colossus, lost. Later, he is thoughtful, taking stock; he will mention that he has heard that Columbia is looking for a Sanskrit professor, but I know, despite my high-pitched encouragement, Joseph will not apply. "You need a degree," he will say defeatedly, as if such hindrances are what keep him off the East Coast. His father was a professor of economics at Harvard.

Mostly, we take cabs to restaurants or downtown to the Lower East Side, when we must attend his poetry reading. For this is the true reason of his visit. He does not want to be seen with me at his poetry reading, because many of his and Arlene's old friends will be there, but he cannot tell me not to come. I maintain that we must eat something beforehand, and since we are early, we walk along Canal Street and look for a Chinese noodle shop. It is a tiny dingy shop with mirrors lining the walls, and crammed with fami-lies slurping from large steaming bowls. We order soup with fish balls and sit side by side at one of the round tables. We slurp in silence. I dab at my chin with a napkin and push his poetry books away so that we will not splatter broth on them. Joseph eats little; he is watchful, not hungry.

The reading is in a basement bar on Mott Street called the Double Happiness. I have imagined walking in with Joseph a hun-dred times; I have urged him not to be afraid, but to feel strong next to me, bold, regal. "We will walk in like men," I say. But I see my mistake immediately, because Joseph pushes down the stairs swiftly in advance of me, and suddenly I arrive from the still-bright outdoors in a room so dark I cannot see where Joseph has gone. I stumble inside and head for the clump of people at the bar, and when I turn, I see that my love has already been absorbed into his group of friends. There will be no introductions. I buy Joseph a beer, just in case, and set it on the table I choose next to the space the readers will occupy. The woman seated at the table next to me is obese, friendly, and chatty and the only one I have to talk to, but I will only remember her later because Joseph reminds me of her—he observes, when he recalls this night, that I sat next to a *fat woman*. Eventually Joseph sits at my table, but fleetingly, his chair pulled well out, before he bolts to join well-wishers at the bar.

He chooses to read without his reading glasses, although the room is cave-like and he has grown slightly myopic in the last years. He stands with his weight on one hip, the other leg thrust out in a kind of ready, cocky stance. He reads a poem inspired by William Blake's "Tyger, tyger," about catamounts in the West (*Felis concolor*), and I finger the amulet of a wooden tiger's head Joseph has given me to keep me always safe; I wear it on a string tied around my neck. He reads several of his Sanskrit translations, which are crowd pleasers, and then a parody of a letter to the editor of a Denver newspaper urging conservation of resources and attention to the infestation of mountain beetles.

The urge to pee nearly overtakes me as I listen and clap and count the seconds until I can find a bathroom.

The reception is polite, warm. But many of his friends have not come. There will be a party afterward hosted at the home of the evening's organizer, who is also an old friend of Joseph from his Berkeley days. The man is Joseph's age, youthful because small and white-haired, and when we shake hands he seems surprised to meet me, looking from Joseph to me.

The man, whose name is Peter, lives in a well-tended apartment on upper Second Avenue. I find the apartment remarkably clean. I know no one at the party, for these are Joseph's poetry acquaintances, some considerably older, some young people just hanging out. Peter offers me tea to smoke, and I agree, though I sense this will be the unraveling of the evening. Peter asks me polite questions but forgets the answer and has to ask my name again. We smoke, we put on music, we dance together. The rest of the party takes refuge in the kitchen.

Joseph will not dance with me; he has renounced dancing in a past lifetime along with smoking weed. He wanders into the living room from time to time to check on me, then returns to the kitchen. "These are intellectuals," he retorts later, when I take him to task for not dancing with me. As if there is a clear distinction! I am tempted to mention that I happen to know Arlene likes to dance, for Darla Worthington has told me. I want to wound Joseph, it's clear: I feel cut out and isolated among these people and he has not brought me closer. In the kitchen he stands for a long while talking to the same woman, who is alluring in a white low-cut T-shirt over full breasts and a well-fitted suede jacket. A small wooden necklace nestles in the inviting cleft of her bosom. I watch her and resist feeling the jealousy well in my chest, making it hard to breathe. And the longer he speaks with the woman, the stronger my conviction that she must be an old lover. I feel murderous, spiteful, and *small*, since I have taken off my boots to dance on the carpet of the living room. There is a tiny hole in the big toe of my stockings. I say something to the woman that is not kind; perhaps I imitate the way she tosses back her hair. They stare at me. On the cab ride back to the hotel, Joseph's face is closed and final.

"How could I ever leave these mountains?" Joseph exclaims, indicating with his ebullient, open-palmed gesture the jagged snowy silhouette of the Flatirons outside the car window. The splendid, naked challenge of them. Peaks called Quandary or Bishop's Prick. "Those unearthly glowing floating snowy summits are a promise to the spirit," Gary Snyder writes. The promise of conquests still to come: would Joseph ever get around to it? Before his incarceration he won't have enough time, maybe one or two big climbs—though not alone, and not with me. His regret is that he hasn't attempted to climb high enough, or chosen the right season, or been sufficiently prepared with proper raingear or enough food and water in his knapsack. He tends to head up the hills on a spontaneous whim, breaking out of the mad, solitary thoughts closing in on him at his desk in his saltbox. He heads straight up wearing his Irish walking shoes and leather jacket, only to get driven back by thirst or a savage sudden hailstorm. What is he after? In the Chinese tradition mountains are masculine, Snyder asserts—vertical, hard, transcendent, resistant. While waters are feminine: soulful, dark, soft, wet. I live near a river and find nourishing its quivery, perpetual hungering; while, Joseph, to maintain a taut sense of self-possession, keeps those snowy summits always within reach.

Curious, I don't remember him wearing his brown felt hat in the West, only in New York. His signature hat, perhaps an affirmation of his essential difference from the contemptible city-dwellers. He does not mind the blasting sun of his desert climate, never applies sunscreen, never replaces his rolled-up long sleeves for a T-shirt. He simply removes his shirt. We hike and I delight in fingering under the straps of his rucksack where warm rivulets of sweat break out along his golden flesh. He wipes his face with his kerchief unknotted from his neck. The higher we climb, the thirstier we grow, the more frenetic he becomes, bounding ahead on the trail like a hyperactive hound on the scent. This will be the summer of little rain in the West: by March the land is already desiccated, brown, brittle. Fires rage as close as Denver, forcing an evacuation of a southern suburb. Flakes of singed creosote waft in the air like Fourth of July confetti. The odor of ashes and apocalypse. But we don't go farther toward the timberline, partly because I am not up to Joseph's practiced exertion. We meet large untethered dogs along the trail, followed by strapping University of Colorado students, and in fright I nearly totter off a ledge. Joseph indicates the Rocky Flats Nuclear Weapons Plant coiled like an innocuous elementary school in the valley below us: he and his classes often demonstrate against the plant. ("Mega Mega Mega death bomb—enlighten!" Arlene would shout.) A succession of scavengers pass overhead like ominous shades: buzzards, carrion crows, ravens. We scan the horizon for red-tailed hawks, but don't find any, not this day.

This is the "long brown land" Mary Austin writes about that lays hold on the affections. I ask Joseph, who is gazing off with a maniacal contentment: Why have you come here, and stayed? Have you come for the names that enchant you: A town called Troublesome, a rock called Elk Tooth, a bar called Rocky Flats? "My friends and my work are here, Frances, my daughter's childhood and stability, the mountains that give sustenance to my work." By way of answer, Joseph talks about Mary Austin, who moved from Illinois to California and finally to Santa Fe, recording an elemental state of nature. I find the quote: "The rainbow hills, the tender bluish mists, the luminous radiance of the spring, have the lotus charm. They trick the sense of time, so that once inhabiting there you always mean to go away without quite realizing that you have not done it. Men who have lived there, miners and cattle-men, will tell you this, not so fluently, but emphatically, cursing the land and going back to it. For one thing there is the divinest, cleanest air to be breathed anywhere in God's world. . . . There is promise there of great wealth in ores and earths, which is no wealth by reason of being so far removed from water and workable conditions, but men are bewitched by it and tempted to try the impossible."

Truly, isn't this the reason why Joseph has stayed? Why he won't come back East and be with me? Tricked by time, tempted by the impossible? In the West he has *reinvented* himself—that foolish word again—broken from his marriage, become the longtime companion of a woman whose legend by association forged his own fame. And he'll perform his reinvention again and again. Is fame an aphrodisiac? I ask him once, and he denies it. "I have been a huge supporter of Joseph's work," Arlene has spoken to me. "I gave him a life. I feel *used.*"

What, then, does the East represent? A degree from a reputable university, a code of honor—an old-world sense of loyalty?

Straight black skirts, heavy-framed glasses?

When Joseph exclaims at the splendor of the mountains outside of our car window, we are speeding toward the airport after our first winter's weekend together. "You will write me at the school, won't you?" he asks, a little anxiously. "Promise?" I am far too distracted by the charming turn of his profile to heed the meaning of his words.

"I HAVE a question," Cathy says, dipping her index finger deep inside her cup of *fromage blanc*. We sit huddled for warmth in the Luxembourg Gardens, unwrapping our lunch items: yogurt, cheese, cold cuts, baguette. It's too chilly to unsheathe my hands from gloves and I glance up hopefully at the midday sun, obscured behind a thick, ominous cloud cover.

"No," I preempt her. "And stop eating like a savage."

"I am not a savage," she replies. "How do babies happen?"

"Now? You want to know now?" I carefully place on the bench the neat parcel containing one of the raspberry tarts we have purchased at the corner pâtisserie: the tart is incomparable in its perfection, firm crust molded into a crisp star with glazed fruit winking at the cluster, and dusted by a delicate scrim of confectioner's sugar. I experience a little thrill, at the sight of the tart and at the question from my daughter, for here is the moment I have been waiting for, not in dread—as I hear from the church ladies, who recall vividly being informed how babies were made by their fifties-era mothers, who tensed visibly at the question then launched into a vindictive theory of sexuality—but with a kind of relish, for there is never such a moment of truth between mother and daughter. How will I relate this story to her? With pleasure? With bitterness? And how will she remember?

"Yes, now," she says.

"How old are you?"

"Seven."

"Is that right? Well, seven," I consider. "Don't you want to wait a few years?"

"Please?"

"Well, all right. Where do you want to start?" I venture, wondering how much she knows or has heard.

"Did you ever see Daddy naked?" she blurts out.

"Sure I have. So have you."

She laughs. She frowns.

"I'll have to explain the way it works first."

I do. She is puzzled, and has many questions. I use physiological terminology to impress her. She squints and knits her brows, attempting to follow me. She looks doubtful, but has had some experience with Momma's menstrual periods and hence follows the trajectory of ova from fallopian tubes fairly well. At this point I recall my mother's own teaching, or non-teaching: that is, my mother was a nurse who once took me to a middle-school evening assembly that discussed mother-daughter issues and sent us home with pastel-colored, pleasant-sounding brochures written in lovely euphemistic language ("the male member is slightly thicker than a finger"). I remember driving home that evening of the assembly horrified at the demonstration about menstruation—my God, I'm going to bleed to death!—involving cumbersome monstrous bandages and the application of straps and ropes like torture instruments, and I fumed to myself, "How could God *do* that to women?" But my mother was calm and noncommittal—*resigned* might be the word. Where was the pleasure, the joy? Sex, apparently, did not interest her. I never could muster the courage to ask any follow-up questions of her and we never spoke of these unpleasantries again.

Cathy is puzzled by the egg and sperm interaction.

"But *where* does the sperm come from to fertilize the egg?" she asks.

"The sperm is introduced by the male."

"Uh-huh."

I can't do it. To impart the actual male-female dynamic would destroy her sense of balance of the world—to admit the necessary violence of penetration—and how will she look at her beloved Abner after this? Her time of innocence is so fleeting, so divine; her virginity is empowering because it is unaware of itself, and once it's lost (or rather, *stolen* from her), I'm afraid she'll become simply mortal like the rest of us.

"The male ejaculates," I say quickly, adding, with textbook generality, "and that means his sperm travels up from vagina to uterus, where it may or may not fertilize the awaiting egg, and thus begin pregnancy."

She thinks for a moment, nods, then decides against asking any more questions for the moment. The word *ejaculates* has stumped her. She frowns skeptically. I am relieved: relieved to keep my innocent one, relieved not to have to tell her the terrible truth.

VII

By the Ides of March Arlene Manhunter has vanished from her house, her town. Joseph is hauled in for questioning. Arlene, pushed to the brink of irrationality by the public spectacle of his treachery, has left a letter to the president of Diamondcutter detailing Joseph's infidelities. She wants validation—retribution! The president of the school is no other than her former husband. She has even thought to write to Joseph's mother, an elderly Bostonian in her seventies, asking: "How could you raise such a son?" Joseph is afraid his mother will drop dead of grief. He is treated as a very bad man and shunned universally on his campus. The students whisper about him behind his back. The innuendoes fly. His three brothers stand by him. At my home I receive many hang-up calls. The line hisses and snaps—the sound of live wires lashing like snakes spraying venom. Harry stands with the receiver pressed hard to his ear, hollering angrily, "Hello, hello, hello!" I yell at him, "Don't answer the phone!" I know to hang up immediately.

I answer Lewis, who passes me the aromatic cigarette made from tea:

"How should I know where she went?"

He watches me, obliquely, thinking himself unperceived. He rests awkwardly against the edge of the sofa. He is a big man, bulky around the middle. It is mid-afternoon, when the rest of the city has shaken off the déjeuner-sur-l'herbe torpor and returns to toil in cars and offices, while we enjoy a delicious sense of *suspension*. We are seated on the floor of his apartment, a narrow space full of shelves stuffed with requisite monochrome paperbacks, inked at the spine in red and black lettering, very Frenchified; comfortably battered furniture, not shabby, though I wonder by the way Lewis moves among the arched rooms strangely denuded of clutter, stiffly as if unsure where anything is, such as matches and glasses and an ashtray, whether this *is* his apartment.

"You sleep here?" I ask.

He laughs (deep belly), coughs, nods, and hands me a glass of wine. Then, groaning a little, he lowers himself to the floor.

"She had some land," he observes, "co-owned with Joseph Pasternak. Called Shad Creek. Ever heard of it?"

"Yes, I have. She told me about it over the course of one of her kamikaze phone calls."

"Joseph never took you there?"

"In fact, no. I didn't realize they co-owned it."

"You didn't—?"

"I mean, he never told me. He called it his land. He tended to leave out certain sticky facts in our relationship," I murmur. "And no, he never took me there." I take the joint and inhale twice. "But you have?"

"During the initial investigation, yes."

Arlene Manhunter takes proud council among her native people, the Arapahoe (her father's heritage—her mother was a blue-stocking New Yorker), at the Gouged Bark reservation in southern Wyoming. She has come feeling abject, sick with shame and indignation. There's a purification ceremony among the elders in the sweat lodge. The men, hovering in blankets, seated in a circle on the cold dirt floor, pass a pipe among them, and to Arlene, cross-legged in the center, bedecked in muskrat fur, her riot of scarves, red-tipped feathers, and colorful beads. She has always met the men on her own terms. She is stunning: tragically downcast face, eyes ablaze with righteous fury, or brimming from the smoke. She coughs a little, her neglected health, and she's not used to smoking, gave it up twenty years before. In her getup she appears to be the Pocahontas she played as a kid at the Greenwich Village Children's Theatre. The elders decide she must remove herself to the hills for three days in order to chase out the bad smell of the demon that is Joseph Pasternak. A vision quest, such as she undertook as an adolescent with the boys of her tribe. She may take food and water, mushrooms for meditation, a little firewood, and matches. No books, no paper, or pen. Which hills? She demands, "I want to go up to my land in western Colorado." The elderly faces confer, shake heads, frown.

"That land belongs also to the demon."

"But it's mine!" she cries. "I loaned him the money!"

They shake their heads. It can't be done for cathartic purposes.

"Then where shall I go?"

Most Elderly Chief speaks slowly, haltingly, a thin high scarcely human voice. Arlene has known him since she was a baby when he spooked the children at bedtime with his eerie animal calls. Learn from the beasts, he would say. Watch them. The others bend in to hear. He points outward with a shaking silvery hand:

"To the dry tearless childless desert," intones he. "To watch the bird roam his piece of sky, seeking his freedom."

Arlene sighs, wonders at the construction of this sentence. (It could be from a poem by her word-swinger friend Gregory Corso, now deceased.) No pen, no paper, not a book to read? Years of sitting meditation with her crazy-wisdom lamas will pay off. She will look within and ignore the aches of her creaking joints. She will wear her headdress.

"I was a powerful woman," she addresses the assembly. "I was a ready woman, a woman with the wares, the whims, the volts. I was a woman who knew how to dry up the semen of senators by my curses, detonate atom bombs! I was a woman who was not made fun of. Now I'm a woman deracinated and destroyed. Do you hear over there? I'm talking. I'm a fifty-six-year-old woman," she says, and bows her head.

BUT SHE does not return within three days, and nothing is found: not an eagle's feather, nor a knapsack, neither a scrap of food nor evidence of fire. No one saw her heading from the Gouged Bark reservation into the "dry tearless childless desert." In fact, she drove away in her twilight-blue Mitsubishi at dust-busting speed.

Where did she go?

"She drove back to Colorado. To her property at Shad Creek," Lewis says.

"But the elders didn't want her to go there," I say.

"Nonetheless, she drove the night of March 15 from Gouged Bark to Shad Creek. It must have taken four hours or so, a long, flat stretch from nine o'clock till one; she made a few stops along the way. People remember seeing her, still wearing her ceremonial robes. And she is a very beautiful woman," Lewis adds, as if I don't know.

"She is. You sound like you knew her, too," I say, trying to resist sounding ungenerous.

"Never met her. But many of my friends in that poetry milieu worked with her in the early days and knew her."

Lewis has put out a book on the coffee table. We stare at the photograph on the cover of an anthology of sixties' poetry that Arlene, fresh out of Sarah Lawrence College, was editing and publishing in the Village. She would recite Edna St. Vincent Millay while cutting an amatory swath through bohemia. Arlene at nineteen: long, softly undulating hair framing her heart-shaped face and disguising the still unformed square jaw that will emerge in later pictures; her gaze direct, challenging, slightly narrowed, shadows underneath the eyes from smudged mascara, perhaps, or pulling all-nighters or smoking hashish. She stands unsmiling, evidently braless; the nipples protrude womanlike through a red-and-black striped tank top, a motley string of beads looping alluringly between them. A beauty, no doubt about it. I imagine Joseph knows this picture of Arlene and fell in love with her from it. Idly I leaf through the book left here to spook me and I find the photograph I like best: a group of naked hippies piled into the apartment of a painter friend for whom they were posing, circa 1972. Amid the myriad white limbs at jokey angles there is Arlene, seated on a sofa to the side with prim sturdy legs, leaning forward so that the hair hangs over her bare breasts, strategically hiding them. The face is unmistakable: her head tilted upward so that the line of the carnivorous jaw becomes more visible, her lips pressed together almost severely, her gaze serious and averted as if she is saying:

"This wasn't *my* idea." I snicker and push the page toward Lewis, who is stamping out the butt of the cigarette in the ashtray.

"Ah, those were the days," he says.

Have I actually seen him inhale? I begin to worry. I wonder if he possesses a file on me. When I smoke I feel radiant, and twist and comb my hair with my fingers. I rearrange my skirt around my legs. I am bedeviled by quick, nervous twitches of my limbs and lips. The narrow, arched room has assumed new historically intellectual proportions: Antonin Artaud's studio, possibly. I am in Paris. Suddenly, I become aware of the humming traffic outside on Boulevard Montparnasse: was it always this loud or is it later than I think and I must rush out to pick up my daughter? For a moment I can't remember where she is. She could be anywhere in Paris, cavorting with strange dogs and careless teenagers. She could be propped on the back of a vélo speeding recklessly around the Étoile without a helmet on. My Eloise. What would Harry say? Abruptly I lean toward Lewis and take his wrist in my hand, examining the face of his oversized watch.

"But it's only after four!" I exclaim.

"You don't have to pick up Cathy at the Luxembourg for an hour," he informs me, patient and solid. He gently extricates his wrist from my grasp. "You have time."

"Right."

We resume.

"She drove to Shad Creek at one o'clock. Then what happened?"

"She parked the car on the shoulder of the road and then took off walking," replies Lewis.

"At one in the morning? And without taking anything with her? Food, water, supplies?"

"Nothing. Nothing was found."

"What was the moon like? Was there light?"

He pauses, his gray, cropped head staring forward, considering. "The moon was full. The terrain is ruggedly uneven, mostly brush, some ponderosa and Douglas fir. There is a spruce forest and some canyons a mile up the creek, full of bobcats, coyotes, and bears, but no water, not by March. Not this fire spring, certainly. The properties don't have boundaries or fences, and she must have known her way around. At night it's nearly freezing, but by midday the sun would be pretty strong, even scorching. But you've been there, haven't you," he says quietly.

It's not a question, but a statement.

"Beautiful country, but inhospitable," I muse, vaguely. "Well, then, where's the body?" I demand, with some exasperation.

"No body."

I push to my feet. Angrily, I cry, "Look, what's the use of this? She's obviously hiding out somewhere. She has a thousand friends all over the world spreading the good word. She's tricked us all. She's in Indonesia, I bet you, hanging out with her third world poets. She's on retreat in Switzerland, she's in Italy—have you searched other places for her? She could be in Paris, for all you know!"

"It's true, Frances. That's why I'm here."

"Then why is Joseph in the holding tank?"

"His car was there, too."

I turn awkwardly at the door. He looms in the threshold, large, square in the shoulders. His eyes are sad; women turn their hearts out for men who look sad. He is shod in socks. He does not bar my way. First one cheek, then the other: he kisses me in the French fashion. I haven't been this close to a man since Joseph and I last say good-bye squeezed against each other in the aisle of the airport bus. I am being sent home, while Joseph must return to his complicated life. My love is snatching a schedule before he leaps off the bus and heads into the parking garage. He offers a slow open-and-closed gesture of his hand to me: releasing me.

"I'll walk to the park with you," says Lewis. "Let me get my shoes."

MY LINE of work has become teaching, by default, I tell Lewis. That is, I never consider teaching until I meet Joseph. Then I want to travel with him and slip away from my home, and I need money. Joseph suggests I consider teaching writing and English, as he does.

I possess the necessary degrees; Joseph reminds me to attend to my aspirations. I have quit my work as a magazine editor in order to take care of my children. But now I feel a new sense of urgency: why do I not have my own bank account? Joseph asks me. I feel shame at my dependence, the same shame I felt when I overheard Joseph speak of Mexican villages I have never visited. My world has narrowed and I feel panicked. My aspiration, always, has been to be independent.

Joseph is an experienced, self-assured teacher. For him it's a calling. He establishes instantly a relaxed and effortless rapport with his class, his students, or the person across the table whom he engages in discussion. Allusions roll fluidly from his tongue, especially after a glass or two of wine. He likes to recount, to amplify, to expatiate. And he has much to relate. I suspect he enjoys listening to himself. He is comfortable standing in front of an audience and receiving the warmth that flows from the free exchange of ideas and impressions. His sense of self and well-being is fed by the approbation he receives in front of a group of eager and adoring students; I recognize this communal affirmation from my own experience with teaching, though I don't necessarily share it. Teaching isn't a calling for me. The transaction I lead in front of my class is rather more antagonistic.

I appear at my classes stiff and overprepared. I teach Freshman Composition at a small, Catholic, liberal arts institution across the county that serves the children of first- and second-generation immigrants to America: Italian, Irish, Hispanic. I have a graduate degree (I admit this to Joseph slyly, almost apologetically) and the school needs warm bodies to teach the lower levels. I wear my glasses and don't show my knees. I expound on the various kinds of expository writing: narrative, descriptive, classification, process analysis, argument, cause and effect, and so on. While scribbling frantically on the blackboard, I knock into a chair that stands near the door. I apologize. There is a clump of boys in the back corner who snigger among themselves and several others in the room fall slumped over their desks. I suspect that many are hungover. They can't keep their eyes open. Over the course of the semester we read short examples of the kinds of expository prose I have lectured on and I ask the class to write a model of each, sometimes in class. The in-class assignments work the best because they give the students something to keep awake for, scratching up their lined, loose-leaf paper, even if they have prepared nothing beforehand. Also, these in-class exercises allow me to make sure no one cheats on writing assignments. One of the students, Nuru, who is older than the others, having flunked the course from the previous year, stares off into space during the writing assignments and then won't let me leave until he hurriedly completes two well-wrought sentences in the last minute. Nuru's eyes are bloodshot and unfocused and he nods off in class; from the subject of his essays (rolling joints, growing cannabis), I imagine that he smokes a lot of dope. For the other writing assignments, I rarely receive them from my students on time, if at all, and I have to make sure they haven't been cribbed from online sites, which the other teachers warn me about.

Once, I ask a young woman student who withdraws from my class, "Why did you leave?" And she responds testily: "Because I don't want a professor like you."

I press her, eagerly, because I want to know: "How—not like me?"

But she won't say, or she hasn't the vocabulary to tell me, and I'll never know what kind of teacher I am exactly or fail to be. Perhaps she means she wants a professor who gives an easier grade without so much effort? Who is rather more relaxed and easygoing in class?

I imagine my students have caught on to my inexperience. I mark up their papers with increasing vehemence and fail six of them for excessive absence. *FA.* But I don't fail Nuru, because he's not a bad writer, and I value that he is not afraid to write honestly about his life.

When I tell Joseph about my new vocation, at a restaurant in Albuquerque outside of our hotel, which is located in the downtown historic district, he cheers me with a glass of wine. I imagine he looks at me in a new way—gaining respect for my mysterious, intuitive faculties. Now I will be like him: a professor, with official duties and even "dear students" to look after and even fraternize with.

However, I can't be like Joseph. There is a time when I lose control of the class, and this is every teacher's worst nightmare. It is not the first semester of my teaching, nor even my second, and I have begun to feel some self-assurance in front of a class. But one spring semester I am allotted an enormous (over thirty students) midday class, containing many who are ill-prepared to write a complete thought in grammatical sentences; they are vociferous, eager to chat, and do as little work as possible, and I sense with a sinking heart that my tidy, well-prepared lessons will not see me through this. They sense it, too, and take advantage at every moment to show me up: "What is the page number? Where are you, miss? Why are you going so fast? Did she say *cinnamon* for *synonym*? What is she talking about? What did you say?" I try to separate the chatterers, but I recognize this is a waste of time since they only make new recruits to their insurgency. They groan at every assignment, and some swear openly and slam the door when they leave the class. When I give back papers, marked up like chicken scratchings they won't read, I see that my hand is trembling under the effort that I cannot let them see. They laugh uproariously at my formal delivery, my two-dollar vocabulary, my insistence on revisions to papers they will never look at again, my taking attendance and checking of homework. At one point, as I ask each member of the class to give an answer, it is clear that none has done the homework. Finally, I am at a loss, rendered impotent, my education proven ineffectual against real-life concerns such as racial discrimination and English as a Second Language. At midterm, I inform several of the insurgents, who have given me scarcely any of the assignments, that I will have to fail them and that it's best they withdraw from the class now before their grade brings down their average.

They snuffle with derision. They trek upstairs en masse to the head of the department and complain about me.

"It felt like a witch-hunt," I recount to Lewis. "It was their word against mine and I had no power in the department, as an adjunct. What happened is that I began to be afraid of these kids—afraid even to give back a paper marked up with revisions because they would erupt from the violence of their frustration. I let things slide."

"But surely the chairman listened to you and supported you?"

"I think he tried. He had been at the college twenty years or more and seemed like a kind, open-minded educator crusader. But he began to have doubts about me when the students complained. I was too exacting. He said it was highly unusual."

"What did you do?"

"I recoiled from them. I ceased wanting to teach this class. I gave them busywork or handouts and had them write the whole period so I wouldn't have to speak to them. I graded their homework. I became a kind of unpleasant scold—I hated going in there. And I don't think I'll ever enjoy teaching again."

"You must have felt terrible," says Lewis.

"You're very sympathetic. I felt inadequate, and my confidence was terribly shaken. This was just about the time that Joseph came to see me for the last time in New York. You see, we always talked about his coming to my house: we will be equal, he'd say, once I see your house. But it didn't happen. He never saw me in my kitchen, with my apron on. Where I stood when I read the letters he had sent me. I could never tell him that I had failed as a teacher."

WALKING THE streets of Paris with my daughter, hand in hand, when she lets me, I recognize what has done me in. We regard the other shoppers and scrutinize what they wear and what they carry, and I am shocked to realize what has beaten me: jealousy. I have become a kind of green monster, thanks to Joseph, or Arlene, or rather to the entire edifice of female competition and envy that keeps us rivaling for affections. Everywhere I turn on the streets of this fashionable city I spy a woman as a potential rival: she has lovely legs, smart shoes, gorgeous clothes, blonded hair, a scintillating scent, and a pretty face. What else? A handsome man at her side. The recognition of my inadequacy (or so it strikes me) in comparison to these women makes me terribly unhappy, and I slump along next to Cathy and scowl and plot to spend money I don't have on flashy accessories I don't need—didn't Darla and I live through this agony as editors at a trendy women's magazine? But I must have something to make me look better, sleeker, more attractive. I have returned to the state of smarting, vulnerable girlhood that marked my first years in Paris. What has happened to me? Arlene Manhunter has succeeded in undermining me, for how could she not? She is superior in every way: age, experience, literary stature, knowledge of the world, legendary lovers, and beauty. After meeting her, and speaking with her, and reading her work obsessively, I can't imagine, frankly, why Joseph would leave her for me. That seems simple. For her part, Arlene can only be jealous of me for one reason I can see: my relative youth. Joseph is an older man whose experience in life attracted me for whatever reason, though I know it's not just because of my age. Arlene, however, hates me because I'm a younger woman. She has, foolishly, disastrously, allowed an upstart to eclipse her. Yet considering her many alluring and accomplished qualities, age seems to me a small and petty concern.

Does jealousy begin in anger, or the other way around? My jealousy toward the other women in Joseph's life surprises me, because I believe that I relinquished jealousy when I got married. What use do I have anymore of jealousy? "Jealousy is destructive," Harry maintains in his absolute, dismissive fashion, and he's right; I agree, absolutely. Yet there are times I feel it acutely, especially in the beginning, when a sense of possession seems a natural outgrowth of a healthy sexuality. In the early days when we are still having sex. For example, at a cocktail party at my husband's office I find myself watching a dark-haired woman in a red dress. She is petite, elegantly turned out, her hair combed to a silky coil at her shoulders, and she wears cherry-colored mules with tiny pointed heels that match her outfit. She is about my age (but then, what do I know? I am younger, newly married, and generous in my views of the world), and she carries about her the desirable confidence of a woman who presents herself always at her advantage. A person who spends whole days shopping for the right color lipstick or cut of dress. I think she has a wonderful nose, a long Roman nose with imperiously rounded nostrils, and vivacious, flashing eyes. She smiles disarmingly, sustains cocktail party chatter as she holds a glass containing a liquid that is the same crimson color as her dress. And beside her, propped against the doorjamb, holding an identical ruby-jeweled drink (cranberry? Campari?), is a man whose confident yet aloof admiration nicely complements her discreet polish. Her English boyfriend, apparently. The woman, I learn, is American but lives in London, and from time to time I detect a lilt, a specific enunciation about her speech, as well as certain expressions she uses, revealing her currency in things English—"knackered" is one. She throws her head back in a clear, merry, not too-loud laugh, and gives a small wave of her hand, a flick of her garnet-polished fingertips.

"Who was that woman?" I ask my husband, when we have returned home and are undressing for bed. We shared the same bedroom then, a smallish space taken up by the double bed. One of our visiting friends—it was Nikki, the pretty blond-head of the spaghetti strapped dress—once remarked at the modest size of our bed: "Do you both sleep there?" she blurted out immoderately. I felt embarrassed that the bed was not bigger—king or queen sized, but simply regular, for regular people.

"The one wearing the red mules?" I pursue.

"Mules," Harry grouses, shaking his head. Then he titters, lightly, carelessly—a rare sound for him that reveals that he has observed the woman, too. "Mules, can you imagine? Walking around New York City in mules!"

I feel the stab of jealousy, because the woman is someone I would like to look like. I feel excluded from his admiration, even if he is being extravagant and speaking off the top of his head. But I get over it, and then again, and soon I cease feeling any stab at all. And Harry, what has he felt? I wouldn't know, of course, because I can't read his look behind his leveled bespectacled gaze.

He stands and appraises and seems to recede behind those lenses. He doesn't say.

I HAVE promised that I will respect Joseph's sacred inner places. That I will not be resentful of the person he used to be (gadabout, devil-may-care, comeback kid) nor jealous of the women he knew. As our tacit agreement of this pledge he sends me an excerpt from John Cage: "love = leaving space around loved one." And that's why he loves me: because I leave space around him.

But I don't. I call his home and leave messages on the answering machine that Arlene is sure to come across. She doesn't, though, because Joseph gets to them first. He is canny and circumspect. He procures a cell phone, a peculiar contraption to own for a self-described Luddite, and invites me to call him whenever I please and without alerting Arlene. I call often and leave breathy messages during the day, when I am feeling lonely and envisioning the feel of his fine downy flanks. Usually he returns my messages right away, between classes or during office hours, and then I am able to reach him directly as he is "out and about" (a sporty Harvardian phrase he likes to use), shopping for groceries for their dinner: I imagine Arlene must be present at the table, too, along with his daughter. Or I reach him in the bookstore, one of the few in Boulder, where he peruses titles of poetry and spends a dilatory evening before taking a drink at a bar, perhaps the Irish pub. We speak while he is driving in his car, on his way to pick up his daughter from the mall or at the tanning salon where she gets a bad burn, or waiting outside the office of his acupuncturist. This winter he suffers from persistent sinus infection and samples different remedies. These calls are delicious because immediate, and I feel almost as if we are living in the same town, a mere mile apart, even if my time is two hours ahead of his. He swims at the Y in the mornings, and often finds a call from me on the cell phone, which records my number even if I don't leave a message. Joseph calls this special feature on his phone the spy-catcher. It is a boon but also becomes a kind of weapon, as we later begin to practice brinkmanship—who calls whom. I wonder that Arlene doesn't suspect he's harboring secrets when he secures a cell phone, though I learn later that she suspects a great deal. "I have known about you for two years," she intimates darkly.

I send him lozenges of bee balm I have found at the health-food store for his sinus infection; I send him the first rose from my garden, a Queen Charlotte that is too ripe and moist and disintegrates in his hand when he unwraps it from the envelope. I should have dried it, of course, as he dried his wildflowers before sending them to me, but I only learn these methods from Joseph after the fact, upon his instruction. I cut out for him articles in newspapers and stories in magazines describing extraordinary trees planted in my area or dictionaries he needs to know about or new Asian restaurants in New York we can try when he comes to visit. I send him pictures of me and the children nestled inside letters, reams of letters, penned with great care every other day, and sometimes daily. In the beginning I write a rough draft so that the letter will convey a concise and beautiful thought. Eventually I learn to rely on my first instincts. I write as if I am making love to him. I write to move him.

In return, his letters grow more violent in feeling and language. It's as if the more I open to him, revealing my situation of sad estrangement with my husband, my tender anxieties about the future, my hunger to be near my lover, the more Joseph feels he is allowed to open up to me. I give him permission to be deeply vulnerable, and he asks me to wound or cherish him. Aren't we beginning to trust? "Maybe I've never had a lover, a dear friend," he writes, "I've felt as comfortably at ease with as you. It makes me shy to say it, as though at our age we're supposed to have experienced vast regions of the world and of the spirit, the highs and declivities—but Frances, the more we speak and touch the more I reach unbearably deep in myself to find those concealed, freshening, open spaces in you." Unlike me, he cannot touch himself; the sensation, he says, is utter desolate loneliness. His bachelor marriage next to Arlene has left him essentially an anchorite, though this sudden wash of desire for me unloosens him, keeps him thrashing in bed at night. The thought of my heart encased in my ribcage like a tiny bird, he writes, makes him want to weep. He is being awakened by a sleeping sexuality, and he is startled, shaken, deeply roused. It is a hunger he had begun to forget and he feels gratitude—yes, and a certain recklessness. For love is making us reckless.

"What have you done to me, Frances?" he wonders, desperate and stung by my messages left at his home phone. Sometimes I can't reach him, and he doesn't immediately return my beseeching call. I am frantic, giving way to jealous gloomings. He is out for the evening—with whom? with *her*—and he has neglected to reveal his whereabouts, his company, his intentions. How many hours do I work my granny's rocking chair, calculating the time difference between Boulder and New York, planning the next call at exactly the time he is likely to walk through his door? And when he answers, or his daughter picks up the phone, or even Arlene, I hear only a roaring in my ears like a surge of water and I have to hang up. The space around him, between us, grows wider indeed. I recognize that I want to be part of his life, and I can't. I am excluded.

"What have you done to me, Frances?" he writes. "I am a frail human creature tossed by winds of karma and conflicting desires, fears, apprehensions, with a strong-headed and willful pursuit of knowledge and ignorance both. When I want something hungrily enough I seem capable of terrific madness—and for a year now I've wanted you. The desire increases, it does not exhaust itself. So I get crazier and my behavior is anything but sage, circumspect, predictable, or clear. I live in a swirl of sensual images and recollected pleasures, all centered on your touch, your voice, your tender beating heart, your infinitely attentive caresses. Whatever happens to us, I would never wish I'd not known these things. You have been *my* liberator . . ."

"Who is this?" Arlene demands, answering the phone.

I've had enough. I am wrung out with worry and disgust. He has been out of touch the entire long weekend over Thanksgiving—he has gone away with her and is unable to be reached. I have left numberless messages. I am frantic. I call his home and insist that he speak with me.

"It's Frances," I reply. Arlene snarls—does the name mean anything to her then? Does she remember me from the wedding? She is annoyed, nonetheless, to be disturbed mid-afternoon at her home. She flings away the receiver.

Joseph takes it up. "Frances?" he responds in alarm. "Frances . . . who?"

HARRY HAS his own reasons for keeping quiet. Stubbornly, he continues to wear his wedding ring, the filigree gold band we bought together on 47th Street's Diamond Row, ten years before. I remember considering the same style in pink gold (imagine what the church ladies would think of a pink gold ring), but I chose the conventional gold because I believed it was more classic and meant to endure. The pink gold, while pretty and feminine, seemed vulgar at the time, yet I wonder if I would have warmed to it more than to the regular gold ring, which I have put away. It even seems to me that Harry suggested the pink gold at the time, a rather daring, uncharacteristic move on his part. Harry's band is a matching gold filigree, also rather slender, and he wears it still, which embarrasses me a little and causes me a slight convulsion when I notice it.

Harry did not take to the effete academics and poets at Douglas's wedding. He remarked on how ridiculous they made themselves over the girlie show at the bachelor party the night before: they had to ceaselessly name, sift through meanings, and analyze aesthetics and couldn't enjoy it for what it was: a striptease by beautiful young women. Harry remembers Joseph from that party of men; he takes pictures (the ones of Joseph are missing because I spirit them away). Harry remembers the guy in black jeans and Irish tweed jacket (at least he puts on a *tie*), with little gold hoops in his earlobes like a girl wears. With a small brush he keeps in the breast pocket of his jacket, he combs his longish salt-and-pepper hair, when he thinks no one is looking. He sips temperately at his Scotch, *neat*, and quotes Yeats and Joyce to show how smart he is. Harry remembers the man knows something about the Viennese

Secessionists, which happens to be Harry's favorite period of architecture and applied arts, and Joseph even demonstrates a goodly knowledge of Herbert Bayer, who lived and worked in Denver. Joseph would also have informed Harry about the house of Bauhaus founder Walter Gropius, located near Lexington, Massachusetts, where Joseph, it turns out, grew up. Joseph will take me there, too, and to the shrine of his youth, Walden Pond. We will swim across the pond together and place a rock at the site of the cabin where Thoreau worked, now a replica of the tiny shed, though impressive still in its austerity. Joseph wears long trunks that seem too large for him, and swims, head up, with a swift, efficient stroke. Nonetheless, Harry already decides on his aversion to Joseph, who won't stop monopolizing his wife's attention at the reception.

"I didn't plan on this," Harry tells me, slumped on the sofa after we have put the children to bed. By "this" he means sleeping on a blow-up mattress in the living room (Joseph's idea—to save Harry's back and the couch springs), building a hut in the backyard, suffering the indignity of his wife's infidelity (with a friend of his friend!), and bracing for an angry, messy breakup. The aim in life is to get married, have children, and live in one happy household for the rest of one's days. "But relationships *change*," I emphasize, and he corrects me: "No, *you* changed." Although it's true that Harry has remained the same unswerving adherent to the status quo, terrified of the rug slipping out from under him, I, too, have proved the same essentially intractable malcontent he married. "Why can't you be happy with what you have?" is Harry's complaint over the course of our marriage. I want to tell him that I am happy with our children, and glad indeed that he was the sire, but that I didn't bank on the Friedanian factors of domesticity such as strangulation and immobility. But these are not words Harry uses. He would refer to marriage and the raising of children as denoting stability and groundedness, not to mention moral virtue and respectability.

Harry is a man of few words. He begins to see a psychiatrist, at Douglas's suggestion. Douglas, his old college friend, now newly married, maintains that if Harry has someone to talk to, he will be able to come up with a wise course of action. Case in point: when

Douglas decides that he is going to leave his former girlfriend, the architect with whom he first moved to Denver, his shrink allows him to shed guilt for not marrying her and giving her babies (she is forty already), but motivates him to move on with his life—specifically, to find someone less screwed up and younger than he. He does: his comely paralegal from Enid, Oklahoma. When Harry begins to see a psychiatrist, he talks to Douglas.

"What do you talk about?" I ask, indiscreetly, irresistibly, adding, as a kind of warning: "You do know that Douglas and Arlene are good friends—you remember her from the wedding?"

"Of course. And I don't think it's any of your business what two males discuss between them."

"True enough"—this is one of Harry's stock phrases I employ—"but this is a special case, don't you think? I mean, I happen to be Douglas's friend, too."

"So talk to him yourself," snaps Harry.

Douglas: my oddball ex-boyfriend. He is cute as a sophomore at Columbia, in narrow-cut jeans and brown loafers without socks, fifties'-style windbreaker, short hair, and literary affectations. Hands always in his pants pockets, fingering his change. Eyes restless and a quick, oily grin at the ready, as he gives his head a cock and swipes his index finger in the air as if hailing a cab. We meet at an orientation mixer, although I am a freshman and try to pass off as older. We are both terribly unskilled about sex, and when I remember him as he was then I see a boy raising his head with hair sticking out at all angles from the bunk of his fraternity house. He begins to write poetry in the deadpan style of Joe Brainard: "Already I am thinking of this as a 'piece of writing,' and wondering if I can get by without really saying anything" ("Aug. 29, 1967"). I do not think that what Douglas writes is so hilarious (ironical, infantile stuff), and we usually end an evening arguing about something inane like how the word *often* is supposed to be pronounced—with the *t* or without? We move apart, he to become a groupie to elderly resident poets, and I to study French literature and spend my junior year abroad. Except I do remember a phrase from one of his poems, "night of magic," about meeting girls. I fancy this phrase "night of magic" to mean a night in which your life is forever changed by love or infatuation—perhaps he stole it from a bottle of perfume. But I think of this line again after Joseph and I meet at Douglas's wedding. When I run into Douglas later at a holiday party in Harry's office in midtown, I carry this phrase in the back of my head, and I feel like laughing out loud because it has become a kind of prophecy fulfilled. The phrase makes me feel triumphant and giddy. But I decide Joseph would rather I be serious and solemn, especially after misbehaving at his poetry reading (this is his word, *misbehaving*), and anyway, there's no humor here, in this steel-and-glass office of tidy desks and closed corner offices, where anything revealing the personality of the occupants has been put away. The place is as monochrome as the faces attending the party. Douglas has become a suspicious, grim-faced lawyer.

He pretends not to see me. Then he cries, "Oh Frances!" as if just noticing I'm there. This is a particular affectation he's assumed from his WASPish clients, I notice. You can't seem too eager to get what you want.

"Hello, Douglas," I say, and roll my eyes.

The requisite kiss on the cheek and queries after the children.

"They are as you see," I reply, indicating the two urchins snatching at sweets from the buffet table. Douglas's new wife, Cynthia, is occupied in another part of the room, nodding and smiling in her gaping fashion, a long, willowy person in an expensive dress—his "type," I have mentioned to Joseph, although the word makes my love uncomfortable. "His type," Joseph repeats, pained by my colloquialisms. Joseph has taught Cynthia about jazz.

Douglas guffaws. "That Cathy," he says, shaking his head as he watches her with snake eyes.

We maneuver around the clumps of holiday chatterers so that we are in a corner by ourselves.

"I hear you've had a change of . . . *situation*," says Douglas, giving a good bite to the word. He talks through his teeth, so that if you are watching him from another part of the room it may appear as if he's always smiling.

"Come off it, Doug. You've been feeding Arlene stuff."

"Stuff? What stuff, Frances?"

"Information. Gossip. How could you? You know she has it in for me."

"I've only told her the truth. That Harry is miserable."

"He's not! Look at him."

We regard my Magyar husband: a husky man of medium height in a navy-blue blazer, broad as a stevedore, gray flannel trousers, white shirt, and striped tie. He bends to catch some food tossed from the table by Bernie, grabs the child's hand, and wipes whatever sticky goo clings to it with a napkin. Bernie slips out of his grasp to trot into the next room, where the computers are, and Harry lunges after him.

"Harry is doing fine."

"He's depressed," says Douglas. "His world is falling apart. He *loves* you."

"You really don't know what you're talking about," I say, marveling at his audacity. "You have no idea what goes on between married people. Harry and I have been estranged for years. Something had to change—someone had to make a move. And he wouldn't."

"It's untenable."

"What is?"

"This . . . situation."

"You must stop giving Arlene ammunition against me, so that she can turn around and scare Joseph to death—"

"It doesn't matter what I say, Frances. This is very serious. Arlene is filing a formal letter of complaint against Joseph Pasternak. She refuses to teach at the same institution. And she is bringing up all kinds of charges of improper conduct between him and his students. It doesn't look good for him."

"What students?" I ask, weakly.

"Frances," Doug whispers hotly, "you have to extricate yourself. This is ruining your marriage—well, if that's beyond saving, think of your children!"

"You're scolding me, Douglas."

"You don't realize the repercussions of your—your—"

"Night of magic?"

He blanches. Hands in his pockets, he rolls his shoulders in a writhing motion, his eyes darting about the room. He, too, has thought of that phrase, but painfully, and he does not smile. His pinched, grown-up face no longer resembles that of the young admirer I knew at school.

Harry waits. I return from long weekends visiting Joseph in Boulder, Albuquerque, Boston, and Harry does not say a word. I take his silence for compliance, resignation. The children have been a handful, they have been sick, they have missed me. The house is turned upside down: mounds of soiled clothes in corners, beds unmade, dirty dishes stacked along the counters and stashed in hiding places in the living room. The children are not allowed to eat in the living room: what is Harry thinking? But these are his dishes, pushed out of sight under the big chair in front of the TV where he watches late-night videos. An empty bottle of beer, bowls with stained rims. In the sideboard I find half-eaten bags of chips, in the refrigerator a jumbo gouged-out carton of sour cream and near-empty containers of ice cream. He gorges on ice cream late at night. But he doesn't say a word when I tiptoe in, at midnight, and drag my airline bag wearily, noiselessly up the stairs. He returns to sleep in the hut. I can't find the phone, removed from its cradle, though I search for it when I sneak into the children's rooms to cover them up and breathe in their smell. Green apple shampoo. Paste. I can't find the phone and so I won't be able to call Joseph and tell him that I've arrived safely home. I toss and flail in the cold sheets, fingering the chafed skin of my sore chin that will begin to scab over in the morning. Before falling asleep I remember that the next afternoon I must take the children for a dentist appointment I have already had to reschedule three times before.

LEWIS SAYS: "There was a car accident. Will you tell me?"

He eases himself onto the sofa in the narrow, densely shelved room. Antonin Artaud's studio. His bum hip aches in the damp weather. He has removed his shoes, secured the window so that we don't have to raise our voices to be heard over the insistent late-day traffic. Straightens the creases of his trousers. Again we are seated here, passing the joint from one to the other in a peace-seeking gesture. I feel warm, radiant, at ease. Have I found in the presence of this kind man the same sort of "comfort and a bit of grace" that Joseph has written about most recently? That he has found without me? The euphemism shocks me anew, and the old pain returns, and with it the desire to cry.

"Surely you know?" I ask Lewis, a little sharply.

He glances at me, wondering at my mood and how to proceed. "I was shown records of auto body work," he says quietly.

"You were shown? Passive tense. We try to use the active voice, to show participation, agency."

"Frances," he says, very gently. "Tell me, won't you?"

"Give me that." I take the cigarette and let my hair fall around my face. "As I was saying: an accident occurred on Sixth Avenue at 12:43 A.M. on the night of October 26. We were sideswiped by an SUV."

"It was your car?"

"Yes, my car—and Harry's car."

"But you weren't driving?"

"No. Joseph was driving."

My love says, "Your orgasms grow stronger the more often we make love." I explain that at first I cannot come directly, too used to the stimulation of my own fingers, and locally, when I don't see him for many weeks. Then we are together again, and our communion is divinely profound. I open to him—he often exclaims, ecstatically, "How open you feel, Frances!"—and I need only the smell of his hair to shudder me to climax. I am explaining these intimate matters to him, as he drives my Subaru down Riverside Drive from our hotel uptown, although he grows distracted by the stately pre-war architecture, the grid of erratic exits, and construction congestion. Why have I allowed him to drive? (How could I capitulate the wine selections to him? What happened to my sense of autonomy?) I wear knee-length boots and a gray wool pleated skirt like a schoolgirl. I am an excellent driver, a daredevil driver, a rude city driver—a driver with the volts!—but Joseph will never know this about me, as he will never see me in an apron in my kitchen, never see me move among the artifacts of my house.

We are headed downtown, although it is late. We embark on an impulse after lovemaking at the hotel. Joseph hasn't visited the city for many years, maybe not since he came with Arlene, though he won't exactly tell me, and the place has changed, irretrievably. The city I know has undergone recent cataclysm, and I feel the need to show him, to make this pilgrimage with my love together. He will remember this transformed city (no longer the city he knew), and with it, me.

Ashes and apocalypse. You know you're in the right neighborhood by the smell. A noxious cocktail of asbestos, asphalt, gypsum, melted silica, synthetics, polycarbonates, and pulverized concrete. A deadly combination. And the oppressive hum of the massive generators for the nightlights set up overhead like the antennae of giant insects for the workers toiling nonstop at ground zero. The area crawls with curious well-meaning folks like us descending to patronize the hard-hit establishments. Fat black rats dart among the parked wheels of cars and along the bottom shadows of boarded-up buildings and gaping lots. I hop along next to Joseph, glad to have worn my boots. Over the all-pervasive thrum of the generators, the air had grown singularly warm. There are firemen at their grim task, a massive display of police cars and fire engines pulsing with blinding lights, and people milling and peering around us. We ingest the acrid odor, we hold each other. We pass the Odéon, though I steer him clear of it, because it used to be Harry's place to eat with his friends from work. I hold Joseph's hand. I try to kiss him under the hot white glare. He says, "Yes, yes," visibly shaken, but he does not look into my eyes.

Restaurants line the blasted blocks of Hudson Street. We choose the Italian place, and while it's late, they agree to serve us. A few parties of diners remain—a group of young women at the table next to us, probably work colleagues or former college roommates who've gathered to talk about their new jobs, new lives in the city. I half-listen to them, a little enviously, wistfully. What are their jobs? What has brought them to this city? Who are their boyfriends? Though I can see that they eye us suspiciously, sniffing at an unseemly relationship.

Joseph orders wine and bottled water, thinking, no doubt, of the contaminated urban sewage system and unhygienic pipes. He is hungry and wants to eat meat. I sense a change: the purge of the old order, the invasion of the new. His eyes are steely, opaque. He seems at loose ends. In New York he seems often this way, uneasy in his skin, and he has called it "Arlene's city," since this is where she galvanized the poetry scene and worked for many years in the early days. I protest: don't I live here? The expression leaves me out. This exclusion is wearing me down.

I ask him: "Will you tell Arlene that you came to New York?"

I need his reassurance, though I know I'm treading on thin ice. I recognize this dangerous look of his. It means I am prodding where he does not care to tread. Yet tonight the look I see in my love's eyes angers me. How can he make this pilgrimage, to this site of Armageddon, and not mention that he was here?

He replies: "I don't know."

The waiter appears. He has tucked his pepper mill inside the waistband of his white bib apron. I point this out to Joseph, and laugh, because it reminds me of how I carry the phone in my house, nestled in the waistband of my pants or skirt, in case Joseph calls me. "You see," I tell him, "I'm always waiting for your call." But Joseph doesn't seem amused this evening; he is forlorn, because I have rebuked him. I stroke the back of his hand as we sip our wine. He remembers the movie that was shot in this restaurant, a film he saw recently, and he launches energetically into his stories. The sinking feeling that all has been lost dissipates.

Then we are hit. We are making our way through heavy traffic up Sixth Avenue. I urge Joseph to drive, unwisely, and I distract him with my hand on his thigh. I say, "Turn left here," and he turns, abruptly, though we are not in the left lane. A towering SUV looms into view and smacks into our left flank. Joseph howls, yanking at the wheel. My first thought is that it can't be true: Joseph wouldn't get us hit. He is an expert driver. He would never crash my car! We make the left turn, the police immediately behind us. We get out of the car and regard the mangled left front fender—metal mashed like accordion pleats, leaving the fender scraping hideously along the pavement. The police belittle us: "Whaddya doing, turning left when you're not in the left lane!" And the two women driving the SUV cry: "We didn't see them!" Reports are written. I stand and fume, scavenging in the gutter for something to tie the fender up with. Angry, unleashed, I yell: "This is just what Harry has always thought of me!" I hiss and kick the fender. The policemen frown, exchange glances. Joseph fetches rope from the corner Asian market and ties up the fender. He is being useful, cool-headed; he talks amiably to the officers, and tries to calm me as I pace the sidewalk. The policeman who writes the report smokes a cigar inside his car; after an interminable wait, he hands us the report and tells us we can go. Still, I won't drive. My hands are shaking.

"I don't know if we made love that night. No, we did," I tell Lewis. "I held his beautiful cock under my shirt, between my breasts, and I said, 'This is where I want you always to be. Next to my heart.'"

"Were you angry with Joseph?" Lewis asks.

The room is dark; it has suddenly become evening without our having to usher in the hours. I am grateful for the comforting presence of this man. Have I been crying?

"Angry? You're seeking a motivation. Yes, I was angry with Joseph because he is supposed to be invincible, superior to other men, namely my husband, to whom I would have to admit this terrible mistake—wrecking the car!—and Joseph murmurs, 'Don't tell him I was driving.' Harry would humiliate me, and Joseph should have protected me. That night was our undoing. I was most angry with myself. I know what you're thinking—I shouldn't have let him drive. I should have ordered the wine, taken control. In fact, I was always angry with Joseph because he didn't belong to me. But I surrendered to Joseph."

"In love you surrender."

"It only works if you're both on equal terms."

"You knew what you were getting into."

"How do you know whether your lover is true or merely a seduction artist?"

"You don't know, Frances. But what's important is what *you* are."

"What *I* am? Is frozen."

"No."

"Oh yes. That's it for me. You don't get many cracks at love in this life."

"You have to wait a little."

"Wait and die. I've searched all my life for the one to complete the fit. My other half. And I've met him, by the way, maybe more than once. But he had other plans!"

"On ne sait jamais . . ."

"And how about yourself, Lewis?"

"Moi?"

"Come off it. You have a girlfriend?"

"I have a woman . . ."

"You have a woman. You sound like Joseph. You have a woman. Do you love her, may I ask?"

"There's love there."

"Oh, fantastic! You're sure she won't look at another man?"

"No," he sounds surprised. We're in Paris, after all.

"You see!"

"What's the alternative, Frances?"

"Children. Children to hop on your bed in the morning and bury their crazy heads in your ribcage. Children with their sweet flesh to kiss goodnight and kiss again—the adorable rascals."

"They grow up."

"I could get an animal."

"All right. We're done."

"Are you hungry? Have I said too much?"

I DREAM, sleeping next to my daughter, her breath warm and rhythmic at my side:

I am seated in the cabin of an airplane that suddenly pitches, begins rocking perilously, then loses altitude. The floor gives out underneath me as if I'm riding in an elevator whose cable tension snaps. There is no one else in the small cabin that feels like a military transport; I am alone. I feel the violent lurch in my stomach, fight the mounting nausea, and stagger to my knees to look out of the small, round portholes. Clouds are trailing through a blue, mindless sky. I'm going down, there's no mistake about that; this is it. I have one gripping thought: Where is Bernard? Then I remember he is with Harry and Cathy and they are safe at home, on land. I brace myself to die. What else can I do? The plane is going to crash, and in a moment—the seconds are interminable—I will become aware of the final colossal jolt and then nothing else. I am not desperate or unhappy at the thought. I fall with the plane. I wait, seated on the floor, readying myself for the terrible impact.

VIII

"You'll like this place," I tell Cathy, who groans and presses the bedraggled Mike to the breast of her anorak. She's also holding the book Lewis gave her: *J'aime lire*, written in the form of colorful comics for kids with short attention spans, weaned on electronic devices. We trudge up six flights of stairs, the last three growing narrower, and I drag both pairs of luggage so that she won't protest too badly. I arrive in a lather. The hallway smells of boiled cauliflower and cat piss.

"I *liked* the bee-day," she objects.

"You'll like the view from here."

The windows are small in our chambre de bonne, but the bathtub spacious and *red*, and there are a tiny galley kitchen, desk, and bed suitably large enough for the both of us. We kneel together on the bed and peer out the dormer windows that give onto the gracious circular front driveway lined with daffodils.

"Do you like it? See, there's the Tour Montparnasse, and behind us, the hospital for sick children—ahem!—and you can probably see the Eiffel Tower and the Invalides from one of these."

"It's okay." Cathy gives up and reclines unceremoniously. She hasn't picked up on my mention of a hospital for sick children and I know she's feeling depressed. "No room service. No TV. That's how I learn *French*," she says, in her cunning dig at me.

"Plus, I can cook."

"What are you going to cook?"

"I don't know. Eggs?"

"Shouldn't I be going to school?"

"Yes, you should. But I'm home-schooling you. Now get out that math workbook and show me some problems."

I unearth dishes and pots and silverware from the tiny cupboards (not too dusty), and I cook up the eggs we have bought. I make a green salad with a dressing of oil and vinegar and mustard, as I have learned from Harry. We sit at the desk together. Cathy chews contentedly and I uncork the wine. She wants a sip. "Resinous," she declares, pursing her lips. The light is gone, but the room is warm, and I make a note to remember to buy some candles.

Later, reclined on the bed like a pasha on her litter, arms crossed behind her head, legs tucked, Cathy demands:

"Read."

"No, you read to me."

"It's your turn."

I settle next to her with *J'aime lire*. "Not French," she says.

"Forget it," I reply and start on a paragraph about la famille Pellerin.

After a while, she asks: "When are we going home?"

"You want to go home?" I exclaim, as if she's never asked me before. As if we just got there. What a preposterous question!

"I miss Abner."

"Only Abner?"

"And Daddy."

"Only Daddy?"

"And Bernie."

"Oh my poor baby."

She rolls her eyes.

"Well? When?"

"Well, sweetie," I begin, gently, "there are some things that happened . . ."

"You mean with Joseph? All right, tell me," she announces with resignation, as if she'll finally deign to hear the secrets of her mother's heart.

"Yes, about Joseph. You see, he was living with this poet lady who happened to disappear one day, while she was walking up into the mountains. So they decided to ask him a lot of questions to find out if he knew why or where she went."

"She just disappeared? How?"

"They don't know. No one can find her."

"Maybe the wild animals ate her."

"Yes, they've thought of that. Cathy, come on, let's just finish this chapter."

"So does he?"

"Does he what?"

"Know what happened to her."

"He says he doesn't."

"Can we go home when Joseph gets out of prison?"

"No. I don't know if he will," I tell her, and then it occurs to me that the thought of Joseph's incarceration is not unpleasant to me, because now I know where he is—day and night—and how to find him. I feel lightened, like laughing. Has this been my revenge, after all, to keep him from straying from me?

"I mean," I add, "we'll go home when Momma finds her way, so to speak."

She grimaces at me. "What way?"

"I don't know. The right way. Right Understanding. Right Ambition. Right Speech. Right Activity. Right Labor. Right Mindfulness. Right Energy. Right Meditation." I'm counting on my fingers. "This is the Eightfold Path out of suffering, according to the Buddhists, anyway."

"What's suffering?"

"Ah, well. Suffering is when your heart aches all the time because you don't have what you need or want."

"I'm suffering because you won't get me an animal."

"Right. We'll keep talking about that."

"Why are you suffering?" She looks at me hard—her wide-eyed, liquid gaze earnest and pained. I meet her look sadly. "What don't you have?" she asks. "Oh, I know. Love and all that," she moans, waving her hand.

"I have you."

She is pleased, returning to her book with a pat on her thighs. "You don't meditate," she concludes, and yawns. Then adds, sneakily, "But Lewis does."

"Lewis? How do you know?"

"He showed me." She scrambles out of bed to sit on the floor and attempts to fold up her legs in a lotus position. She rolls her eyes back in their sockets. "Except he can't cross his legs completely because of an old football injury," she says.

She snuggles back next to me on the bed. "Baby," I say, "I don't know if we can see Lewis again."

"Of course we will."

She's sleepy and has stopped listening. I caress her head of soft brown curls, inhale her gamy rough-girl smell. We begin to breathe deeply together. And I dream again of Joseph: I am cradling his slender, fragile form, eyes slitted against the morning sun; he grows smaller and smaller in my arms as I rock him, until I am suckling Bernie, my big-headed baby, and he is sweetly sleeping at my breast.

WE HAVE to be careful where we are spotted now: a grown woman with evidently no pressing pursuit and a prancing child in tow who should certainly be in school rather than gazing into sewer gutters to examine their contents. As we speak English between us it's hard to remain inconspicuous. Then one morning it happens, as we sit inside a dark café situated among a medieval configuration of streets near the Musée Picasso, which is one of Cathy's favorite haunts. We have ordered *oeufs anglais* because Cathy is hungry and tired of croissants; she likes to drag strips of toast through the mess of runny yokes and fill her belly. I have opened numerous white paper napkins and stuck them about her person, under her chin, in her lap, on each side of her plate, so that she wears a festive, convalescent air as she munches and gesticulates, flinging food to the floor. I see she's done it on purpose to attract the hound, and I'm about to get mad: the slow-moving German shepherd gets up arthritically and begins to drag itself toward us. I would be horrified, given its snout size and crazy guard-dog eyes, but a woman enters the café, sending off the gentle chime of the doorbell. I sit instantly at attention.

She stands at the bar and orders a coffee. I examine her profile: a solid figure, not tall (she's not sporting heels), wearing a head scarf, sunglasses, and loose-fitting, silky clothing. She speaks French with the proprietor; they seem to know each other, since he offers a kind of louche, familiar grin. It's hard to detect an accent from her, and I can't make out her face; she won't turn her head and look around the place, which seems odd to me; she's ignoring us rather too purposefully. I feel a flutter of panic, and turn my chair (without scraping the floor) to one side, away from the bar. I lower my head, letting my hair fall over my face, and eat the eggs on my plate, sunny-side up. When I sneak another look her way, the woman's gone.

But no, she's there, on the other side of the bar. I whisper to Cathy to wait a minute—I'll get the salt and pepper. I throw off my napkin and vault to the bar, where the mysterious lady stands sipping at her café expres. I even venture perilously close to the jaws of the salivating cur, who guards her ankles. I give my command succinctly to the bartender, and the lady, detecting my accent, her interest momentarily aroused, turns to look me full in the face. Our eyes lock. Her great brown eyes of Picasso's weeping ladies. I even reach to brush her arm—I *seize* her arm. The lady might be she, not quite as stunning nor as awe-inspiring; she glances over at Cathy, festooned in napkins, and laughs. Then I know for certain it's not she—not our Manhunter, with her inimitable warbling from the infernal depths. I would recognize her laugh anywhere.

Later we run into her again; that is, it could be the lady or almost the same strong, grounded silhouette, clad in garments of a faintly Eastern flavor, a beaver-fur coat, head scarf, long, scraggly tresses dangling down her back. Sometimes she seems tired, standing in line at the boulangerie, with change in hand to buy bread, her back sagging unselfconsciously; or she's dressed more stylishly in the art galleries, clunky heels and black slacks, lipstick, and jewelry. Her broad Indian cheekbones catch the light and give her away. She is always alone; I keep her in the periphery of my vision. We hustle with the crowds deep into the somber crypt of the Panthéon, and meander under drafty Neoclassical vaulting to view sarcophagi of writers I have wept over in my youth, such as Jean-Jacques Rousseau. I recall, a little sadly, that the one book I gave to Joseph was Rousseau's *Reveries of a Solitary Walker*. He seemed pleased, at the time, murmuring that he had always wanted to read these romantic essays about taking solace within oneself, and had even been urged before to read them, by mentors. He also meant to read Montaigne, he declared, especially at this reflective time in his late middle-age, though I don't think he ever did, as these writers smacked of some kind of elitism I could not quite fathom. (I imagine, moreover, that reading Montaigne, that staunch essayist of man's limitations, who wrote that "irresolution seems to me the most common and apparent defect of our nature," would have helped cure the ills that ailed my love.) Yet we never spoke about the *Reveries* again, and I suspect that my love did not find the time to read the book, and also he was a little embarrassed by this Eurocentric thrust of mine, which was, for him, a gulf in my experience he felt uncomfortable about, indicating some kind of class deficiency. These rueful thoughts fill my head as I gaze half-blindly (from tears, murky light—I don't see well in the gloom) between the thick Doric columns. I haven't seen Cathy for a while, but I'm keeping the lady in the beaver coat (a little worse for the wear) always in the corner of my eye. I turn, amid the clusters of tourists, and find her, swimming in the shadows, in conversation with my daughter.

What I won't do is run over to them and break the spell. I stand, simply, and watch them in what the theater people call the cheating-out profile. I beam Cathy an alarm signal with my eyebrows, but she doesn't heed. What can she be saying? She has been warned not to talk to strangers. Yet she nods briskly to the lady, and even leans in for a kiss, before she spies me. Then she trots to my side, smiling her secret, traitorous smile; most shocking of all, she throws me a thumbs-up sign. I have no idea what this means. I will berate her, threaten to disown her, withhold treats, and refuse to speak to her again until she tells me, but it's no good. She keeps her secrets.

"It's all good," she parrots an expression she has picked up, and not from me.

I SEEK her out. I've searched the poetry websites to ascertain where she will be reading in New York. I hardly admit to myself that this is what I aim to do. I set out one raw March night, having ensured that Harry will be home to put the babies to bed. I dress carefully—jeans I manage to repossess from my closet, black jacket, and heavy-framed glasses to disguise my face—I've rehearsed every step. I can always turn around and stay home, I tell myself, but I don't do it. I drive to Brooklyn, my old neighborhood; I arrive at an old converted warehouse near the water. There is a benefit for the Diamondcutter archives and I wouldn't miss it for the world, especially since Arlene Manhunter, it has been posted, is reading. The hall is cavernous and cold; the amorphous, motley crowd moves with a slow, near-hypnotic restiveness. This is not a fussy crowd, but sure of its purpose, artists and poets and the like, a little scruffy, uninhibited. I find a step to sit on in the back of the hall, and as poet after poet reads from prepared pages, I watch a young couple seated in front of me preen and simper: the woman continually turns to her partner and caresses the side of his head with her fingers. She has short dark hair and wears a cowl-collared black sweater; she lifts her thin arm and rakes her nails along the nape of her boyfriend's neck. She smiles dreamily, though he does not return the touch. I watch them and hardly listen to the speakers, and it is a long while before Arlene is announced. Then the place erupts: a thunderous applause explodes in the hall, and everyone sits up a little in his or her seat. Arlene appears, wearing a fire-red Chinese silk smock that hits just past her ass, long black leggings, and high heels; her hair is loose and wild around her shoulders. She paces the stage. She seems thinner, taut, edgy; she launches into a chant without a word of introduction. The first word she spews is "Fire!"

I skulk out. Her torment hurts me. The pain of her every movement: her jittery laugh, the thrust of her long breasts against the silk of her shirt, the tight, nervous flip of her hand to keep the hair out of her eyes. Her glorious hair has dulled, I see, her beauty sharpened by grief. Her voice trembles in a low, menacing crescendo, and then she begins to wail. The crowd is mesmerized. She shouts, she shrieks. Is this part of the performance? The room incinerates. I run.

JOSEPH IS sleeping late, as he does. I have been wandering the house, peering at the surrealist collages on the wall, snooping in the refrigerator for coffee. But there is only a bag of beans in the freezer, and I'll have to hunt for a grinder and make a lot of noise to rustle up a cup of coffee. I give up and return to the small, side bedroom where Joseph sleeps, ensconced in his separate chamber for the last ten years. I compose a haiku with one of his pretty pens and leave my message on his table:

> Morning sun falls heavily
>> On her red-rimmed eyes—
> He turns away.

Joseph sleeps, despite the urgent twittering of the birds, the stark, bright light in the room; he doesn't bother with curtains, since he can sleep anywhere. I wonder at this ability or need to sleep long and deeply, which I've lost since having children; his sound, babylike slumber, the sheer unperturbed length of it. It is the sleep of a child or an old man—here my own thoughts chide me. For Joseph is more than ten years older than I am, his hair and beard are graying, his face creased from exposure to the sun and the weathering of unkind elements, though his body is youthful and sleek. We have not allowed the discrepancy in ages to become an issue between us, especially since Arlene is older than he, and it would be tactless to compare. Yet when I watch him sleep I wonder at the years that separate us, years filled with experience and living that I know nothing of—years I have not shared with him. Arlene has. The last ten years with her have made up the period of his prime, as these are the years of my prime—the adult years of productivity and achievement. The decade with Arlene has turned his hair gray, left him beat. While the time with me allows him to sleep. How *can* he sleep with me beside him? How can I? For I am anxious and awake since dawn, ready to restart love and get on with it. He has *troubled my sleep into waking*—inscribed into a book of poems he has given me. His sleep is self-indulgent, luxurious: doesn't he see how he squanders the little time we have together? But Joseph's sleep is for restoration. Already he has lived long and hard and needs his rest.

"Frances, what are you doing?" he asks, groggily, maybe a little suspiciously, from the bed. I am poking in his bookshelves, viewing his rows and rows of rare poetry editions, his collaborations with Arlene: two entire shelves dedicated to her own writing including her first book, *Shaman Woman*, which catapulted her to howling fame at age twenty. That was in the late sixties; the picture on the back cover shows a wired-eyed, braless fair-haired angel.

He is a little alarmed, imagining I have invaded Arlene's lair upstairs and rifled through her things—he is getting to know me better, and wouldn't she certainly be able to sniff out an intruder? I reassure him, and after a pot of tea he needs to talk as avidly as I absorb. We return to bed. The more he tells his stories, the quieter I grow so that he will never cease unless I press my lips against his or paw at the buttons on his chest. Does he notice my silence and occasional mewing, or has he grown mesmerized by the sound of his own voice? This is the drawback of teaching, and Joseph is a consummate teacher, possessed of a polished, commanding delivery, confident, unfaltering manner, open, solicitous attitude toward his "dear students" who sense he cares deeply. (He does not relish reading student papers, however.) Through teaching he has grown aware of the impression he makes on people, suave and politic, and he knows to watch his back.

But this morning Joseph holds forth on his early years living in Berkeley (have I asked?), when he manages a well-haunted bookstore in town, and he starts up a funky literary magazine with another poet which segues into the first fledgling publications of his own. He writes poems about his bursting new father's pride: he makes the rounds at Berkeley with his plump baby girl in her harness, strapped to his lean, strong torso. He is happy during these years, still experimenting in life. His learned adviser at the university makes the inevitable pronouncement that Joseph is not cut out to be a scholar, which he accepts fatalistically. "I don't have the discipline," he admits, "I always hated school." He is a lover of women and wine, a singer of songs. He meets Arlene Manhunter at a Buddhist symposium (she is married to her son's father at the time), and she invites Joseph to Boulder to become her personal assistant. Does he understand what this entails? He does, my darling gigolo at heart; he totes along his wife and three-year-old daughter. He gives talks on Sanskrit poetry at Diamondcutter, begins to teach, and fashions a Buddhist studies department under Arlene's umbrage. Then takes off to India one spring accompanied by the doyenne herself, although he neglects to tell his wife with whom he's traveling. I learn this fact later from Arlene.

The mood of the morning is melancholy. Indigo. He inserts a CD: a lady jazz singer softly crooning. I am feeling fragile after love. His revelations affect me distressingly: I feel touched by his candor, but powerless to receive his scarred, raw experience. What should I do with these details? He will tell me of near-fatal drug use at rock concerts as a teenager in Boston, or awakening as a very young man in a filthy hotel room in Mumbai to a rat gnawing on his hair washed in coconut shampoo. Joseph does not cry, but I do.

"Frances, are those tears?" he asks, aware for the first time that I have grown quiet next to him in bed. I wear my charcoal silk pajamas and cover my face with my hands.

"Joseph, my heart, do you remember telling me that Belinda"— his still-pissed ex-wife—"is thinking of going back to California to live after all these years because she believes that life there was happiest for her, when she felt simply most herself before your breakup and it was the time of her life?"

Joseph nods soberly.

"And don't we all hold some period in our lives dearest to us because it represents a time when we were most truly ourselves? A time when Belinda was most Belinda, before the anger set in, and Joseph most Joseph? I think that's what you're telling me, love, that the time with Arlene was *your* time—"

"I don't think—"

"That very brilliant time for you that can't be regained or paralleled. But, you know, darling," I add bitterly, because he looks stricken and lost as he does whenever I cry, "I haven't had my time."

We stare at each other. Later we'll have a silent breakfast and enjoy a little love.

WE DINE in an Italian restaurant in town: a real one, not hidden away in the hills where no one can see us. This is before Joseph begins using words like *fearful* and *destabilized* to describe his personal situation, before he finds excuses to keep me from coming out to see him in the form of forgotten board meetings and faculty retreats at Zen centers twenty miles outside of Boulder. And we are dressed for dinner: Joseph wears a jacket over his ubiquitous jeans, even dons a tie, though I try to dissuade him. I suspect he is trying to impart a certain respectability by appearing in a tie with me. Am I so scandalous? I wear black with the scarf he has given me for my birthday, slung around my neck. It is deep violet and fuchsia silk, though I don't know how to wear scarves; I wear them clumsily. Joseph says when he gives it to me, "I've learned how to find presents for women," and I laugh, gaily, giddily. Tonight we feel festive; it is almost Christmas, and Joseph has moved out of Arlene's house. Our gaiety masks the sense of impending doom that the season carries in its merry current.

I am staying in a B&B up in the foothills outside of town, because Jan is around, and I am not yet allowed to meet his daughter in their saltbox, which is their small, echoey new Cape Codder. I am safely stored out of sight.

"It's too soon," Joseph tells me, when I ask.

What he doesn't know (and when have I begun to keep my own secrets?) is that I have seen Jan, even spoken to her. His pretty, straw-haired teenaged daughter, whose face in her bright school picture is framed on the front table and first greets the visitor to his home. I spy her in the bookstore as I'm killing time before meeting Joseph in the late afternoon: I recognize her immediately, crouching at shelves in the children's section. She wears tight jeans, a beat-up suede jacket, her hair long, straight, and swinging. I notice with an ache that already at fifteen she has a full, heavy bosom. She has begun attracting older boys, Joseph tells me, with deep voices and importunate, manly bodies, and Joseph is often beside himself with anxious worry. I move swiftly toward her, take a quick peek around to make sure he hasn't brought her in himself and is loitering nearby, handsome and leather-clad.

I poke around the shelf above her head.

"Excuse me," I say, and frown. I have lightly brushed the top of her hair with my arm. "I'm looking for . . ."

"A children's book?" She is lovely, the voice I recognize is high and sweet. The eyes, the nose: they are Joseph's.

"A video, actually. Something for Christmas for my children. Do you know any?"

"At the home where I babysit they watch *The Snowman* about a hundred times a week. The kids love that one."

"I don't know it."

"It's animated, and has no words, just pictures and music. It's about a little boy who builds a snowman that comes to life and he takes the boy to visit Santa Claus at the North Pole. It's actually kind of sad," she says, considering.

She runs over the selections with her long, slender fingers. Her hair moves with a life of its own: thick, spongy, wonderful hair. I imagine it swept up in a ponytail, or sectioned into pigtails, as she wore for her starring middle-school role in *Alice in Wonderland*.

"Here it is!" she cries, handing it to me. "How old are your children?"

I am overcome for a moment, and stammer their ages.

"Oh, they'll love it."

"Are you buying presents for the children you babysit?" I manage to ask so she won't see me blushing.

"Yes, they're four and *twins*," she says, and by her theatrical grimace I guess that they are hard to manage. "But I can't spend a lot of money," she adds.

"Do you know the Frances books? About the little girl badger and her family?"

"Uh yeah, I think I know that one."

"There's a little gift set over here," I say, leading her to a display table. I gauge her height: I have measured myself against the highest pencil mark ticked into the frame of the kitchen door at Arlene's house. "Frances has a birthday, Frances only eats bread and jam, Frances is always singing to herself."

Jan laughs. "How cute. But these twins are boys."

"Oh, everybody loves Frances."

She thanks me. I resist the urge to embrace her, moving away quickly with a wave of my hand.

At the restaurant, candlelit and rather gloomy, Joseph leans forward to eat, one arm anchored lightly on the edge of the table, the other hand poised with a fork. His napkin rests in his lap or perhaps left at the side of his plate, his back straight from learning to sit for long hours of meditation. The posture of a man who often eats alone. Or someone alert to having to make a quick exit, as firemen do. He chews slowly, looking down thoughtfully or across at me. His gaze, however, seems far away. The dining room is fashionably elegant, warmed by an open oven and spacious, though mostly empty of customers; there is a party of older diners to one side that keeps looking over at us in curiosity, and I'm never sure why we garner the attention we do: does he look so much older than I? Is it because I often break off talking to lean over and stroke his face? We speak of Christmas cards (as this is the season) and Joseph grows somber.

"We always used to send a poem," he explains his holiday ritual quietly. "One of us would start it, the other finish or rework it, and we'd have it printed up and sent out to a list of friends."

His eyes assume a grayish opacity in the muted glow of the candles; I can't tell if the expression is hurt or angry. In any case, he is devastated. His usually warm, tawny eyes grow steely and hard. He has glimpsed the bridges burning and all that is lost to him forever. His eyes grow narrow, gazing off, and I wonder at the pain they hide. What has he given up to be here with me tonight? To leave the longtime shelter of Arlene's bungalow and find and furnish a place of his own? He has confided that he does not like to come home to the empty new house. His new saltbox does not have a fireplace, as did his homes shared with other women, Belinda and Arlene, and Joseph is fond of making a fire. He notes, sadly, that most of his friends own their own house.

"And this year?" I ask tentatively. "What did you send as a Christmas card this year?"

"We wrote about the victory over the communications tower," Joseph says, lowering his head. "We often collaborate. But I didn't really send any cards," he adds, defeated.

We pause to eat, gnocchi and tagliatelle in neat little piles on great oval plates. We sip at a bottle of wine Joseph has ordered.

"Do I ask too many questions?" I say, a bit coyly.

"We haven't spoken openly about the pain involved," Joseph replies. He is pondering the grief of breaking up a family—for he and Arlene had made a home, a family. Does he consider the grief he has caused in my own family—the breakup of my marriage?

"We've ruined each other's life," I say.

He laughs. It's true. He has told me more than once.

"I haven't lived alone for over twenty years," Joseph remarks.

"It's time, don't you think? An exciting time to be on your own."

He trains his flinty eyes on me. Am I serious? Oh yes, I am. His look is dangerous. I back off. He has told me that he moved out "for us, for the . . ." but he doesn't finish his thought. For the future, for what might be? He has always told me that he has to do things his own way. Then, once resolved, he would move quickly. He *has* moved quickly, but did I believe him? No, I did not. I recognize the chagrin in his face.

"You're not comfortable here," I say.

Next time, we'll stay home, he promises, and I add: We'll *cook*.

"Baby," I murmur, backtracking, leaning forward to stroke his beard. I administer tender, mollifying caresses, as I do, as women invariably do. I desire only to return to our sweet bedroom rites of hours before. "We are caught helplessly in this collision," I tell him, "this fatal course of two . . ."

He reminds me: "In the end you're alone."

WE HAVE begun losing things. First, the "2" sweater, left on the seat in the métro. This is bad enough, and Cathy cries when she realizes it's gone. She loved wearing it. It made her feel grown up. It was a new item, and not chosen by her mother, hence it possessed special properties independent of me. Then El Tigre disappears. The amulet that Joseph has given me to keep me safe while I travel. What could have happened to it? I look through my luggage, the pockets of my pants, blouses, even inside my shoes. I wonder if I have hidden it somewhere in a frantic, mad (drunken) moment and now I can't remember. I suspect the Algerian maid in the hotel on Montparnasse found it on the floor in my closet while cleaning our room. She sensed the power that emanates from this ferocious tiger's head hand-painted on wood and she pocketed it secretly to add to her household icons. I'm angry, horrified at my carelessness. Joseph gave it to me for protection over long flights across the country, and by losing it I am guilty of taking his love for granted. This bodes disaster for us, surely. The end of the end. I sit on my bed, dazed and uncomprehending.

"What's wrong?" Cathy asks, looking up from her primer, *J'aime lire*. She's been sounding verbs out, making sentences, motivated, no doubt, by Lewis's gentle tutelage.

"I can't find the amulet. El Tigre. I can't find it anywhere."

I must sound pathetic, or scarily desperate, because she helps me look. We sift through the luggage over and over. We find stale croissants and museum ticket stubs and maps. We scour dusty corners, under the bed. The more I peek into the hidden recesses of the room, the less I like this place. I sit on the bed and cry. She comforts me.

"Don't worry," she says, "we'll find another one."

"It won't be the same," I lament. "He gave us those things, my friend Joseph from Denver. And we keep losing the things he gave us. Isn't that weird?"

"No," she replies, considering. "Sometimes you want to lose things."

"What do you mean?" I ask sharply.

"Remember the story you used to read to me about the dog that hated the sweater with the roses he had been given by his owner's aunt? And he tried everything to lose it—like leaving it on a park bench, but somebody was always returning it."

"No, I don't remember that story."

"*You* read it to me."

"So what of it? No one is returning our stuff to us!"

"That's sometimes better. I mean, in the story the dog finally snags the sweater on a branch and unravels it as he runs and the birds use the yarn for their nest."

"That's a beautiful ending," I concede bitterly.

"That's not the ending."

"Now I'm remembering."

"The aunt gives him another sweater. But it doesn't have roses on it and the dog loves it."

"You've got potential, kid."

THIS ROOM I recall most fondly: mud-brown tiled floors and ornately grooved Spanish furniture, and a bed of such vulgar capaciousness that I exclaim to Joseph: "But we won't ever find each other in it!" I prefer smaller quarters, where I can cling to my love while breathing into the pit of his arm. From the windows: views of low-sprawling downtown Albuquerque, an old trader town accustomed to the cycle of boom and bust, and beyond, the violet corona of mountains.

We drink wine immoderately (Joseph reminds me I am dehydrated after traveling) and eat Mexican food heaped with beans. In the elevator we frighten a convention of young people in a Bible group because we are fooling around in drunken play. But there are very few people to be seen at all.

On this trip Joseph lets me drive. He admires the art deco diners along old Rt. 66. We head out to Santa Fe, but he doesn't feel like sticking around because it's a town Arlene visits periodically and has friends there; we push on to Taos, passing rocky pastures in which goats are resting under the shade of fruit trees. We stop at an Indian pueblo, although seemingly deserted; we slip into the tiny adobe chapel and rest quietly in the coolness of the interior on rough wooden benches. A crude plaster Jesus hangs forlornly over the altar. Joseph crosses himself as we leave and I whisper, "Joseph, why do you cross yourself? You're not Catholic." He smiles, my bearded naturalist, my student of neolithic arts, and replies: "But dear Francis, I assume the religion of whatever people I am among."

The sun is setting behind the Sangre de Cristo, a blood-red sphere sinking into a miasmal cauldron. I exclaim to Joseph that we must hurry and we scramble on top of an adobe wall we find near the Old Town Square. He hoists me up, precariously—he is not a large man, nor particularly strong, and I don't recall his ever lifting me or carrying me—and we watch together the flaming disk making its descent with alarming haste into the embrace of the mountains. I feel in the midst of this wide-minded sky, bathed by the glow of the sun, as close to being free as I have ever been. We shout out—we sing in exultation! And nearly weep at how evanescent the moment. We are left sitting on a cold wall in darkness. Later we drink margaritas at a tavern and listen to a Mexican musician play folk tunes on his electric violin. I think of Cathy and how my daughter would love to hear these curious sounds from an instrument she has been schooled to regard as rather more stately and orthodox.

"Jan always wanted a sibling," Joseph resurfaces, from deep in his thoughts.

A startling admission. "A sibling? My heart, do you want to have more children?"

"Always wanted to . . ." he murmurs.

"A baby would solve all of our problems," I reply, gamely (another child? who would take care of her?). But he remains serious and quiet and wisely does not pursue this avenue.

When we must leave this place where we have tasted our liberation for the last time, I am almost convinced that we will make a go of it together. That we can find a way out of our separately sticky situations and we will find the will to blend happily and maybe even have another child. Everyone will forgive us if a baby ensues. I am almost content as we drive out of town, then we see the dog lying on the side of the road near a shopping mall. We are headed out to the Albuquerque airport. "Look at that dog," I say, artlessly. "How can it be lying there amid all this traffic?" For I believe the dog is resting in the sun. But Joseph recognizes the specter of death.

"The dog is dead."

ONCE, WHEN I leave Joseph sleeping in our hotel room in the city in order to drive home in the pre-dawn hours, I arrive at my suburban street and come upon the most amazing scene. There on the lawn is a wild, assorted menagerie cavorting under the uncanny brightness of the moon. A deer meanders across the street, unconcerned for the presence of my quietly humming vehicle, while two sisters of her herd loiter on my grass, munching on the tender leaves of my hosta plants with what seems to me an utterly serene obliviousness to my existence. (Am I really here? Am I awake or sleeping?) Some kind of roly-poly prickly creature scampers in front of my headlights, probably a porcupine (though I've never actually encountered one) or a skunk; I flick off my beams in astonishment. In the periphery of my vision I glimpse a few other furry beasts making their brazen pre-dawn raids— raccoons, rabbits, maybe the neighbor's big-bottomed muskrat venturing boldly up from the stream to join the party. There is about this scene a magical harmony I am loath to disturb: I inch gingerly into my driveway, turn off the ignition, and sit for a while. I listen, marveling, a privileged observer to the secret life of animals. I want to hold the clarity of the moonlight next to my heart with Joseph's smell from our love bed. I sense that it's Joseph who has brought this nocturnal wonderland to life for me. This night is my benediction.

WE'LL FIND another sweater for her, I tell her. The same kind, dark blue with a zipper up the front and racy stripes lining the sides. No, even better: a yellow one (her new favorite color), with diagonal bars in red, orange, purple; a turtleneck, perhaps, with fringed sleeves like the teenagers wear. We'll find whatever she wants at this flea market, this marché aux puces at the Porte de Clignancourt, in the northern suburbs, where we have traveled interminably by métro on a gray Sunday afternoon. We mingle seamlessly with other Parisian families, seeking diversion, bargains, junk to cram into apartments and houses, stuff to be hauled in cars, dragged back into the orifice of the métro, lugged up innumerable stairs and dumped into rooms, piled with more detritus and throwaways, furniture, accessories, relics of lonely voids gathering dust from years of disuse. We'll find it here! A new old not-very-clean sweater, whatever she likes, I'll buy it for her, if I can see her laugh again, show that big wide boxy baby-smile of four-years-old (still her first teeth!), just like in the photo I have of her, hanging in our snug little brick Tudor back in New York. We'll find her another mother while we're at it: a mother who'll play with her whenever she wants, who won't snap, "Wait a minute!" when she needs something, to be read to, a Band-Aid for her knee; a mother without unseemly desires, who won't leave her—won't leave her brother behind!—a good mother who doesn't lash out when angry, frustrated, hurt by a careless affront to her nurturing abilities. A mother who desires nothing more than being with her. We'll find her! I tell Cathy, amid the teeming anonymity of this foreign place.

"What are you staring at? Are you staring into space?" Cathy demands, having recently learned a new expression. "Come *on.*" She pulls me out of my dark thoughts. I unclench my fists. She tugs at my sleeve and propels me through the throng into a stall on rue Jules-Valles jammed with dresses hanging like scarecrows, distressed leather coats, and gypsy scarves. The proprietor is a large woman in voluminous robes like a fortune-teller, seated on a small stool. She wears black gloves without fingers and gives us a wan smile. American tourists, *c'est adorable*. We rifle through crates of clothing and I extract a few items that might fit my girl. "How about this one? Or this?" I suggest, holding it against her virgin-willow frame. The day is raw, the sky dun under the shadow of the Périphérique, and I need a cup of coffee.

"Yuck," she says, grimacing.

"Take off your coat and let's slip it on."

It's a fancy-sleeved sweater, silvery blue in a scratchy wool material, outrageous, yes, but once she puts it on she is transformed and suddenly I see what I haven't seen yet or couldn't notice: that she is going to be a young lady soon and she is lovely. The metallic hints against her pale peach tone bring out her flashing eyes. The baby roundness to her face has contoured into strong, supple shadows, like her father's face. Freckles dotting the nose still forming, the cheekbones tenderly emerging. When did this happen? I stand back and feast on her and feel my throat tighten. But she hates the sweater, pulls it over her head, and turns on her heels. I continue digging through the bin and look up to see her approach a couple walking between the stalls with a large dog—no, a pony—smooth, short fur the color of desert sand, an elegantly sloping ribcage revealing black hardy teats, a snout the size of my daughter's skull. A Marmaduke dog, large but not evil, I surmise. My Cathy has no fear, raises her arm straight from her side to let the dog sniff the back of her hand. Well, good: she's learning some-thing. I meet the eyes of the dog owners momentarily, those sleek, gilded Parisians, and smile a wary that-better-be-a-nice-dog smile. Then I lower my head back to the task of rummaging through the unsavory pile.

"Stay close," I call to her.

"What are you seeking?" the lady vendor asks me, in French.

"I'm not sure. A sweater, I think, bright and warm, *exotique*," I add, though I'm not sure what I mean.

"Is that your daughter? She's very pretty," replies the knowing lady, moving among her wares.

"She plays the violin," I sniff.

She brings out some children's clothes but I see right away that they will meet with disapproval: castoffs with glued emblems of dated cartoon shows that American children have evidently jettisoned for more fashionable stuff. Hardly *exotique*. I want my daughter to look sensational, stylish, not like the other kids she knows back home. Abner, for example, in his sports T-shirts and baseball caps. Cathy would live in a baseball cap if I let her. But having seen her in the smashing sweater, I feel the urge to find her something thrilling, electric, and I nod and frown, digging a while longer, then smile at the woman and thank her for accommodating me. I turn to leave.

But I can't find Cathy. I turn one way between the crowded stalls, then another way, return finally to the stall with the woman in the fingerless gloves.

"Have you seen the little girl?" I ask her. "She was petting the dog"—but in my confusion I don't remember the word for *pet*, so I say, *touch*. The woman offers her Gallic shrug and fierce crimping of the lips.

"The little girl," I say louder, attracting the attention of a few bystanders distractedly stroking some hanging garments, "who was right here. She was touching the *dog*—my daughter. You saw her." The woman is blank. I wave my arm and point to the spot where she was standing. "She was wearing a yellow coat"—but then I see that I am still holding her anorak and I am at a loss to recall what she was wearing underneath. We have lost the "2" sweater. "No, she has short dark hair," I cry, gesturing at my own face with my hand. The verb comes swiftly to me: *caress*. "The little girl!"

Now I am angry. I stare at these strange faces, which stare back at me, closed, startled, unyielding. They are appalled at the sight of this shrill madwoman. You don't belong here, they are saying to me. Why are you destroying the serenity of our Sunday afternoon with your hysteria? Why have you come to our country to lose your child? They do not intend to help me. Indeed, it seems to me that their faces have masked a kind of malevolence all along, and I imagine they are asking me what right I have to complain, being in their country, as they have plotted all along to snatch my child. But I haven't seen the writing on the wall until now; I haven't been vigilant enough. Why did I come to France, this nation of critics? Why didn't I flee to India, where love songs are holy? And I begin to shout, "Cathy! Cathy!" despite what they think, what I might look like to them, this nutty American lady, flapping the yellow anorak in my arms and lunging frantically among the stalls of junky housewares, antiques, sewing supplies, crazy shoes. I knock the French citizens out of my way. They raise their hands in defense. "Where are you, Cathy?" I cry in English—what do I care about their fine, exalted language? I can curse in my own fucking language, and I do, snarling as they turn on me their shocked, hostile faces that leave me utterly desolate. But I see no dog, no Cathy's dear face of dazzling joy and mischief. I know at last I'm alone.

IX

Joseph translates an ancient Sanskrit poem for me in bed: "Oh you silly women always chattering of love—of sweet kisses, lingering caresses, heavy sighs! Once my lover touches my breast, I swear I remember nothing at all." How familiar and fresh these sentiments! I, too, am acquainted with the agony of longing. Delicious, tortuous: the longing for my lover whose embrace banishes the memory of loss and loneliness. When we come together my other life falls away and I am nothing but a vessel to meet his desire. Our rapturous limbs entangle so that we no longer know whose body is whose, who is crying out—he or I? Our love sighs mingle as one. But what I do remember is every kiss and breath and caress exchanged, and nothing else. That is, my other life is far, far away, and I don't recall how my children are growing up in front of my eyes, or other friends I no longer see, or ambitions I have let go of. At what point does longing become its own torture, of waiting, sitting, counting? I wait for my lover's calls, his exquisite silhouette to appear outside the arrival gate, his letters in my mailbox daily, and his sweetest words to transport me once again to that place of joined oblivion. I wonder if I am ever truly happy knowing him: whether love is a form of willful sabotage. But Arlene Manhunter will put me straight. She is a warrior of love, full of scorn and fury: scarred, battered, and bent on smashing worlds smaller than her own.

"You're living a dream," she tells me. "A beautiful dream."

"What else is there?"

She snorts. "He doesn't love you."

"I won't listen."

"You have to listen. There are others."

I will hang up. The voices of my children playing outside in the street alert me to danger. From my bedroom window I scan the street for Harry—for who is supervising them in case of a passing car? The cars whip around the block, without looking for small children on bicycles, skateboards, scooters. Then I see him, holding aloft a hockey stick, racing around the shade of a forsythia bush where he has leapt to retrieve the rolling puck.

"You'd say anything to hurt me," I reply, angrily.

"He tells me. He has a new friend."

"Come on!" I say, and laugh. "You can respect me a little here!"

"He told me her name."

"Who? Sunflower?" She thinks she's got me.

She scoffs. "No! A board member at the school. She is my age, maybe older. But no grandma, let me tell you—Meadows is flashy, keeps in shape. We've all know each other for years. She's rich," Arlene intimates, "comes from a rich family, and has an Asian art collection that impressed the hell out of Joseph when we had dinner at her house. She's an adult. *Her* kids are grown up."

"That's impossible. He told me to wait for him. He would never—"

"He's sleeping with her."

The tension snaps, the cabin collapses. I am plunging to my death. There is no heaven, no hell, simply a relentless human suffering to be transcended by emptying the mind of ego, consciousness. I fall through the vacuum, a free-floating body through a sphere of gauze.

"What do you know?" I challenge her. "I'll talk to him."

"This is reality, Frances. You have to get on with it. Real life. Be there for your children. Can't you make it up with your husband? Douglas says—"

"Don't insult me!"

She laughs, a deep, demonic rumbling. Then promptly changes the subject. "I'm headed out to Shad Creek shortly."

"Why?" I ask.

"Because I have to penetrate the force field of his arrogance," she retorts heatedly, falling into her rhetorical flourishes, her lyrical recitation. "I have to stomp and bow and *kill* this discursive thinking. I have to gather the energy of muses, goddesses, and energy fields and I have to propitiate the gods. I must go pay homage to Gaia. Reestablish the rightful place of Semele, Earth, after she was displaced by Patriarchy—"

"Why would you go there when there's a chance of running into Joseph?"

"He wouldn't show his cowardly face. I'd kill him." She growls menacingly. "And you?" she demands.

"Me?" I echo, stupidly.

"Are you coming to Boulder?"

"No. I have to go," I say quickly. "Good-bye, Arlene."

I have cancelled my plane ticket to Denver this weekend because Joseph has forgotten about an important board meeting he must attend. He must not neglect official duties, he tells me, in light of the accusatory letter Arlene has written, and given his precarious position at Diamondcutter. This seems highly irregular, and I know that he's lying. I plead with him. "I want to come," I tell him, but he insists. "Frances," he warns me, revealing the truth, "it's too hot. You can't come here." He does not relent. But I must see him; I've thrown down my gauntlet. And with Arlene's words, I am resolved. I repack my bag, kiss my babies, who cling to me, confused; I give a silent parting wave to Harry, who believes I am taking the train to LaGuardia. Once in the city, however, I rent a car. When interrogated later, where I am this long weekend that becomes an absent week of my life, my husband replies, "She has been here, at home, with her family."

I set off, across country.

WHAT I love about Kerouac's *On the Road* is the speed. Back in the car, with wild Dean smacking the steering wheel and yelling "Whooee, here we go!" his friends and fellow passengers are ecstatic that the journey's begun all over again. It doesn't matter where they're going, just that they're going: "We were all delighted," muses good old Sal, "we all realized we were leaving confusion and nonsense behind and performing our one and noble function of the time, *move*."

I'm going. As long as I'm in motion, I feel good, I can do this, I tell myself. My nerves are sharpened to needle points. I listen to the radio and don't have time to hear the reproaches in my head. I don't even hear Arlene anymore. I'm angry, it's true. Smoking out of my ears. I'm angry and driving so hard that the toll operator on Rt. 80 across the tedious swath of Pennsylvania stares through his booth window, then winks. I nearly swerve when I notice that wink—what is he thinking? But then it occurs to me that that's the way the world operates. The world operates on sex and people are motivated by it, make their decisions by it, their life choices. Well, okay. At least that's honest. I should lighten up, get into the game. But grief is choking me, and as it begins to get dark out and harder to see through the swimming headlights, I'm finding it difficult even to breathe.

I don't sleep with the Harrisburg boy I meet at the truck-stop diner under the shadow of converted steel mills. He catches me crying (just like in the country-western song playing on the jukebox), buys me a beer, then another, and I smoke his cigarette and leave a brûlée stain of my lipstick.

On my lover's thigh.

But I am mad and chugging past limp, busy Cleveland, burning from his contempt—how many others? I don't feel like sleeping.

The radio goes something like this: "Sweet-talking, love-stealing, low-down son of a gun."

I don't sleep with the driver in a pearl-gray BMW who flirts with me in and out of traffic till Chicago. When he pulls into the rest stop I catch a glimpse of his butt-heavy build and find the thought of touching my slender gigolo maddening.

I am weeping again.

I don't sleep with him, sniffing all around Lake Michigan, feeling double-crossed, the radio spinning spiritual hymns.

I don't sleep with the truckers at Joliet—all those tattoos make me dizzy and the smoke, the good smells of hard real men, when my lover comes precipitously and leaves me cold.

(He drove a warehouse truck once and knows how to talk to them.)

I don't sleep with the elderly man at the hotel restaurant in Rock Island, where I finally take a room, bleary in both eyes, no lipstick. I get a little lost, and he is nice, a widower, and would make love to me: "I'll suck your toes," says he, seeing my weariness.

(He has another lady with him in the morning at breakfast.)

The accents are broadening out with the land. Crossing the Mississippi I'm clear of the East and I rejoice, getting closer to my target.

I don't sleep with the guy who changes my tire in Des Moines: he drives a white truck and pulls over three lanes to stop. Cell phone at his belt, teeth emitting warm rays. He warns me that a snowstorm is coming over those farmlands and maybe I need a place to stay.

I do.

I don't sleep with him, but I should, mystified by his kindness while my own lover is all cold knocks and aren't I tired of begging for love?

I am lonely in passing Omaha.

I wonder if I'll see some real cowboys. But I don't sleep with any of them, though they move me, and wave, seeing my New York license plate, and I blush, gazing into those blue blue eyes like the American continent I cross bravely.

My lover's eyes are not blue.

He always wonders why I don't take a lover closer to me, a carpet cleaner, for example, that's what I need, a good fuck who lives next door, not 2,000 miles away, what idiocy! And it might have kept me quiet.

A wide-open verdant morning in North Platte, fertile as the Nile.

Signs for Hastings, Nebraska—I don't turn around.

I don't sleep with Mr. Sousa (his shirt says), who pumps gas in my car. "Hi," I say, real friendly. "What do you do in North Platte?" Maybe he'll take me back inside the garage for a ride on his hydraulic lift. "You from New York?" He squints, as if I'm an extraterrestrial, and I feel lousy, just wanting to be one of the girls.

I'm always too married. Too mother. Soon too old, and it's my lover's fault. He ages me: what am I doing with a man ten years my senior?

But Mr. Sousa doesn't ask. He must be all of twenty, smooth baby skin and a little tussock of hair at his chin.

I don't sleep with Marlon, Don, Jaime, nice men all along the way.

Then the plains turn suddenly brittle and serious sagebrush sprouts, and sad meditations. My bushwhacking anger reignites and I spot signs for Colorado:

"Color red."

I don't sleep at all.

Drive into Larimer Street and get a drink.

I have found the house by taxi. It's located in an older Boulder neighborhood, a suburb Joseph once points out to me where the wealthy parents of Jan's friends live. A Frank Lloyd Wright cedar-shingle with wide-flying porches and great drooping cottonwood trees attesting to the house's age and venerableness. Wood the color of buckwheat honey, gleaming by twilight. A majestic dwelling unlike Joseph's modest rented saltbox where he hammers out his shapely poems for little reward. A yard well tended by an army of Mexicans, tidy beds of extravagant grasses I would never know the names of. There are lights on in the house, allowing the viewer from the street to spy a vaulted entranceway, spacious front rooms in which the curtains have not been drawn, where the inhabitants move with the spatial familiarity of people comfortable in their skin and have nothing to hide. Little did I know what his longing glances meant as we drove through this neighborhood months before, maybe even passed this very house. Did he know then that he would be master of the place?

I ascend the front porch, pause at the front door, and hear music: jazz, sultry elongated horns and hip-rolling percussion.

And then I smell it: the sweet, herbaceous aroma of burning piñon. Somewhere an exquisite, cozy fire is being prepared with loving attention by the aficionado. My love, my infinitely adaptable love, has bartered his Sweet Girl for a comfortable hearth.

The lady of the house answers the Zen door chime.

"I need to see Joseph, please."

She is just as I have imagined, though not as tall, perhaps: blonded chin-length hair in a good cut, tanned skin, jewelry flashing in the light of the porch sconces. The effect overall is tasteful and very expensive. She wears creamy, light silks as befits a teacher of Chinese calligraphy. A sturdy figure kept firm from hiking, scuba diving, skiing in the winter on vacation with her grown children. She is smiling at first, a tight, officious smile she offers to her workers and others who serve her and ask favors: money, contributions, her presence at benefits and philanthropic functions. She patronizes charities that save trees and Tibetan monks. I have read that she comes from old money; her previous husband owned racehorses.

Then she seems confused.

"I beg your pardon, miss?"

Miss, she calls me. Not *ma'am*, and I am secretly pleased at the distinction she is making in our ages.

"My name is Frances. I need to speak to Joseph, please. I know he's here. I see his car."

I motion toward his dusty Subaru parked down the street. Her mouth opens. Then he appears behind her, in a hallway lined with many rare and beautiful objets d'art. An inestimable Asian art collection that Joseph couldn't stop marveling about when he first came to this house with Arlene for a faculty dinner four years before. He is here, my love: wearing his jeans and rough-hewn shirt, and I feel an absurd relief that he has not replaced his clothes for fancier garb ("Beware of all endeavors that require new clothes": Thoreau). He steps out from behind her, sees me, and the blood color drains from his face. "Frances," he breathes, and I am backing up, beckoning him outside. He speaks swiftly, in hushed intimate tones to the frightened woman, pressing her back into the house. Then closes the door behind him.

He glances around. Is anyone watching this scene on the porch? He looks nervous, runs his hand through his hair. His little gold earrings twinkle in the evening light.

"What are you doing here?"

"I came. I had a ticket. I came in spite of your—board meeting? How's it going, Joseph? Are you getting some business done, in there by the fire?"

"But you can't. I can't see you."

"Yes, I see."

We move into the shadows of the great shaggy laurels. The grass is moist and spongy, despite the earth-cracking drought of the season. Cataclysmic fires inch toward a suburb south of Denver. The air is raw with grit, and sharp smelling. The membranes of the nose are rendered so desiccated that it hurts to breathe, and so tender and raw that nosebleeds are common.

I pat the sodden ground.

"Didn't you warn me about watering my lawn in this drought?" I wonder, but he looks so defeated I give it up. "Is that Meadows?" I ask, though of course I know the answer. I want to laugh. What a name! A Hollywood name. Or a former husband's pet name for one of his favorite horses.

"It is. Oh Frances. Arlene called you." He is hanging his head.

"She always calls me to tell me what you're up to. To throw her poisoned darts at me. To tell me what you can't tell me. And why can't you? What grief you've put me through, Joseph! I wish—I wish—I had never met you."

I want to hit him. My love with the heart of a gigolo. I want to feel my fingers strike the fine bones of his face. I want to scrape my fingernails into the flesh of the face I adore and make him bleed at my feet.

He looks as if he is going to crumple to dust. I start to cry.

"Please don't cry."

"Why? Why do tears scare you so much? Tears are pure, cleansing. When have you ever cried? You can't—you could never reveal yourself honestly."

"Frances, I cry," he says quietly.

We sit on the grass. His car keys fall out of his pocket.

"Frances," he says, and takes my hand, "I can't be there for you anymore. I'm collapsing under the pressure of comforting you and then having to live and work here. I'm wrecking you and me with this longing, these vague hopes and dreams. Loving a woman who is so far away, and who is still married—albeit estranged—" he adds quickly, silencing my objections, "and with two small children. Part of the reason it didn't work with Arlene was the tension inherent in getting along with her son. I wasn't good at it, Frances. I failed."

"My babies would love you. They would come to love you. Cathy already does."

"Frances, I can't move East! My work, my friends, my daughter's upbringing, these mountains I love—are all here. And your frozen situation at home—"

"You don't know what I wouldn't do for love of you."

"You haven't done it!"

I am left breathless and staring at his rebuke: I didn't see it coming. He regrets it immediately, touches my hair.

"With time, patience, ardor," I plead, using the magic passwords from his own letters. For hasn't he written: *Wait for me?*

"Frances, I can't bear it."

"It's Arlene, isn't it. She's a witch. She's cast a spell on you."

"She is . . ." he pauses, gazing off sorrowfully, "very powerful."

There is a sound from the house. He leaps up, pulls me to my feet. Kisses me. Our time is up.

I HAVE studied the maps of the Colorado terrain that hang in Joseph's saltbox. I know how to reach Shad Creek, and even if I can't see well at night I have the ghostly face of the moon to guide me. Joseph's car is the same make as my own, though an older, larger model of Subaru, and very dusty inside. ("A clean car is the sign of a sick mind," he has cheerfully recited to me.) I explore the contents of the glove compartment. There is a bottle of Tylenol I once deposited there (the high altitude and wine always give me a headache in the mornings), as well as a small brush bearing strands of salt-and-pepper hair (he rakes it over his skull when he thinks I'm not looking). I smell the brush and return it to its place. Wearing gloves, I am careful to disturb nothing. I put on the radio, which is tuned always to Joseph's alternative jazz station. I have pulled the front seat forward slightly, since my love has long, climbing legs. His rucksack rests on the back seat, and I know inside I will find a flashlight and rope, among other trusty items (candles and corkscrew!), because Joseph travels prepared. Bottles of water cradle on the floor of the passenger seat.

The radio plays: *Everything is illusion, but I am confident that all is well.*

I can't see much: flat, arid land and occasional boulders along the route that must have been kicked there in play by some neolithic giants. The sky is clear and luminous, though I detect erasure smudges in the spangled design and I know these signify smoke. I sense the impassive solemnity of the mountains, snow-capped and lethally spiked: I will get out and look at them, like a good naturalist and traveler, even though it's very cold and I'm apprehensive about encountering the great outdoors without a guide—without my mountain man at my side. I drive and sing and swig from a bottle of water; I wish it were wine. Sometimes I can't see the road well; that is, I stare so hard at the bright white center lines that my vision begins to swim—it must have to do with optical illusion— but since there are few other cars, I drive somewhere in the middle. I'm afraid of hitting an animal (bison? antelope?) or running over a passing tarantula. Joseph has mentioned the annoyance of these. I haven't brought a proper coat for the chill at these climes, and I'm freezing; I keep the heat going full force at my feet. The engine gulps and protests: the thermostat has probably never been hiked this high because the owner can't tolerate the heat.

My cold-blooded lover.

Everything is illusion.

A couple of hours outside of Boulder I see signs for Shad Creek. There are a few small houses with fenced land and an occasional barn and rickety billboard that advertises services twenty miles away. Wide-open, gently ascending land culminating in a barrier of impassable mountain ranges: Did Arlene and Joseph plan to build a house someday on this property and move out here together as a kind of literary retirement for their golden years? It's a thought that has never occurred to me, and plunges me into a sad meditation. "The fact that we never had a child, never married," Joseph bemoans, in an effort to explain his unwillingness to commit to the woman who became essentially his common-law wife. He doesn't complete his sentence. He senses all along that he carries a diminished role alongside her, unavoidably, as she is an implacable, avalanchine presence. A star. Douglas once remarked that every relationship contains a "star" and then the other person who is not—chooses not to be, for whatever reason; in Douglas's case, of course, he is the star, and Cynthia, for all her length and youth, can't displace him. But for Joseph it is time to pull away from Arlene's energy field, her mighty gravitational pull, time to forge out on his own. And he does (don't I liberate him?), except that his solitude frightens him and he turns and runs.

I amble up the road looking for a creek, because that's where Joseph says his land is (his and Arlene's land), but I remember that the creek is dry. I despair of finding his lot in the dark, #43 Shad Creek, until I see a car, a twilight-blue sedan panting on the road's shoulder. Silently fuming, crouched, and ready to leap. It's Arlene's car, unmistakably. I pull up behind it and leap out, startled by my own surge of adrenaline though nearly knocked unconscious by the blast of frigid ash-smelling air. I half slide into a deep gully off the road, probably full of quiescent rattlesnakes. I creep up to the sedan, thinking to catch her swigging from a bottle of moonshine, shelling nuts, and pounding the dashboard with rhythmic war cries. But the side door is locked, the hood cold, and inside I glimpse all manner of detritus on the seats. I recall the state of her aerie upstairs in her house—boas, books, mail—and wonder at the clutter she likes to harbor in her mind.

I peer closer, touching the glass with the tip of my nose. There is a flicker of color, a sudden movement, then a face, painted, terrible, appears at the window. A ghoul uprights itself from the horizontal. The apparition is so unexpected that I shriek and fall backward onto the uneven pavement. The door flies open, nearly hitting me in the face.

A figure steps out in full battle regalia. Feathers, beads, war paint. It is she.

Crazy Horse.

"Where is he?" she thunders, glancing briefly behind me before stepping toward Joseph's car to get a better look. Her silvery trappings at ankles and wrists clink menacingly as she charges. She flings open a door and searches inside. Then slams it and scans the horizon in each direction before turning back, shoulders squared accusingly, animal teeth chattering at her breast. She has a leather strap tied around her forehead, her hair long and braided at the sides of her fiercesomely streaked face. I manage to stand on shaky legs.

"Where is he?" she demands of me.

"If you mean Joseph," I breathe, "he's with his new dear friend, just like you said."

She leans toward me with blazing eyes, peering closer at my face. "You!" she exclaims. "Frances?" She gives me a long, hard once-over. She looks furious, then skeptical, disappointed, no doubt that I don't present a more worthy opponent. She makes a threatening step toward me. I recoil.

"You don't have a gun, do you, Arlene?"

She scoffs, disgusted. "Bah," she says. "I am a nonviolent person."

"Excuse me, but I have a hard time believing that."

"Did you get a look at her?" Arlene considers quickly, as if talking to herself. "A pretty face, and she keeps herself fit, but I don't know about the hair, and she's not very smart. It won't be long before Joseph leaves her for a younger woman . . . What do you want here, anyway, Frances?" she says, glaring anew at me. "Does your husband know you're here?"

"I beg your pardon. Did you husband know when you ran off with Joseph to India?"

"Of course. I told my husband immediately."

"I want to know why you had to turn Joseph against me."

"I didn't have to," she retorts poisonously. "He was tired of you, Frances. He was trying to get rid of you."

"Ah, well. I've been forthright with you all along. Haven't I told you what you want to know?"

"Look, lady. He's sick. He's a womanizer—a pathological liar. It's one lie after the other. He's lied about everything—he's lied to me the last ten years! It's a pattern with him . . ." Arlene launches into a decade of Joseph's dissembling, the details of which I have mostly heard before. She construes various theories for his chronic duplicity: that his private and public sides are irretrievably conflicted; that his father conducted a long-running affair outside of his marriage and never told his sons the truth. I'm amazed at her relentlessness, her ability to stoke her layers upon layers of grievances to a rare, pitched flame of vengeance, and I see it won't stop—she can't stop herself. Making amends is not sufficient; she wants him dead.

"But Arlene, we have a certain responsibility in this, don't we? Each of us does. I do, and I regret my role, I really do, but Arlene—"

"If he had seen a therapist," she resumes, not hearing me. "If he had maintained a more modest course of action when all of this broke out before Christmas—"

"I mean," I continue, speaking over her, "if it wasn't me, then it would have been some other chick, right?"

"Then I have you to thank, don't I."

"I don't mean that. God, no. I'm sorry. I mean—but don't you carry some responsibility here, too?"

"For his cheating on me? The victim is responsible for her rape?"

"Arlene," I say levelly, "you didn't love him."

"What are you talking about? That's ridiculous. Of course I loved him."

"You didn't take care of him. You didn't cherish him. I held him, didn't I? Doesn't a woman know? He felt unloved by you, left out of your schemes to save the world. Emotionally you were absent—far away. And that's where I stepped in."

"You don't know anything about me! I am a flame, I am a mountain on fire, I am a boulder on her way to join the sea . . . And I've had enough of this."

She wrenches open the door to her midnight-blue sedan and snatches up items of clothing, namely her resplendent headdress, which she adjusts on her formidable crown. She slams the door and vaults over the road's gully and up the hill. She moves with startling animal swiftness and surety. She stomps away, and I am too amazed at the sight of her fantastically proud retreating figure to call after her. But then she turns at the crest, abruptly, shaking a finger at me. The silhouette of an Aztec goddess. I see by the phosphorescent moonlight that her face is smeared, glistening—wet.

"I did love him," she calls, and sets her jaw squarely.

I let her go. Rather, I decide to wait for her on safe ground. Certainly she'll be back, I tell myself, as it's too cold to go tromping off into unfamiliar hills, too late, and she wouldn't leave her car. I feel suddenly terribly sleepy; the weight of a week's dreamlessness drags on my limbs. I return to Joseph's car and get in to keep warm. I recline the driver's seat and wait her out, hoping that sleep will overtake me and soon it will be morning. Arlene will have come back, cooler, more reasonable, and retrieved her car and driven home.

But she doesn't come back. An hour passes, maybe more; sleep eludes me. I close my eyes but can't rid my mind of the terrible image of a mountain on fire. A boulder hurtling toward the sea. How could such a magnificent chief as she be brought so low? All of us despoiled, tainted by our monstrous hubris? Should I leave her be, should I let her go? Why am I here if not to help her? Then I summon the will to move: I take the rucksack from the backseat, fish out the flashlight, and stuff inside a few bottles of water. I'm wearing hiking boots, I thought of that before leaving home. And enough wool to keep me warm if I keep moving. It seems even colder now that I've been sheltered in the car. I shine the flashlight on the ground in search of a path, and there is one, leading, I hope, to the creek, or what once was a creek, swelling with the newly released springs rushing down from the snowy peaks. Only ashes, silt, and fine brown dust remain. I start out along the path, in the direction where Arlene stomped away, the rucksack strapped to my back. I am humming loudly one of Cathy's Suzuki tunes to keep up my courage—and alert any night critters who dare to dart out of their crevices and into my way. I'll look for a walking stick. I'll try not to keep guzzling at the water bottles.

After a while, I call her name, "Arlene!" tentatively at first, because I'm afraid of waking up the wolves, but then louder to embolden myself: "Ar-leen!" My mantra. The path has grown smooth and steeper. I don't imagine she's in good shape for hiking: how far could she have gone? Yet she carries within her genes the survival lore of ancient civilizations and knows how to get along in the wilderness. The trail ascends for what seems like miles— hours—and then I see the creek, or what once was a creek, two steep banks and a deep, dry ravine running like a scar along the earth for as far as I can make out. I scramble up the bank and trek along the seam, poking with my stick and listening hard for sounds of life. I hear an occasional telltale hoot-hooting and a strange, incongruous lowing that must be cattle somewhere in the neighboring properties. Along the ground I spy dark shadows like ponds of oil, or cow pies or the coiled bodies of sleeping snakes, but upon closer inspection I see that they are scraps of abandoned clothing: first a necklace of beads, some red-tipped feathers, a woolen native poncho, scarves, a robe of elaborate hand-dyed texture. Each item I pick up and examine carefully and sniff—patchouli and feminine unguents. I remember her smell from a robe at her house I once donned, in curiosity: it was silk, printed with a smoking dragon design, though it felt heavy, oppressive from the oils of her skin and perfume, and I quickly took it off and put it back in the closet before Joseph could see me. I fold each piece of clothing, even the underpants and socks, one by one. I sniff these, too, with a forlorn sympathy. I place each item carefully in the knapsack.

Then I find her headdress: she must be naked, freezing to death, or maybe she has taken shelter in a cave. I don't smell fire. But I know better. I recall how Mirabei, the legendary, fearless sixteenth-century Indian singer of holy songs, persecuted by her in-laws, who desired to take advantage of her popularity by forcing her back into the life of wealth and privilege she has forsaken, meets her death in her early fifties: she vanishes from a shrine where she has taken refuge for the night. She leaves only her robe and her hair. What if I find Arlene's hair, her raven hennaed tresses? She's been here: I feel my own hair tingle electrically at the back of my neck, and sense how Joseph must have felt when he hiked into the territory of the catamount. I have to sit down on a rock next to the sadly desiccated creek. My heart murmurs sickeningly. I have found her headdress and I know it's the last trace of her I'll unearth.

What is her state of mind at this moment of abnegation? Is she angry, resentful, resigned at last? Her plight—a postmenopausal woman cedes her allure to a younger, fertile female—is my own, and every woman's: it will happen to me. A woman's power is manifested discretely over successive stages of her life, from lissome girl to rainbow maiden to mother to hag; she knows at some point she will lose one kind of power to gain another, though the transformation will feel like a death. If I have the power to steal her man by my charms, she has the power to keep him away from me. I can't pretend that I didn't see her take Joseph's hand in her protective gesture at the Cruise Room in downtown Denver; I can't pretend that I didn't hear Joseph say of the woman who was his longtime companion, "But we're not married," as if he were free to love another. He wasn't free. I knew but I didn't heed. What I wanted was to gain an ecstatic state—steal from her—elevate myself. It was my time. I wanted Joseph; I took him. I wanted my lover's heart to soar.

But it's done and she beat me. I tenderly crush her headdress and put it away in Joseph's rucksack. She's vanished, received into the arms of her grandmother Gaia, to return to elemental nature. She's acquainted with vision quests into the mountains; she was initiated like the boys in her tribe and she knows what she's doing. It would be disrespectful, downright patronizing, to thwart her now. And she'll visit me again in my dreams, I'm sure of this, maybe a little apprehensive, too. In fact, I haven't slept for days. The sky has changed colors at the edges of the horizon, grown a bleak and sorrowful gray; the luminousness has diffused, burned off. The stars have fled. I rise unsteadily. The water is gone from the bottles, and Joseph hasn't packed anything to eat. I feel stiff from the cold and light-headed in this altitude, unsure, now that the terrain is revealed in the nascent light, where I have come from. Where are Harry and his sense of direction when I need them? I wouldn't know how to find the car. I follow the sound of cattle solemnly lowing, and keep following the creek. At some point I'll strike something—a road, a body walking—and ask the way.

I am confident that all is well.

I DON'T have to find Lewis. A child has been lost. Lewis strides through the mob that has gathered in the intersection of the marketplace. The people stand around and conjecture, gesticulate, assign blame. Where is the child, where is the mother? He emerges like my dark angel in his long raincoat and conservative cuffs. He is neither smiling nor frowning, but wears an assured air, as if to say he knew all along how this might turn out. The bells of Sacré-Coeur toll the hour. The crowd makes way for the hero. At his side strolls a smaller figure, licking an ice cream cone: my daughter. Or who must be Cathy, looking vaguely like the child in photos I have of her back home, as she is wearing a garment I have never seen: a dark brown shearling coat that flairs to her ankles, with fluffy ragged fur at the sleeves and collar, framing her small face, and colorful folksy stitching across the breast. A sylph, she could be, a little mountain sprite. She tongues around her raspberry-squashed mouth, oblivious to the attention she earns, intent only on the ice cream. She sees me and smiles, the eruption of her mischievous girl-woman grin, as she clutches the coveted sweet that her mother cannot take away from her because Lewis gave it to her. She holds it up for a moment, a trophy for her temerity, as if to say, "See, I knew we would see him again."

"The coat," I stammer, "you'll smear ice cream on your lovely coat."

Lewis says, pressing his lips to my tear-stained cheek, "Frances, are we ready to go home now?"

El Tigre arrives in the mail after the passage of many full moons when I have put away imagining that anything wondrous could ever happen to me again. There is no return address, no note to me. My name and address scribbled by a strange savage hand in black ink. The postmark: Denver. I hold the amulet in my hand. It feels hot. I bring it to my nose: pungent odor of mammal. Cathy asks me what you do with it. She laughs. Bernie places his finger in the tiger's mouth: "Ouch," he says, and draws his finger quickly away.